Birth
of the
Angel

THE COVID MURDERS MYSTERY: BOOK ONE OF TWO

CONAL O'BRIEN

Conal O'Brien

The COVID Murders Mystery: Book One of Two

Soft-Cover ISBN: 978-1-09835-562-3
eBook ISBN: 978-1-09835-563-0

Go to conalobrien.com to learn more about this book and other Bookbinder Mysteries

for Gwen

Contents

Prelude

Thursday, February 27th, 2020

Raphael Sharder was eighty-two years old and had always been a careful man. He pulled a tissue from a nearby leather box and held it under the lip of the bottle of fine cabernet as he poured himself a third glass. Dressed in a dark blue cardigan, white button-down shirt, and his oldest worn jeans, he looked like a chubby, but well-preserved, country lord. Only, instead of a castle in England, he had the grass dunes of Long Island and the vast ocean before him. He sighed as he stared out at the last light shining across the sea. He was grateful that the weather was better. It had been a difficult winter with too many storms sweeping up the sound from the south. And, since December, a coronavirus had spread with alarming speed throughout the world. Five weeks ago, the first case was reported in Washington state. At least there were no reported deaths in the United States. Yet. But maybe the President was right. Yesterday, he said COVID-19 was like the flu, there would be a vaccine soon, and the risk to the American people remained very low.

Raphael wasn't sure he cared. He felt old and tired. And after what he had set into motion, he wasn't sure that he would be around much longer anyway. He sipped his wine and smiled. It tasted like rarified time.

And after all, spring would come again, and his house would still be standing. And it was a lovely old place. It was too big for just him—that was certain. It was called *The Arethusa* and had once been featured in a prominent architectural magazine and was listed in the National Register of Historic Places. It was a dinosaur that cost him vast sums to keep up, but he didn't mind. He had lots of money, and it was his pleasure to fuss and maintain the property, decorate it with wonderful art pieces, and guard it with a state-of-the-art security system. And because of that, though he was alone in his twenty-acre estate, he felt protected. He'd always felt safe here in Southampton.

Raphael shook his head. After all that effort, and all it had cost, he was standing in this amazing place alone. This house had been his joy, his obsession, and his excuse for all the strange things he'd gotten involved in. Tonight, the cost of what he had done was heavy on him. He sipped his wine and turned toward the large painting over the fireplace mantle. The low gentle flames lit up the greed in his eyes as he walked closer to the canvas. It was a landscape—a sunny cliffside village in Greece, a little impressionistic. It was pretty good. He should know. It was, after all, his life's work to be the darling of the gallery set, and *the* art dealer to those in the know.

He pushed a light switch plate, and it popped open, giving access to a small numbered panel. He keyed in a code. Like the movement of a fine watch things happened: the roller shades came down covering every window, the Greek village painting slid up and disappeared into the ceiling, revealing a large, dark void in the wall, from which light slowly grew brighter until that space became vivid color and form. There, from the secret recess, a painting slid forward slowly, a very famous painting, which only he, Raphael Sharder, could ever see.

The lust of victory he had once felt was still there. But it was different now. Now he was old, and he'd come to feel that it was time to let the world know. Maybe it was regret or guilt; he wasn't sure. He only knew that his time with this masterpiece would soon be over.

He settled his chubby frame into a large leather chair, put his feet up, and stared at it. The tiny sailboat in peril in the storm, the followers reacting in panic: some looking to the broken ropes, some to the dark, wild sea, and some to the Christ figure sitting quietly in a strange, knowing light.

Raphael Sharder smiled, raised his glass, and murmured a toast to his stolen masterpiece:

"To you, Rembrandt, you amazing fucker. Did you have any idea how much this would be worth today?"

"I doubt it," said a voice behind him.

Raphael spun around so quickly, he spilled red wine across his arm.

"He was only twenty-seven when he painted it," she added.

"Jesus, you scared me," Raphael managed after a moment. "I didn't expect you...."

He got up and went to the bar, where he wiped off his sleeve.

"Some wine?" he asked the visitor.

"No, thank you," she said quietly, moving closer.

Raphael refilled his wine glass. "So, what do I owe you for this lovely but unexpected visit?"

He froze as the cold barrel of the pistol touched the back of his neck.

"You owe me... your life."

Chapter One

It was too early for this meeting, but Artemis was doing her a favor because she had a flight to catch. He handed over her signed documentation, recapped his fountain pen, and replaced it so it was perfectly aligned with the right side of his leather blotter.

"Oh my God, you're so neat. I don't know how you do that," she said.

Professor Artemis Bookbinder watched as the pretty young woman stood up and shoved her papers roughly into her backpack.

"It's true," he admitted freely. "I'm a real Felix and always have been."

She stopped packing and looked at him completely puzzled.

He could feel the cool early morning light shining on them through the large windows of his Columbia University office. Outside, the glass needed a wash, as always. The grit and gray of New York City had been darkening them on and off for over a hundred years, but inside, he was satisfied that the glass was clean, almost antiseptic, because he took care of that himself. His desk was set out in perfect piles of pads and folders, his laptop set in the exact center, all perfect again, now that his pen was back where it should be.

"Like Oscar and Felix, *The Odd Couple*," he explained. "You know, one of them was sloppy, the other super clean and neat, like me." She still looked at him with wide-open non-comprehending eyes.

"It was a movie, then a TV show," he said flatly, wondering if she really was smart enough for a master's.

She smiled politely and said that she'd have to hurry if she was going to make her flight.

"You're not worried…?" he asked gently. "You know, it's just a matter of time before the borders are closed."

"No, I'll be fine." She shrugged. "Besides, I can't think of a better place to get stuck than in Italy."

"Right. Well, I hope you have a wonderful time," he said and smiled.

"Thank you, Dr. Bookbinder. I'll see you in the fall."

He watched his office door close behind her. She was a good kid, and he liked her, but he had to admit that it was a relief that she was gone.

Is she just too young to know better? Or, is it me… again?

Artemis took a sip of coffee and set the mug back down in the exact center of a square stone coaster. He looked around at his office. It was a sign that he was in favor here, that he'd been given such a choice space. It provided him with a feeling of wood-paneled protection. Or did it?

It was years ago when it had first started. He was just twelve, and it was bad. It was after his parents' death, and he was living with relatives in Brooklyn. His childhood obsession with order and cleanliness devolved into germophobia until one day Artemis refused to leave the safety of his bedroom. Professional help, and the patience of his relatives, had helped him return to the world outside. By the time he left for college, he believed he had everything under control.

On his desk was a framed photo of Emily and him on their honeymoon in the Caribbean. That was fourteen years ago, and they looked so good together. He smiled.

She still looks that good. Probably will till the day she dies.

Artemis felt lucky all the time about having Emily in his life. She accepted him for who he was and steadied him. In the photo, she was laughing with her arms around him. And he was grinning, so pleased with himself.

Artemis opened his laptop and returned to the report he'd been reading before his meeting. The pandemic had spread to fourteen countries. Italy had over eight hundred cases.

He got up, straightened his vest and tie, and went into his private bathroom. He looked at his face in the mirror and sighed.

His eyes were still piercing blue, but little creases and lines were sneaking in around them. He was thirty-eight years old, tall and thin, with light brown hair, always kept neat. The clean features of his distinctive face made him someone people noticed, and listened to.

But what about now? Are we prepared?

It had all come down to a compromise and promises made for the sake of the family. To create a new life for them away from danger. And it seemed to be working. After all, wasn't their home in New Jersey safe and clean? And wasn't Emily happy in her job? And even Silas…? Well, his brilliant son Silas was a twelve-year-old odd duck, just like Artemis was at his age. But he seemed to be fitting in as well as could be expected.

Artemis rinsed and dried his face, refolded and replaced the hand towel, and went back and sat at his desk. He opened a lower drawer and pulled out a bottle of single malt and poured a healthy slug into his coffee. It was too early, but his vacation had officially started last night, so he was off the clock. The plan had been for two weeks in the Caribbean. But now it would be a staycation in New Jersey.

He sipped his coffee and put his feet up on his desk, being very careful that his shoes were perfectly placed on a pad of paper. He'd throw out the top sheet later. He shook his head. Even here in the quiet of his own thoughts, he knew that he was just too strange.

His cell phone rang. He checked the ID and smiled. "Ray...?"

"Yes, son. It's been a long time."

"Too damn long. How are you?"

Special Agent Ray Gaines had been working for the FBI for many years. He'd once headed up the Boston Office, but these days he worked out of Washington.

"I think we found one of the Gardner pieces," Ray said.

"Say what?" Artemis whispered as his dark blue eyes lit up. "Tell me where."

"Southampton. You with me?"

Artemis thought for the briefest of seconds of promises made, and the risks involved, before he answered, "Absolutely."

"Good." Ray sounded relieved. "Drew Sweeney's onboard, and she'll explain how she fits in on the way. She's arranging a chopper from 34th street. She's waiting for your call."

Artemis took a long breath as the news filtered in.

"A Gardner piece... I'd almost given up," he said very softly.

Ray's voice warmed. "No, son, that's something I'd never believe."

Artemis almost laughed. It was like waking up after a long sleep.

"Thank you, Ray, I'll see you soon."

* * *

"You're where, doing what?" Emily's slim cat-like body was still damp and wrapped in a towel from her shower. She closed their bedroom door for privacy.

"Artemis," she didn't care if he could hear the fear in her voice. She sat down on the edge of their bed, gripping the phone so tightly her knuckles were white.

Artemis pressed his cell hard against his ear trying to hear her over the noise of the NYPD chopper blades starting up overhead and spoke louder. "Drew and I are heading out to Southampton. But it's not like I'm back on the force, I'm just consulting. It's temporary."

"That better be true. And what's that noise? Are you on a fucking helicopter?"

"Yes, we both are."

Drew gave him a look to ask how it was going as they climbed into the back and belted themselves in. Artemis shrugged.

"Em," Artemis was shouting now to be heard over the noise, "I need you to understand—"

"Like you're giving me a choice?" she shot back.

"Emily, it's from the Gardner. You know what that means."

Emily lay back onto the unmade bed, pulled a pillow close, and hugged it tightly. She did, in fact, know just how much finding a Gardner Museum piece meant to Artemis.

"Emily?" he shouted. "Are you still there?"

That was certainly the right question. She sighed.

"Yes, I'm still here."

She ran her fingers slowly through her long hair, closed her eyes, and took a breath.

Finally, she said, "It's okay. I understand."

"Thanks." He half smiled over to Drew.

"Artemis, promise me that you'll be careful," Emily demanded.

"I always am," he answered.

"Give my love to Drew, and tell her I expect her to take care of you."

"Emily loves you and says you're supposed to take care of me," Artemis shouted to the woman beside him.

Drew smiled and shouted, "Fuck that, and give my love back to her."

"She loves you too," Artemis shouted into the phone, "and I'll see you later."

Artemis was smiling as he hung up. They put on their headsets, and Drew told the pilot to take off.

They lifted up from the 34th street NYPD heliport with crisp precision and in seconds were high above Manhattan's East River, heading off into the midmorning sun.

"I told you she'd understand," Drew said through the headset, her voice resonant with her usual command. "So, tell me the truth, cousin, you've really missed this, right?"

"Yes, I really have," Artemis answered truthfully.

*   *   *

"He's gone back to police work? Mother of God!" Aunt Delia's fear and disapproval could not be mistaken, but because young Silas was sitting there at the kitchen table busy with his laptop, she was trying to control herself.

Emily, now dressed, simply nodded and looked away. She looked at the clean lines of the crafted wood cabinets, the colors of the dishes and glasses, and she remembered the care and time she and Artemis had put into selecting everything here. She felt the protection of their two-story suburban house all around her, so lovely in its fresh blue paint, sitting on two acres of yard with gardens and trees. And beyond their land were good neighbors, nice shops nearby, and schools. The town was called Halesburgh, and they had moved here only five years ago when Silas was just seven, when they decided that New York City had grown too dangerous.

Delia watched her niece for a moment. Then she pulled her shoulders back, smoothed her apron, grabbed a mug, poured a cup of coffee, and handed it to Emily.

"Thanks." Emily smiled, aware again how dependent they all had become on her Aunt Delia.

Delia Twist Kouris was Emily's only living relative, and when she first moved into their home, some four years ago, she was just a bossy handful. But Emily knew how difficult Delia's life had been, and so she helped to smooth the way. Things calmed down, and soon Aunt Delia was doing all the housework and most of the cooking to express her gratitude.

Delia was still a strong, solid figure of a woman who admitted to being fifty, though they all knew she was closer to sixty. She always wore her brown-gray hair pulled back, which showed off her wide forehead, high cheekbones, and mysterious dark eyes. And when she smiled, as she was doing now, those eyes projected a feeling of strength and purpose.

Emily felt all of a sudden too fragile. Her gentle green eyes filled with tears. Aunt Delia answered with a soft tap on Emily's cheek, a sign of understanding and support.

"One day at a time, right?" It wasn't often that Delia used one of these sayings, but Emily didn't mind. She was proud of her aunt's four years of sobriety. Delia tilted her head toward Silas, indicating that they must both carry on for his sake. Emily sighed and nodded agreement.

"Alright, that's enough technology. It's time for breakfast," Delia announced to Silas as she scooped scrambled eggs onto plates.

Silas looked up at Delia, making an effort to return from his thoughts so far away. He pushed his glasses back up into place on his nose and looked confused. Firmly, but kindly, Delia explained it to him:

"Breakfast. Ready. Now. You must eat so you have strength for running, and so your brain can grow and you can get even smarter, though I don't know how that is even possible."

Silas smiled at himself and closed his laptop. "All right, Auntie Dee, I got it."

Emily watched the way Delia handled her twelve-year-old son. There was a time when Silas wouldn't have answered at all. And now, because of Delia, he actually spoke. Still, Silas never said much. When he was a year old, a wise old doctor had told Emily that Silas was a special child. Emily was, at that time, an administrator at a special needs school in Manhattan, and her heart sank. But the doctor saw her reaction and shook his head. He told her that after so many years of watching babies grow up, he could tell that her son was unusually smart, and that she must always be patient with Silas and understand that genius children have special needs too. Emily often wondered how the old doctor could have known so much about such a young baby. But he was right.

"And no bacon for the boy who can eat no spices," said Delia as she set plates before them.

"Thanks, Auntie," Silas answered.

"Just like your father," she added as she sat down to eat with them.

"Thank you, Delia, this looks great." Emily was smiling, but her worry was still clear.

Delia nodded to herself once, swallowed a bite quickly, and happily announced, "There's just no getting around it; winter has been here too long, and I'm just in the mood to clean this house from top to bottom!"

Emily almost laughed, knowing exactly what Delia was doing. "Thanks, you're my favorite aunt ever."

"Because I'm your only aunt." Delia smiled as she reached for the coffee pot to top them off.

Silas looked up suddenly fascinated. "Can I have a cup of coffee?"

"No!" Both women surprised themselves as they answered him in unison.

* * *

"So, what do we know about the victim?" Artemis asked through his head-set as they flew east, high above the Long Island coastline. "He was an art dealer…?"

"Yeah, his name was Raphael Sharder," Drew answered. "Had two galleries: one in Southampton and one in New York City, on East 64th Street."

Artemis nodded. "Which is in your precinct and why Ray Gaines could call you in."

"Well, we all go back a long way on this thing," she said truthfully.

Artemis smiled grimly. "I know that gallery on 64th Street…"

"I've sent one of my guys to check it out," Drew said.

Detective First Grade Drew Sweeney of the NYPD Criminal Intelligence Section was Artemis's cousin, and six years older than him. She was a tall, fit woman with large swimmer's shoulders and strong hands. Her self-assured voice and movements reflected her military background. She had served in the Middle East before the NYPD. She was very aware that women in command positions in both those worlds were still a new commodity. So, she was dressed, as always, in proper police-business attire: black shoes, dark pants, white dress shirt, black jacket. Her dark brown hair was short and neat. Her aggressively handsome face was balanced by her clear and kind hazel eyes.

There was a time, when Artemis was just a child and she was still known as Mary Drew, that their fathers were NYPD detectives together. One of the cases they worked on was the Gardner Museum robbery, investigating possible links to mob figures in New York City. Because of that case, both of Artemis's parents were dead. But Drew's father, Mathew Sweeney, survived and rose through the ranks, becoming a captain before he retired just a few years ago.

At first, people suspected that Mathew Sweeney was responsible for his daughter's quick rise through the department. And maybe he had helped some. But Drew was a solid cop, with good command of herself and others, and she became a respected detective on the merits of her police work.

Artemis Bookbinder wanted to become a cop like his father. But his uncle Mathew insisted that he go to college first. There, Artemis excelled and stayed until he earned two degrees: a BA in criminology and a doctorate in art history. When Artemis finished his studies, he joined the NYPD, with the support of his uncle Mathew and his cousin Drew.

Artemis's quick, intuitive mind, and his specialized knowledge in art history, helped him solve a major case for the Metropolitan Museum some five years ago. The recovery of *The Sword of Ormond*, a strange and notorious artifact, brought much press attention to the then Detective Second Grade Artemis Bookbinder. Suddenly, reporters wanted information about Artemis, and stories appeared about the detective with a PhD in art history. And about his father, Nate Bookbinder, the detective who was killed years ago while investigating the Gardner Museum robbery. Artemis admitted, and it was printed, that the still unsolved Gardner case was very much alive to him.

All the attention made Artemis feel exposed and vulnerable. He and Emily, and their young son, Silas, were living on the Upper West Side, only a few blocks from the place where his parents were killed.

Artemis decided he would give up police work and retreat to the safe private sector. His return to teaching at Columbia had been greeted with tearful relief by Emily. At the time, five years ago, he was sure that he was doing the right thing to protect his family.

But right now, he was thinking about his son. That quirky little version of himself.

What would Silas think of me if I just gave up?

"That's it, sir," the pilot's voice, cracking through the headset, broke his thoughts. "They call the place The Arethusa."

Below them was a vast track of land bordered on the south by the ocean, where a high sea-wall with steps, and a security gate, ran the edge of the property. From there, a wooden walkway winding through tall dune grass led to the formal gardens. The plantings, still winter-wrapped in burlap, seemed to provide a barrier, protecting the wide lawn, covered pool, tennis courts, and the house itself. The Arethusa was an imposing New England–style mansion covered in cedar shingles and trimmed in clean white edges, reeking of wealth, privilege, and seclusion.

Circling to land, they could see the north edge of the property, where a long serpentine driveway led through tall evergreen hedges to a security gate. There, two local police cars were parked to keep onlookers away. The pilot set them down on the open lawn next to a stationary FBI chopper and more official vehicles.

Drew and Artemis hopped out, ducked under the slowing but still spinning blades overhead, and started for the house. As they straightened up again, Drew took a moment to adjust her jacket and attach her gold-blue shield to her belt. And Artemis felt what he often did when he was around his cousin Drew. That although Artemis was six feet tall, Drew's extra inch and greater physical strength somehow made him feel short. But he didn't mind. Drew had always been there for him when he needed her most.

As they approached the large slate patio, the French doors opened, and they were greeted by their old friend Ray Gaines. Ray had been an FBI agent for a long time, and though his years of service showed in the careworn lines on his face and his thinning gray hair, he still carried himself with a powerful, understated authority.

"Great to see you again, Ray," Artemis said warmly.

"It's been too long, son." Ray smiled back. "I'm glad you're back in action."

Artemis started to say that he was only a temporary consultant, but Drew cut him off:

"We all know that you love teaching about paintings and all that, but this is in your blood, Artie."

Artemis turned and looked squarely at his cousin. "I hate when you call me that."

Ray laughed and clapped Drew on her shoulder. "I'm just happy you're both here because I need your help."

With that, Ray turned and led them into the mansion.

Inside the door, another older, dark-suited agent stepped up to meet them, self-consciously buttoning his jacket over his expanded waistline.

Ray smiled and introduced them to Special Agent Bert Rocca, saying that he was someone he'd been through far too much with.

"It's really great to finally meet you, Dr. Bookbinder." Bert Rocca's gravelly voice carried a definite Boston accent.

"Please, call me Artemis."

"That was some damn good work on that Met Museum thing back when," Bert Rocca added.

And there it was again, and Artemis all at once felt too exposed. He managed to smile as he said, "Well, never believe everything you read."

"This way," Ray said, taking charge, "so far we've got no prints and no gun." He led them down a hall and into the room where Raphael Sharder lay dead on the floor.

*   *   *

Lucille watched Paul's intense lavender eyes become focused with purpose. His bare muscular chest lifted and dropped against her chest, making her nipples hard. She felt him so deep now inside her, his hips so perfectly meeting hers, faster now, almost desperate as he pounded into her. She, for the first time in forever, began to surrender and let go to the force of a man. Her eyes teared, and she let out a soft, uncertain moan.

Above her, Paul's eyes focused on her, and his hips slowed down. Suddenly, alert that he needed to be assured that she was alright, she thought back to the kind of things she'd said before, back then. She whispered,

"Yes, Paul, please… fuck… me… hard."

Paul grinned at her, like a boy really, she thought, as he bore down on her again.

"Good girl…," he growled.

Then she saw his eyes grow cold. His jaw clenched, his back arched, his hand slid up her chest, and his fingers tightened around her thin throat. Her eyes opened wide, a mix of fear and trust, as he came so deep inside her. She gasped and moaned in pleasure.

Paul watched her as he slowly released the pressure on her throat. His eyes softened, and that almost feminine smile returned. She carefully reached up and ran her fingers through his short soft hair. With a sigh, he gently lay his body weight down on her, pressing her deeply into the bed.

Inside her, she felt him grow softer, and his breathing slowed down. Lucille felt victory. So many women wanted to be here with Paul, but she was here. She couldn't wait to tell her sister.

And she felt grateful. After the mess that her life had become, after the ways she'd been treated by men… Here, now, she felt primally protected. Paul's perfect body covered her. It was a miracle.

With a sigh, Paul shifted his hips, and his penis slid out of her. She felt an overwhelming sadness and loss as he rolled off and lay beside her. He closed his eyes.

She lay as still as she could and listened as his breath grew more even. She smiled to herself, wondering if it was right to be sleeping with her doctor. She never thought this would really happen, though she had been fantasizing about it since their first meeting. And that was only three weeks ago. Ida, her sister, had read her the riot act and insisted that she see an old friend of hers, a respected Upper East Side psychiatrist, Doctor Paul Marin. He was thirty-six years old, taller than average, trim, muscular, and so nicely groomed and dressed. Only three weeks ago, and so much had happened since then.

From their first session, she had simply surrendered to his eyes—those powerful, strange eyes. And he was so handsome, almost pretty, with his soft, curly dark hair cut short, proud Greek nose, strong jaw, and almost cruel mouth—except when he smiled—which made her want to do anything for him. Anything! Lucille looked at the leather cuffs lying on the bed table and her red wrists and wondered just how far she would go for him.

He finally called last night, so late, in the middle of the night. He was so worked up. He really needed her. She smiled, feeling a kind of ownership of him. No, not really. It was just sex; she knew better. Still….

She watched him sleep. Such a male when he was awake. And so female when he slept. So cute, and so… scary. Just being here in Paul's bedroom seemed unreal, and a little confusing. He was her doctor, prescriber, teacher, mentor, and conduit to something he called *Sacred Voices*. It was a strange new world. To her, Paul Marin was a savior. She felt like she was standing on a bridge above the mess that her life had become, and for the first time she could see something in the future that was good.

Lucille looked around at the expensive furnishings, so tasteful and neat. She got up carefully so as not to wake him. Naked, she walked over to the large windows, stifling a shiver in the still chilly morning. Outside, the large tiled balcony framed a world-class view of Central Park, the Reservoir, and the buildings of the distant Upper West Side. Everywhere out there she could sense new life; soon enough winter would end, and then new buds on countless trees would be born. It was so quiet. This high up, there was no sound of traffic even though Paul's penthouse was on Fifth Avenue. She breathed in and felt so lucky to be there.

She walked across the soft carpeting to a full-length mirror.

Who else but Paul would have a full-length mirror in his bedroom?

She smiled at the thought.

He's sensitive. Like me.

Cautiously, Lucille lifted her eyes and looked at herself in the mirror. She shook her head in disbelief. She was proud of herself, that somehow at thirty years old she still looked so good. Her face was thin, elegant, almost fragile, with large trusting blue eyes and full lips. She ran her fingers through her long dark brown hair.

Maybe I should have my tits made bigger.

She turned slowly and looked at herself critically.

I bet Paul knows somebody good. Maybe he'd even pay for it...?

"You are so fucking hot standing there."

She jumped at the sound of his voice. Paul was sitting up on an elbow, watching her.

Pleased and self-conscious, she laughed as she knelt on the foot of the bed close to him.

"Sometimes you look like a cat." She smiled.

"Do I?" Paul watched her amused.

"A cat with the most beautiful lavender eyes," she said and suddenly felt awkward and unsure of herself. Carefully, she crawled next to him and put her head on his chest. Paul wrapped a protective arm across her bare shoulders. She breathed in.

"I love the way you smell," she whispered softly.

Paul smiled but said nothing.

"I just can't believe that I'm here, with you, in your bed. So many of the others want this, they'd be so jealous...."

"Little Lucille, don't go there," he quietly but firmly commanded.

She nodded in quick assent, adding, "Sorry, Paul, I'm just grateful for all you've done for me."

"You're welcome," he answered simply.

"Have you always had the gift?" she asked.

"Gift?" Paul smiled widely and said, "You mean the way I rocked your world last night?"

Still not sure of herself, she answered, "No, yes, no… I mean your Voices, the guides who talk to you."

"I knew what you meant," he gently ran his fingers across her back. "I've heard The Voices all my life, ever since I can remember."

Like a respectful child, she asked, "So, who are they, are they angels—"

Paul cut her off firmly. "I never talk about them."

She nodded quickly, eager to please. She looked up at him. "Well, I'm just very grateful to be allowed into your school."

As if called, Paul looked away from her, up above and to his right. This was the place he always looked when he was listening to his Voices; Voices that no one else could hear, and not even he could see. He smiled and nodded to them in agreement.

Looking back at her, he said, "They say that you are most welcome in The School, that the sacred number of students must be maintained, and since we lost one girl, we can welcome you in."

"And that was Beth something, right…?" she added, trying to be helpful.

"Who told you her name…?" He focused on her eyes.

"My sister," Lucille almost stammered. "Is that all right?"

Paul sighed and smiled gently. "I am too lenient with Ida, I always have been, but we have known each other a very long time."

"Since college, right?"

"Yes." Paul finished the subject with a nod and said, "I do hope you will take the class seriously."

"I will. I promise!" she answered devoutly.

"Good," he said to her as he turned his face up to hear The Voices again. He spoke softly, repeating what they were saying:

"They said that you are a *Being of Light*, dear Lucille. It will be for you to lead them out of their darkness and into your light." He closed his eyes and smiled.

Uncertain as to how to respond, she said, "Thank you, Paul. Um, please thank them for me…."

He opened his eyes and kindly whispered, "They hear you."

"Oh, yes." She so wanted to say the right thing to him. "I like the people in the class. They seem so dedicated to you and the work."

He just continued to watch her.

"And I will be too…. And, so far, they all seem to like me."

Paul smiled avuncularly. "Who wouldn't like you?"

Emboldened, she added, "And Roxie is so great…."

"We don't use our outside world names. We must protect The Sacred School," he instructed her patiently.

"Oh, right." She made an effort to remember what Roxie's name was in class. She focused her mind to recall the gem pendant necklace that each class member wore. Remembering, she carefully asked, "How long have you and *Ruby* known each other…?"

"A very long while," Paul answered with finality as he turned to check the time.

"How long have the classes been going on—"

"No, no, my little Lucille," he cut her off cheerfully, "no more questions about the classes."

"Yes, Paul." she said apologetically. "Sorry."

"It's okay," his voice grew light and playful, "your curiosity is one of your best features." He leaned to kiss her ear.

She giggled and rubbed against him. "And what else?"

Paul smiled. "Your tight body, your perfect little tits…."

"I'm too thin," she whispered.

Ignoring her, he continued, "Your sweet blue eyes...."

"Make me look like I'm a child, so foolish—"

"Stop that," he quietly commanded her.

And like a child who wanted to have the last word, she added, "And I'm too sensitive. I am. And you know it."

Paul lifted her chin up, and she looked into his eyes. He said quietly, "Don't put Lucille down. She has been through a lot, and she has survived. And survival is something to be honored. And there is no such thing as too sensitive."

"I just still get scared, you know, when I'm by myself," she whispered. "I'm afraid I won't be strong enough to really stay with it and stay clean."

"Trust me, Lucille. I will help you."

"Yes, Paul, I trust you," she said, looking at him with a kind of devotion. "I trust you more than I've ever trusted anyone."

"Good." And that boyish smile returned to his lips. "Because trusting your doctor is vital to your recovery. Okay. Let's get going." He swung himself away from her and got out of bed. "I'm so late! I just have time for a shower and to get to the office. Big day, a new patient."

She watched his perfect naked body walk off into the bathroom. The door closed, and she was alone.

* * *

Artemis, now wearing blue nitrile gloves, which he'd brought along because he was allergic to the latex ones the cops use, was kneeling over the chubby body of Raphael Sharder. Near him, at the foot of the bar cart, was a broken wine glass on its side and a dark red stain on the antique Turkish carpet. Leaning close to the body, but being careful not to touch anything, he examined the bullet hole at the base of the neck. He studied the wrinkled face of the victim.

"He looks kinda surprised, I think," said the man kneeling next to him.

"I agree," Artemis murmured absently, off in his own thoughts. He leaned to examine a folded white tissue on the floor near the body. It was stained with dark blotches. He breathed in and detected the stale scent of red wine.

"I'd guess 9mm, but we'll have to wait for confirmation on that," the man added.

That second piece of information brought Artemis back from his mental journey. He looked up curiously at the man next to him. He was in his late twenties, wearing jeans and an FBI field jacket. His compact body seemed full of energy, but he was completely still. His friendly face was turned toward Artemis, and his clever, intelligent eyes seemed to be waiting for a response.

"Who are you?" Artemis asked.

"Makani Kim, sir," the agent answered with respect.

"Call me Artemis. You're Hawaiian?"

"Yes. Born there. My parents are from Korea."

"Okay…," Artemis processed this. "It's nice to meet you, Makani. Did Ray assign you to me?"

"Yes," the agent answered, "and everyone calls me Mak."

"And I agree with you about the gun," Artemis continued, "definitely 9mm. And I'd be curious to know if the bullet can tell us the gun's country of origin."

Mak considered that for a second before he asked, "Because?"

Artemis smiled. "Because of that beautiful thing," he answered as he got up and went over to the large painted canvas over the fireplace.

"And you're sure it's the real thing?" Ray asked, as he and Drew watched. "No question," Artemis spoke quietly, almost reverently. "Stolen on March 18, 1990, this is one of the thirteen missing pieces from the Gardner

Museum in Boston. This is *Storm on the Sea of Galilee*. More than five feet tall and almost as wide. Rembrandt van Rijn painted this in 1633."

With his eyes still fixated on the masterpiece, he added sadly, "It has cost us all so much to be here today. Thank you, Ray. I appreciate your calling me in."

Ray came up behind Artemis and spoke softly. "Your father would have been so proud of you today." He placed a hand on the younger man's shoulder. Artemis flinched, and Ray let go.

"Still got that monkey on your back, son?" Ray asked, not unkindly.

Artemis smiled a little. "Well, you know. The world's got a sickness."

"I guess," Ray shrugged, "but there's always some damn thing somewhere."

"So, how did you get here so fast?" Artemis changed the subject. "I know the FBI is good, but the guy was killed just last night."

Ray nodded in agreement. "So, here's the thing. Yesterday morning, Raphael Sharder called the FBI in Washington and talked to me. He said he wanted to negotiate a deal to return one of the paintings stolen from the Gardner. The deal was for no names, no information. And he didn't want the museum's reward."

"That's a lot of cash not to want," Drew said as she joined them.

"Hell, he didn't need any more cash. Look at this place." Ray scoffed. "Raphael Sharder just wanted immunity and no questions asked."

"How did he sound...?" Mak Kim asked.

"What do you mean?" Ray said, turning to include the young agent in the discussion.

"Was he scared, being pressured...?"

"No, not frightened," Ray answered. "He sounded tired, old, and kinda... guilty."

"And you set up a meet?" Drew asked.

"Not an official one, no. I needed approval first, but we were already en route here by chopper when I heard that he'd been killed." Ray sighed.

"Who found the body?" Drew asked as she turned and looked at the dead man on the floor.

"The maid, when she arrived this morning around seven," Mak Kim answered. "She's pretty upset."

Artemis knelt down again next to Raphael Sharder. "What time yesterday morning did he call?"

"About eleven thirty," Ray answered.

"Seems news traveled kinda fast," Mak murmured.

"I agree. Too fast," Artemis said very softly as he studied the dead man's face.

"Ray?" Bert Rocca's respectful voice broke in. "We've got the maid in the kitchen if you're ready for her? She's calmed down enough to talk to, I think."

Ray nodded, signaled Artemis, Drew, and Mak to come along, and headed off to the very large, clean kitchen.

"This is Patty Figgins." Mak introduced them to a non-remarkable, late-middle-aged woman of undoubtedly Irish descent. She was sitting at a large stainless-steel table, slowly wringing her well-worked hands. She was dressed in a simple green-striped house dress. Her hair had come undone, her round face was blotchy from crying, and her eyes red. Patty Figgins flinched in quiet panic as they sat down around the table.

"That's all right, Ms. Figgins." Ray took charge. "We just need to ask you a couple of questions about what's happened here."

"Oh God, oh my God," she whispered, her eyes darting from face to face.

"I'm FBI Special Agent Ray Gaines, this is my associate Special Agent Bert Rocca." He indicated Bert, who alone remained standing near the door. "And Agent Makani Kim. He'll be making notes on what we say here, okay?"

Patty nodded but seemed vague. Ray continued:

"This is Detective Drew Sweeney of the New York City Police Department."

Patty Figgins looked at the woman sitting across the table. Drew nodded at her, a small gesture that conveyed authority. Patty flinched again and looked confused.

"And this is Dr. Artemis Bookbinder from Columbia University," Ray said, watching her carefully. "I've asked him here to identify the painting over the fireplace."

"Yes, sir," the maid managed in a reedy whisper, clearly overwhelmed.

"Let's start there," Ray said. "That's some painting Mr. Sharder had over the fireplace. Do you like it?"

"I've never seen it before in my life." Her voice was quiet but trembling with emotion. "I saw it this morning; it's never been there before. I came in and there he was on the floor, dear Mr. Sharder, who was always so kind and gentle. And then I saw the blood…" Her voice cracked and fresh tears came.

"That's all right, Ms. Figgins," Ray said soothingly.

Across the table, Artemis breathed in slowly and just barely nodded. It was a gesture that only his cousin Drew noticed.

Still weeping, Patty managed, "He was so nice to me, and just so old… Who would do such a thing to him…?"

"That's what we're going to find out. Try to calm yourself," Ray answered.

Quietly, so as not to distract Ray, Artemis got up and went over to the sink. Selecting a clean glass from the drying rack, he filled it with cold water from the tap.

"So, I understand that you got here this morning at seven. Was that when you usually arrive?" Ray asked.

"Yes," she whispered, "Almost always at seven."

"What do you mean?"

"Well, I mean that I get a day off, Mondays usually, and holidays off, of course. Mr. Sharder was always so kind to me...." She looked as if she might start crying again.

Artemis set down the glass in front of her and speaking gently said, "Here, Patty, drink this."

She took the glass in her shaky hands and sipped a little. Then she looked up at Artemis and nodded a small thanks.

Artemis asked, "And did Raphael Sharder live here alone?"

"Yes, yes, he did. He said he liked it that way. A very private person... he was."

"All alone, in this huge house?" Artemis asked in a knowing way.

"Well," she smiled a little for the first time, and spoke directly to him, "we used to entertain here a lot. When Mr. Sharder was younger, there was always a party here, and lots of house guests, and fun.... But that was years ago. You know how it is, we all get older. Nowadays, Mr. Sharder liked being alone, liked the quiet, reading books...."

"You've been here in this grand old house a long time, I'm guessing." Artemis smiled at her.

"Almost twenty years," she said proudly, her Irish accent suddenly stronger.

"And now," Artemis asked as he worked his way back around the table and sat, "any special friends of Mr. Sharder ever show up as house guests?"

"Not so as I'd remember." She shrugged a little nervously.

"A man who loved art this much. He must have had someone to share all this with," Ray picked up seamlessly. "Maybe there was some special woman in his life...?"

Unexpectedly, Patty Figgins chuckled, "Oh, God, no!" Then realizing she had said too much, she snapped her mouth closed and focused on Ray warily.

Ray asked, "So, was he gay?"

Patty swallowed once before she answered, "I really don't know. Probably. Well, no, maybe. It's not really for me to say.... You see he was very discreet, in an old-world way." And then in a rush she added, "He was charitable, very well liked in town, he liked going there, having a nice meal, maybe at the Primrose. It's a nice place. Do you know it?"

"Not yet, but we will," Ray promised.

Patty Figgins collected herself and took in each of them: the young Asian-looking agent taking notes, the heavier older agent standing like a guard at the door, the scary strong-looking woman cop sitting across from her. And next to the cop, that very thin, handsome man, who was kind enough to give her water. Her eyes settled on Artemis's sympathetic dark blue eyes.

"I should have been here. Last night." Her voice was raspy. "But I got a text from my older sister Mary. She lives in a home in Amagansett; she's got the Alzheimer's and is in a bad way. She texted me around four in the afternoon and said she needed me to come out right away. She's not knowing who she is half the time, and so when she texted, I just had to go. I asked Mr. Sharder, and he was so kind, as always, so kind to me. He said I should go and that he'd be fine with some scratch-together meal. I do always leave something in the fridge for him... Well, I always did."

"Can we see that text, Ms. Figgins?" It was the woman cop, Drew Sweeney, who asked the question. The quiet command of her voice seemed to surprise Patty. She nodded and pulled her cell out of her purse, which was by her feet on the floor. Controlling her trembling hands, she found the text and handed the cell to Drew, who read aloud:

"Dearest Biddy Socks, I need you right now."

Patty shrugged at Artemis.

Drew continued: "They are trying to steal my money." She looked up to Patty. "And I'm thinking no one steals her money there, right?"

"No," Patty smiled a little, "but it's a regular fantasy in her poor mind. The nuns that run the place are the salt of the earth and always so dear. By the time I got there, Mary had forgotten the whole thing. She forgets who I am too, for the most part," she added sadly.

Artemis smiled. "Uh… Biddy Socks?"

Patty smiled back. "She's called me that since I was born. Seems it's easier for her to remember way back, than now."

"Okay, so you left here, what, around four thirty?" Ray picked it up.

"Yes, sir." She turned back to the older man.

"And got back here when?"

"Oh, no, sir," Patty shook her head emphatically, "I never came back here. I had dinner with my sister Mary in her room around seven. And when she fell asleep, I left. Let me see, that was maybe around ten thirty or so. I drove back to Hampton Bays, that's where I live, and stopped off at the Antlers. It's a nice little pub near my condo. I stayed there a long time talking to Sal, the owner. After that I went straight home to get some sleep."

"You drove yourself home?" Drew Sweeney suddenly sounded like a cop.

"Well, no," she answered carefully, "Sal is a friend, a really good friend, and he doesn't let me drive if I've had a nightcap."

"Or two." Ray smiled.

"Yes, you're right there," she admitted. "So, what's the harm as long as I don't drive. Sal closed up the place and took me home."

"And did you ask Sal in…?" Ray followed.

Patty looked at him suspiciously. "That's kinda personal, don't you think?"

"We need to know where you were last night," Ray explained patiently. "And if this Sal can confirm your whereabouts, it will only help you."

29

Patty Figgins sighed. "There are no secrets in the world anymore. Yes, Sal and I have been friends… Yes, that kind of friends for a long time. We keep it quiet. It's a small town, and people got nothing better to do than get in your business. And yes, he stayed with me last night."

"All right," said Ray with a look to Mak Kim, "we'll check that out. So, are there other staff members here?"

"Well, no permanent staff." Patty Figgins was speaking more freely now. "There's a gardening company that comes once a week in season. But there's been no work yet, it's still a little too early. Mr. Sharder liked to cook for himself, or I would make something simple for him like meatloaf or a stew and leave things for him in the fridge."

Ray nodded. "But there must have been gatherings here? Friends, or businesspeople?"

"On the rare occasion we were entertaining a group, there's a local woman who comes in. She owns a little restaurant here in town, and she'd bring in food and help serve."

"That would be the Primrose Restaurant?" Mak asked, referring to his notes.

"Yes, that's it," she confirmed. "And her name is Maddy Griffin."

"And when was the last time you had a big function like that here?" Ray asked.

"God… it really has been a long time." Patty smiled wistfully. "Maybe a year ago, last spring. There was a big event at Mr. Sharder's gallery in town, and he hosted a small cocktail party afterwards here."

"Who came?" Artemis asked.

"Oh, a few press people, and some longtime customers, and friends of the artists." Her brow furrowed as she remembered. "A real mixed bag. I don't know names or anything much about that crowd. I always keep myself to myself and stay out of trouble."

Ray asked Patty for her address and number and that of her friend Sal's. Artemis gave her an encouraging smile, got up, and quietly left the kitchen. Intuiting where her cousin was going, Drew likewise got up and followed him out.

Artemis went back into the living room and stood in front of the Rembrandt. He felt Drew approaching, but he continued to stare at the painting, lost in thoughts of the past.

"It's not enough, you know," Artemis said quietly.

Drew did know exactly what he meant. "It's just a start; there are still twelve more stolen pieces out there somewhere."

"Yes. And it will never be enough, will it?" Artemis whispered.

Drew sighed. She chose to change the subject. "This hide-the-painting rig is really something. We'll have to find out who installed it and when."

Artemis nodded in agreement but said nothing.

After a moment Drew asked, "What do you make of the maid?"

"She's nervous," Artemis quietly mused. "But at least part of her story is true, she was drinking last night."

"I thought I saw you get something." Drew smiled. They had known each other a long time.

Still only half present in the room, Artemis continued, "Patty Figgins had three, maybe four drinks. Whiskey and soda, lime."

Drew shook her head. "It's just freaky how your nose can tell you that."

Artemis, still far off, nodded to Drew and walked away, stepping outside through the tall Baroque doors.

Outside, the air was cool and salty. It was still morning, the light soft and changing as the sun came and went behind swift moving clouds. Everywhere teams of FBI agents and Southampton police were searching for the murder weapon. But Artemis was already certain that they wouldn't find it.

He walked slowly across the lawn toward the pool house and the still covered in-ground pool. There he stopped. Something suddenly bothered him.

Artemis took a deep breath to clear his head, and using a technique he'd learned from his father a long time ago, he let his eyes just wander freely across the scene to see if anything jumped out at him.

And then, something did.

Agent Makani Kim was the first to happen upon him standing unmoving, staring at the pool house.

"Uh, Dr. Bookbinder…?" Mak asked gently. "Are you okay?"

"Artemis," he corrected, his gaze fixed, his voice far off.

"Right… Artemis. Um, Special Agent Gaines wants to know if you are up for talking to the press. He thinks you'll be better at it than him. And I've seen the old man with the press, and trust me, he's so right." Mak smiled, though Artemis didn't see him.

"Tell Ray no," Artemis murmured.

"Oh. Okay, I'll let him know…" Mak broke off and turned to study the area that Artemis was finding so fascinating. There was the pool house, a couple of doors, with two big empty garden pots on either side. And mounted above the doors was an old weathered ship's wheel.

"So… what? The wheel…?" Mak asked carefully.

"Yes. The wheel." Artemis took a long breath and started to return to the world around him.

"Not sure I get it," Mak said respectfully. "That kinda fits here… You know, old nautical things, ocean-front house, boats…."

"Exactly." Artemis turned, his eyes now alive and focused on the young agent. "First of all, Raphael Sharder was an art dealer, his house is full of expensive furniture, fabrics, antiques, and not to mention one stolen Rembrandt masterpiece. He appreciated *things*. Knew how to display things, how to care for them. He was orderly and careful. Did you see the tissue on the floor near the body?"

"Kept wine from running down the bottle when he poured, I think," Mak answered.

Artemis smiled and continued. "Right. But this"—he gestured to the ship's wheel—"he hung here, outside. How big would you say that is?"

"About three feet across, I guess," Mak said softly, trying to follow.

"So, it came from a large ship. It's old, well crafted, made of teak and brass…. And here"—Artemis moved closer and pointed to the middle of the wheel—"something has been removed."

Mak came closer and looked at a small indentation in the wood around the center brass hub.

"Maybe the name of the boat?" Mak offered.

"Yes." Artemis nodded. "Or a manufacturer's label…."

"Or maybe it just came this way, you know, from an antique store, or something." Mak shrugged.

"That is possible," Artemis answered. "But could you have your people take a look at it and see if they can tell where it came from?"

"Yes, sir," Mak answered before he could stop himself. Then with a smile he corrected, "Sure, Artemis."

"Thanks," Artemis said. "And I'd be interested to know if Raphael Sharder kept a boat around here."

"Something kinda large." Mak smiled. "I'm on it."

"So, he was eighty-two years old. Any relatives?" Artemis continued as they looked around the boathouse together.

"Nothing we've found yet, but we're just starting."

"His state-of-the-art security system?" Artemis asked.

"Yeah, that must have cost a fortune, and it's been recently updated I think," Mak answered. "It was turned off at the terminal at the front gate. There was no break in."

Artemis stopped and looked at him. "Somebody knew the code?"

"Yeah, seems possible," Mak nodded.

"The Arethusa," Artemis quietly mused. "Historic house, built in the 1920s. Know where the name comes from?"

Mak shrugged. "I kinda think Greek mythology...?"

Artemis smiled approvingly and turned to look at him. "Good. Arethusa was a nymph. She was the daughter of Nereus, and her story had to do with water and fountains. Percy Bysshe Shelley wrote a poem about her." He turned to look at the old mansion, his voice floating further away. "But this place wasn't named for her. Arethusa was the name of a schooner used for bootlegging during Prohibition. The owner became a very wealthy rum runner. He built this place in the 1920s."

Artemis walked away, deep in thought.

Mak watched him make his way past the parked helicopters, the wrapped-up gardens, and onto the wooden walkway that led toward the beach. Mak turned back to look at the old ship's wheel mounted above the pool house doors. He took out his cell and took a series of pictures.

At the edge of the property, Artemis came to a tall metal security fence and a gate that barred him from going down to the sea. A few feet beyond the fence, a rusted steel seawall dropped away to the eroded beach below. This created a man-made cliff some fourteen feet high. The top of the wall stood a few feet higher than the land, and its edge was ragged metal, as sharp as razor wire. At the base of the wall, where the ocean's rough waves were breaking, rocks and riffraff had been piled up, making the area below impossible to navigate.

All that effort.

Artemis wondered if Raphael Sharder ever really felt safe here. With a sigh, he turned and looked back at The Arethusa, the magnificent old mansion across the dunes.

The security system was coded off. Did Raphael Sharder know his killer?

* * *

Lucille Orsina sat in a small booth in a tiny luncheonette on Third Avenue and 66th Street, with a half-eaten English muffin and a coffee in front of her. An old sign above the door read: Eat Good Here. Grammatically incorrect, but for the most part true; the place was crowded with professionals hurrying through their lunches. Lucille checked her watch. Her sister, Ida, was late, as usual. Her office was just a few blocks away on Madison, but she was always overbooked. Ida Orsina was already running a respected practice when, a few years ago, she'd been featured on a TV News exposé as one of the five best dermatologists in New York City. That had been the work of her prize client Paula DeVong, the host of the show.

Ida Orsina banged nosily through the door, called out a greeting to the older waitress behind the counter, asked her to get her a coffee, spotted her sister, and pushed her way across the small, crowded space. Ida sat down with a thump, pulled off her stylish vintage plaid jacket, dropped her bright green leather bag on the tiny table, and too loudly greeted her sister. Lucille inwardly winced but smiled. Ida had always been so good to her.

Ida was thirty-six years old, some six years older than Lucille. They were all that was left of their family. Ida was attractive in a controlled bohemian way. Her hair was straight, short, and startlingly red, dyed regularly with henna. Her pronounced nose heightened the determined look of her sharp eyes. Her now signature look was somewhere between a dramatic page boy and an Egyptian queen. She took a deep breath, smiled, and focused completely on her sister.

"You look well," she said and then, forcing herself to speak more quietly, added, "Are you?"

"Yes," Lucille answered and smiled back, so ready to tell her about her and Paul.

"Good." Ida nodded. But before Lucille could go on, Ida said, "Sorry, I've only got a half hour." She turned away and called over the waitress.

Lucille waited quietly.

The waitress came over and put down a coffee. Ida ordered a tomato soup and a ham sandwich and, without asking, ordered the same for her sister.

"We have to get some meat on your bones, and you have to eat more than just an English muffy and a coffee," she announced as the waitress left. Lucille nodded again and shifted in her seat. Ida laughed at herself. "Sorry, I'm just being me. I think you look great. I really do."

"Thanks," Lucille answered and pulled at the cuffs of her shirt.

Ida never missed much. "What's with the long sleeves and cuffs? I thought you hated having your wrists covered?"

Lucille giggled, the sound happy and unexpected. "I'm just trying new things, that's all," she deflected. Then, like a child busting with good news, she added in a euphoric whisper, "I slept with Paul last night!"

Ida's eyes became hard and clear, but a cautious smile spread across her perfectly made up red lips.

"Paul is a god," Lucille added in quiet triumph. "I already trust him so much!"

"Well, good," Ida said very quietly. A long moment of silence passed between them.

"Good, good," Ida finally managed to continue. "You do know though, that Paul is... well, Paul. He has always had lots of... friends around."

"Like the women in his class, you mean?" Lucille asked.

Ida paused again before she answered. The waitress arrived and put down their food. Ida asked for a couple of waters, and the waitress went off.

"We don't talk about the class out here," Ida said not unkindly.

"Right, sorry." Lucille nodded obediently.

The waitress returned, put down their waters and went away.

Suddenly remembering, Lucille opened her purse and took out a small bottle of pills, shook out two, and popped them into her mouth.

Ida nodded with approval. "Paul prescribe those?"

"Yes," Lucille answered as she washed the pills down with water.

"Look. You are the most important thing. I'm so proud of you, the way you've gotten yourself sorted out," Ida said.

"So far, so good." Lucille smiled hopefully.

"And, you know, I'm glad that Paul is helping you so much. But remember, this is about you. It's your time. Your life."

"Did you ever sleep with Paul?" Lucille asked, too quickly.

Brought up short, Ida smiled and sipped her coffee. "Well, we've known each other a long time."

"Since college, yes," Lucille persisted. "But did you?"

Ida sighed. "Yes, but that was a long time ago."

"Okay then." Lucille nodded, accepting the news. "Is that why you're being so cautious about me and Paul?"

"No, I wasn't thinking about me," Ida stalled.

Lucille bit her lower lip, and Ida could see the new worry in her eyes.

"Look, eat something, and I'll try to explain," Ida commanded. Lucille lifted her sandwich up and took a small bite, watching her sister.

"Okay. I know I said that we can't talk about class," Ida began, dropping her voice, "but you need to know how things work there. Paul's work with us is sacred…."

"Yes," Lucille whispered, "I love that."

"And the work," Ida continued, "requires Paul to relate in a personal way with all of us. A very close, personal way. Especially when someone is new to the group, like you. Understand?"

Lucille looked stunned. She folded her hands on the tabletop.

"Look, Paul is a guy," Ida kept on, "a powerful, sexy guy. We all get that. And he's also the conduit to a higher power. So, he does things his own way. And if you mean to be part of the group, you have to be okay with that."

"I thought I saw something between him and Roxie," Lucille whispered.

Ida gave her a warning look.

"Okay then, between him and *Ruby*," Lucille said, her eyes filling with tears. "So, is he sleeping with all the women in the class?"

"No." Ida reached across the table and grabbed her sister's hands. "No, I'm not saying that. And I'm sure that Paul has real feelings for you, otherwise he never would have invited you in."

"Didn't you arrange that?" Lucille looked confused.

"No, only Paul can invite people in." Ida's voice was now warm and reassuring. "I sent you to him because I knew he was the right professional to help you get through your... hard times. I didn't know he was going to invite you into the class, but I am really glad he did."

"It was only because that girl Beth Schaefer left and there was a space, I guess," Lucille said sadly.

"No"—Ida gripped her hands tighter—"That was just the door opening. You had to be there to walk through it. You are the important one here, okay."

Lucille looked at her powerful, strong sister who was trying so hard to support her. Then, after a moment, she said, "Thanks. I'm okay." It lacked conviction.

"Good." Ida nodded and cautiously let go of her hands.

Lucille took a sip of coffee.

"It's cold," she murmured softly.

"Eat something." Ida smiled.

Lucille sipped her tomato soup, and Ida started eating quickly.

"Can I ask you something else about the class?" Lucille said gently.

"I guess," Ida answered.

"And can I use their real names?" Lucille asked, suddenly sounding like a child.

Ida smiled. "What the hell, help yourself."

"I know that in the class we represent something to do with sacred numbers. And there's Paul, and all of us women...."

"Right, we and Paul make up the *Sacred Six*," Ida confirmed.

"So, what's with that guy Greg? How did he get in the class?"

Ida answered factually, "Paul said that The Voices told him that Greg was the exception."

"Because he's gay...?" Lucille asked, with a hint of a smile.

"No, Paul said that we needed a man to serve as the *Holy Protector*," Ida answered patiently.

"Greg seems a little precious for that, don't you think?" Lucille smirked.

"Yeah, I guess." Ida smiled back. "We women are the inner circle. Greg is other. That's why he doesn't have a gemstone."

"Oh." Lucille tried to sound like she understood what that meant. "And when will I get a gemstone?"

"Whenever Paul deems it the right time," Ida answered with finality. "Anyway, Greg is a good guy, pretty funny too, when you see him outside of class. *Ruby...* I mean Roxie Lee brought him along maybe three or four years ago. He works at TVNews, too."

"I know that Roxie is Paula's boss there, right?"

Ida barked out a sharp laugh, then dropped her voice and said, "Don't let Paula DeVong hear you say that. She's the on-air talent, the face that everyone sees. And she knows it. Roxie is her producer, and Greg and Deni work behind the scenes there."

"Deni, too. That's a lot of television people in class...." Lucille sipped her soup.

"Yeah, I guess so," Ida answered and then turned to flag down the waitress, signaling for the check.

"Well, it feels pretty impressive to be in an esoteric class with Paula DeVong," Lucille admitted.

"And speaking of the face everyone sees, Paula is my two o'clock, so I'm out of here." Ida got up, pulled on her jacket, grabbed the check from the passing waitress, threw down a tip, and, leaning over, kissed Lucille on the top of her head.

"I really am so proud of you," she whispered before she abruptly turned away, marched through the still crowded restaurant, and paid the bill at the register. With a quick wave, Ida banged through the glass door, and disappeared down the always busy street.

As she watched her go, Lucille's smile faded, and she hugged herself.

*   *   *

It was a half block off Park Avenue and called the 64th Street Gallery, a name that described its location as well as the simplicity of intent. It was known as a good place to buy very expensive minimalist modern art: mostly paintings, collages, and some small sculptures. Situated down a few steps in a beautifully restored old townhouse, it had large rounded bay windows that allowed the passersby to see the art within.

A young Black man with a strong build, close-cropped hair, and sharp eyes approached the door. He was dressed in an overcoat, jacket, and tie; and on his belt was the gold and blue shield of an NYPD detective. He pushed the door but found it locked. It was only midafternoon on a Friday. He knocked loudly on the glass.

Inside, he sensed, more than saw, movement. And then, from the back of the shop, a figure appeared. She approached the door with obvious fear. She was a good-looking woman, with dark blonde hair pulled into a neat ponytail and dressed in the casual elegance expected of a high-end art gallery worker. She came to the door and said in a loud voice that the gallery was closed.

"I know that," he replied as he lifted up his badge for her to see. "NYPD. I need to talk to you. Could you please let me in?" His tone was friendly but commanding.

She looked past him to the sidewalk and the construction scaffolding of the building next door. Assessing that he was alone, and taking the time to look closely at his badge, she nodded, unlocked the door, and let him in.

"I'm Detective Jerome Clayton Collins," he identified himself as he closed the door behind him. He looked around the well-appointed gallery and at the art pieces. He didn't like them much but knew not to comment. "You work here?" he asked.

"Yes, I run this place," she answered. She looked at his friendly face and volunteered, "My name is Beth Schaefer."

"Nice to meet you," the detective answered. "And this place is owned by Raphael Sharder, is that right?"

She breathed in a short sharp breath and nodded yes. Tears welled up in her eyes and ran freely down her cheeks.

"I see you've heard the news, then." Detective Collins sounded sympathetic but was watching her closely. "You okay?"

She nodded again and walked away. She eased herself down, sitting on a gold upholstered chair by an antique desk. Beth put her hands over her face, her shoulders rounded forward, and she began to weep. The detective sat down across the desk from her. He spoke kindly:

"I'm sorry for your loss, I am. I can see he meant a lot to you."

After a moment she was able to collect herself. She wiped away her tears, pulled herself together, and looked up at the cop. "What can I help you with?" she said.

"Well"—he pulled out his pad and pen—"I guess the first thing would be how you heard the news? Raphael Sharder was killed last night, and the news hasn't been released yet."

"I got a call this morning. From my brother. He works at TVNews. And you're right. Raphael meant the world to me. He was always so kind." She swallowed hard to keep herself from more tears.

"And what's your brother's name?" he asked.

"Greg. Greg Schaefer," she answered, opening the desk and finding some tissues.

"And how long have you been working here?" he continued.

"About six years now, I guess. I applied for the job of sales assistant, and Raphael and I just sort of hit it off. A few years ago, he decided that he wanted to spend more time out in Southampton." Beth gulped again to steady her voice. "And I got a promotion and became full-time manager here."

"He must have trusted you a lot, then." He smiled.

"Oh, yes. And me him. I can't believe anyone would hurt him." She began to cry again. "Did he suffer much?"

"No," he answered, suddenly aware that he wished he could make this easier for her. "He apparently died instantly."

"How?" she asked simply, looking up and finding the detective's eyes for the first time.

"Shot at close range," he answered carefully and truthfully. "From behind."

She took in the news with difficulty. "God have mercy on his soul," she whispered. "Have you caught the fucker who did it?" she added sharply.

The contrast of her sorrow and this new voice of raw, quiet anger surprised him, but he understood it. "No, but there's a lot of good people on this. We will."

"Thank you," she said sincerely. "You're being very nice to me, Detective…?" She looked apologetic that she couldn't remember his name.

"Collins"—he smiled at her—"Jerome Clayton Collins."

"That's a lot of name." She nodded as if she'd like to remember it. "So… they call you Clay?"

"No, Collie." He was still smiling at her.

"That's…," she seemed unable to process, "that's…cute."

"Nah, just messing." He laughed, a quiet, gentle sound. "They call me Clayton."

"That's better. Clayton,"—she smiled back at him—"nice to meet you."

"Me too."

Having opened a line of trust with her, the detective continued to ask questions. He learned that Raphael Sharder mostly stayed out in Southampton, where his other gallery was. But occasionally, he'd come into the city and stay at his apartment, which was only a few blocks away. He took down that address.

She said that she didn't know anything about Raphael's friends, his social life, or his past. And that she hadn't heard anything about the stolen art piece.

Clayton asked for and got a printout of the 64th Street Gallery's clients, of past purchases, and a list of artists whose work was displayed currently. Finally, he took down Beth Schaefer's contact details and where she lived in Brooklyn. She said that she was also a painter, hopeful of one day having a career, but in the meantime, she mostly painted at home in her free time.

"Nice meeting you, Beth. I really am sorry for your loss," Clayton told her as she walked him to the door.

"Nice meeting you, too."

"We'll be in touch." He smiled and left.

Beth locked the door and watched him go. And when he was out of sight, she quickly went back to what she was doing before he arrived.

In the back room of the gallery, the door of the small wall safe was still open, and her purse lay on a table nearby. Moving now in controlled panic, she took out a large envelope containing cash and shoved it into her purse. She closed the safe, pulled on her designer jean jacket, slung her purse over her shoulder, and walked quickly out through the gallery.

At the front door, she looked back with sadness. She turned out the lights, let herself out, and locked the door behind her. Taking a deep breath, she went up the few steps to the sidewalk and turned to walk under the construction scaffold. There, without warning, a large, dangerous-looking man stepped into her path. She let out a small yell before she realized she knew him.

"Jesus fucking hell," she gasped, "you scared the shit out of me, Ladimir!"

The man waited until she calmed herself and said nothing. He was a foot taller than her, with big shoulders and arms, a strange pale face and odd eyes. His left eye was much bigger than his right. She had met this man a few times before, but then he was always smiling and friendly. This new persona was quietly terrifying.

"You really did scare me," she repeated, now sounding small and fearful.

"Good," he said grimly, his Slavic accent strongly coming through. "Now I know you'll listen. I hope you do. It could help you to live a long time."

"What...?" she managed.

"I think you should leave. Today," he said quietly.

She was afraid this would happen. Raphael had warned her. She started to tremble. She thought that her legs might give out from under her.

"I am. I'm going away tonight, I swear it," she whispered urgently.

Suddenly kind, the large man reached out and took hold of her shoulders. "That's all we want, Beth Schaefer. Never to hear from you, or about you, ever again. Do you understand?"

Beth felt the power of his large hands on her shoulders. Tears started down her cheeks again, but she found the courage to look up into his strange eyes. "I promise. You will never hear from me again."

"That's nice." He smiled darkly at her.

He let go of her shoulders, and she stepped quickly around him, heading for the corner of Lexington. Without looking back, she hurried down the crowded avenue, went down the subway steps, and caught a train heading to Brooklyn.

Daylight was just starting to fade as she came up from the Prospect Place station. She almost ran the few blocks to her four-story walk-up apartment. Inside her home, she threw some clothes and supplies in a suitcase. In the kitchen, she grabbed her checkbook and some papers. She wrote a short note to her landlady and left it on the old wood table. From the bureau by her bed, she dug out a small jewelry case. Opening a few buttons of her blouse, she looked at herself in the mirror. On a silver chain around her neck, she wore a single large pink gemstone. Forcing her hands to stop trembling, she undid the clasp, carefully placed the necklace in the case, and tucked it into her suitcase.

With her few possessions gathered, she headed to the door. There, Beth turned back and took in the little apartment. She had loved living here. Under the skylight, her easel was still set up, a water color seascape, left there unfinished. She sighed at all that she'd have to leave behind.

Then an idea occurred to her, something she could do in the name of honor. With purpose, she went over to the painting on the easel. She opened a tube of dark blue paint and with a fine brush added something to the lower right corner of the painting. She looked at it for just a second and smiled. Then, with a worried look at the time, she regathered her things and left.

Outside of her building, she hailed a cab, got in, and told the driver to take her to LaGuardia Airport, Terminal B.

From across the street, a very fat man saw her go and smiled. He took out a cell phone and hit a button.

"She's gone," he said and hung up.

* * *

Paula DeVong's live news program was shot in a modern building on the Upper West Side of Manhattan, at Columbus and 64th Street. It was six o'clock Friday, three hours to air, and the large studio on the seventh floor was busy with crews doing technical setup: cameras and lights being checked, the news desk wiped down, and in the control room, staff were reviewing graphics.

Stairs along the double-heighted studio wall led up to the floor above. Here, on the eighth floor, the newsroom staff was moving in controlled frenzy, preparing for the last show of the week. The central area of the large open space was patterned with work stations and short half-wall partitions. At opposite corners were two glass-enclosed offices, and from one of these a short, chubby, olive-skinned middle-aged woman holding a mug rushed out. Anna Canneli looked out of place in this world of intense young professionals. Her beady, close-set eyes grew dark as she saw that two people were in her way at the coffee station. Without a word, she pushed them aside and filled her mug with coffee.

Greg Schaefer, one of the pushed people, looked down at the top of Anna Canneli's head and wondered why she always wore her hair pulled back and greasy. She was balding, and that look just wasn't helping at all.

"I hope we're not in your way?" he said pointedly, but Anna ignored him and went to stand by the reception desk. There she could see the elevators through the glass walls. There she would be ready to greet her boss Paula DeVong the moment she arrived. Anna checked her watch and bit her lip. Paula was late... again. And people were starting to notice.

"She looks like a faithful dog," Greg smirked to the other person who Anna had pushed aside.

"Waiting to hear her master's voice… *woof.*" Deni Diaz laughed and shook her head.

With a ding, the elevator doors opened, and Paula DeVong stepped out like a star, and Anna Canneli ran, being careful not to spill the coffee, to greet her.

Paula pulled off her expensive jacket, revealing her trademark rose quartz necklace, making sure that everyone in the large office space had noticed her arrival. Paula was described by some reviewers as mousey, spoiled, slightly chubby, and shortish. But maybe they were just jealous. Her fans liked her ambitious, non-threatening yet aggressive presence: the way she interviewed people, her sharp sense of humor, and especially her track record of seemingly always being at the right place and right time when important news events had happened. That, in particular, and the ratings that came with it, is what had caught the attention of the hierarchy and earned her a show of her own a little over a year ago.

She took a sip of coffee and winced.

"Cold," she commented unhappily.

"I'll get another," Anna simpered.

"Never mind"—Paula sighed—"it'll do." She tossed her jacket at Anna and started for her office.

"You look wonderful, your skin so… fresh!" Anna gushed happily as she followed.

"Thanks. Ida Orsina is a fucking god," Paula proclaimed, and as they passed Greg and Deni, she ordered: "Meeting in five, round up the troops."

"It was supposed to have been five minutes ago," Deni said sotto voce to Greg.

"And thanks for showing up, your Majesty," Greg added quietly.

"And do we think Anna Canneli can get her nose any further up Paula's ass?"

"Nope, probably not." Greg laughed.

In the year or so that they'd been working together, Deni and Greg had become fast friends.

Deni Diaz was a fiery up-and-coming twenty-eight-year-old news writer. She was attractive in a petite, athletic way and was a dedicated workaholic who was respected for her endless energy, a trait that helped her survive the continuous, grinding schedule of television news.

Greg Schaefer was more relaxed about himself and his career. He was an openly gay man in his thirties, of medium height, with shrewd blue eyes and a kind open face. Always careful of his appearance, he dressed in fashion-forward business attire, which suited his role as assistant to the executive producer.

"Well, we live to obey." Greg smiled and poured a cup of coffee. "Time to tell the boss what's going on."

"For the A Segment, we're still going with the first US death reported," Deni confirmed as she walked him to the foot of the stairs that led up to the executive offices.

"Yes, unless Roxie gets her source to confirm the other story," Greg said with a nod.

"I bet she does. Why else would she have sent Moira out to Southampton?" Deni looked at him hoping he'd say more.

"Well, until Roxie gets the goods, the A Segment stays put." He smiled. "Though I'm not sure the country really gives a shit about a virus."

"I know." Deni sighed. "But the interview should be hot. I just talked to the Senator, and she's ready to rip the President a new asshole for how he's handling this thing."

"Excellent." Greg laughed.

"And how's our Brit Twit tonight?" Deni asked, dropping her voice.

Greg shrugged. "So far, so good, I guess." And he started up the stairs.

"But for how long, I wonder."

Greg stopped, leaned close to her, and said very quietly, "Hush, if he knows I told anybody…he'll have my nuts in a sling."

Deni couldn't help herself. "Lucky for him!"

"I know." Greg laughed and promenaded up the steps. "And that so will never happen."

Paula DeVong stood looking out her glass-enclosed office at her busy staff. It had taken so much to get here. And her show was doing well, getting notice and praise. But she was worried about her future. Nothing was more temporary than television, and she knew it. She knew that she was still pretty, but she was starting to feel that it was taking longer and longer to keep it that way. Her highlighted brown hair, her perfect makeup, her stylish clothes were starting to feel like just so much work.

Somewhere behind her, she heard the drone of Anna Canneli listing her messages. With a sigh, Paula walked to her desk, opened the top drawer, took out a chocolate, and being careful not to spoil her lipstick, popped it in her mouth.

Anna audibly gasped.

"Shut up," Paula commanded gently and closed the drawer loudly. "There has to be some fucking reward for all this work, right?"

Anna nodded and too quickly said, "Absolutely! And nobody deserves it more than you!"

"All right, all right." Paula smiled at her faithful assistant. "Where's Roxie?"

"In her office, and something's up. She's been asking for you." Anna smiled hopefully.

With an imperious wave of her hand, Paula dismissed her assistant, who retreated to her small adjoining cubicle.

On her way across the newsroom floor, Paula noticed a particular empty desk and frowned. That Moira Weyland was never where she was supposed to be. Paula wondered if Roxie had sent her out on something. Across the room, Paula could see Roxie in her glass-walled office. She was on a call, pacing. She looked upset. Paula went up the three steps to Roxie's door, knocked once, and walked in.

Roxie's office was nicknamed by her staff the Watchtower because of the way she could keep an eye on the whole newsroom from here. Also, it was on the outside corner of the building, so she had a commanding view of Lincoln Center across the street, the constant traffic, and the busy tourists.

Roxie waved Paula in and indicated she should close the door behind her.

Roxie Lee, the supervising producer of Paula's show, was a beautiful, tall, powerful woman with striking features—very dark black skin, clear sharp eyes, strong cheekbones, and a sensual, almost too perfect, figure. She wore her hair short and natural. On her ears were simple silver earrings and laying perfectly in the low cleavage of her dark jacket and open white shirt was a single ruby on a silver chain.

Roxie exuded a constant adult-in-charge professionalism, which had earned her much respect. Together with Paula, this relatively new show of theirs had become a force to be noticed.

"Thank you, sir. Thanks, as always," Roxie said as she finished her call. Upset, she turned away from Paula and looked out the window.

"You okay?" Paula asked.

"So many people out there," Roxie mused as she collected herself. "Where the fuck are they all going?"

"Dinner before a show, of course," Paula offered quietly, waiting for Roxie to say more. And when she didn't, Paula added, "So, you sent Moira out on something?"

"Trust you to notice that." Roxie turned back to her friend with a smile. "Yeah, I did. Something's up. Something big."

Up one floor on the executive level, Greg Schaefer walked into the office of his boss, Executive Producer Jock Willinger. Jock, an older gaunt man, was dressed like a character in an old British sci-fi film: a dark gray suit, a button-down white shirt, a thin black tie. His pale long, oval face was topped with carefully combed over white and black receding hair. He wore thick-rimmed black glasses and had a habit of repeatedly pulling on his very large ears when he was nervous.

Greg set down the mug of coffee and brushed off the cigarette ash that had fallen on Jock's suit sleeve.

"I thought you'd given that up… again," Greg said pleasantly.

"Such a shite," Jock muttered, his reedy voice thick with his Liverpool accent. Shaking his head, he stubbed out his cigarette and took a gulp of coffee.

In England, Jock's oldest friends called him Taffy, a jovial moniker from his school days. But it was a long time since he'd been home. Here they called him the Brit Twit or the Slimy Limey, but never to his face.

Jock's office was directly above Roxie's and had the same views of the oncoming night in New York City. But Jock never looked out the windows much anymore. His desk was piled high with files, and the shelves behind him were crowded with mementos of a long television career.

When he first came to America, some twenty years ago, his Liverpool inflections had made him quite popular. There were still enough people around to remember the Beatles, he would joke, which was helpful as he had come to the States seeking a fresh start. He had come up through the ranks of news television in London, but after some early success, he had a string of failures. So, he'd burned his bridges and come to America, where he caught a break and was picked up by a New York news program. He determined then to learn how to become a survivor in corporate television.

Through time, Jock Willinger had learned two ways to treat people. To the hierarchy he was always polite, smiling, and eager to flatter. His other managerial mode was reserved for his staff and crews in moments of crisis: often yelling at the top of his ragged, panicky voice every fucking obscenity he could string together. This had instant results of obedience but made him hated by the rank and file.

But to Paula DeVong, his rising star, and Roxie Lee, his next in command, he was always respectful and supportive. He also extended this courtesy to Greg, his assistant, because he knew he was a close friend of both women. And they, after all, made him look good to the Network.

In the past few years, he'd watched as Paula DeVong went from being a good on-location reporter to a minor cultural phenom due to her uncanny abilities. She had miraculously been on the scene when an illegal drug factory was raided in New Jersey. And when a small terrorist cell was captured in the Bronx. And when a shipment of drugs being smuggled into the port of Newark was dropped from a crane and broke open, and arrests were made.

So, it was a good moment for Jock Willinger, executive producer. Or it should have been. He was all too aware that the *shite* was about to hit the fan.

As Greg followed Jock down the steps and through the newsroom, he filled him in on the night's rundown. Jock nodded his approval as they went into the bullpen, a large workplace with a long table and a dozen chairs, all facing a couple of whiteboards covered in notes.

"Evening, Jock," Deni Diaz said respectfully as she rushed in with her laptop and took a seat. Jock nodded a little but said nothing. The group that was assembling noted the silence and sat down uncomfortably. Sitting next to his boss, Greg caught Deni's eye and gave her a supportive shrug.

Like comic relief, Anna Canneli bustled in, in her usual self-important way, carrying a pad and pen in case her hero Paula DeVong uttered anything important.

Then Paula and Roxie entered, and Roxie swung the door closed behind them. Roxie looked at Greg and gave him a quick nod. Then she addressed the group.

"The A segment is changing. The Senator will still go on, but everything slides," Roxie said with quiet authority. "Deni, have your team find us a graphic of a painting stolen from the Gardner."

Jock Willinger sat up and said with happy surprise, "Really?"

Paula DeVong looked him square in the eyes and smiled. "Yes. Really."

"Holy Fuck Me," was all he could manage.

Paula, her eyes now gleaming like a big hungry cat, said, "Exactly!"

From the back of the room, the whinny voice of Anna Canneli broke in, "What's the Gardner...?"

Greg looked at Deni and rolled his eyes. "1990, Boston museum, art stolen, never recovered... Read a damn book!"

Anna, embarrassed, flushed red and stared at Greg with hatred.

"Greg, play nice," Roxie commanded though she was smiling.

"How many paintings?" Deni asked.

"Just one, as far as we know," Roxie answered. "One of the Rembrandts: *Storm on the Sea of Galilee.*"

Greg whistled softly, and Deni nodded to one of her staff, who rushed out to hunt down a graphic.

*   *   *

It was a little before 9:00 p.m. when Artemis Bookbinder pulled up in the driveway of his New Jersey house. He turned off the engine. It was quiet and foggy. He got out of the car and took a long breath of cold air. The house before him was over a hundred years old and had been completely restored. It was a fine house with strong stone walls and large windows. The clapboards of the upper story were freshly painted blue and the trim white. There was a yard with trees outlined by an old stone wall. Even now, in the dead of winter, it looked so safe.

Artemis sighed and entered the house through the back door. In the kitchen he found the ever-dependable Aunt Delia cleaning up.

"You hungry?" she asked. "I've a plate warming for you."

"Thanks, maybe in a bit. Where's Emily?" he answered.

"She and Silas are watching the news." She turned to take him in. "Maybe a glass of wine?"

"A single malt would do better." He smiled gratefully.

"Right you are," Delia said with understanding. "I'll bring it to you."

"You sure?" he asked kindly. He respected Delia's dedication to AA.

"It's not a problem." She smiled. "Go sit down."

Artemis nodded his thanks and walked down the hall to the living room. Emily and Silas turned and saw him. Silas muted the television. Emily got up and wrapped her arms around Artemis. He breathed in and held her. She always smelled so good. He had been worried about what to say, how to explain. But now that he was home, with her body pressed so tightly against him, everything felt all right again.

Delia came in and gave him his drink.

"Dad," young Silas called, bringing everyone's attention to the television, where a graphic of the Rembrandt painting was filling the frame. Silas turned up the volume, and they watched as Paula DeVong reported the murder of an art dealer in his mansion in Southampton. And that they had positive confirmation that one of the stolen art pieces from the Gardner Museum had been recovered.

In Dr. Paul Marin's penthouse apartment on Fifth Avenue, two people had joined him to watch the same program. Paul sipped his drink as he watched Paula describe the history of the Gardner Museum theft.

"She looks good." Paul nodded approval.

"Can I pop a zit or what." Ida Orsina shook her head of henna red hair and smiled.

Laughing too loudly, the third person there, Ladimir Karlovic added, his Slavic accent pronounced, "Is that all you do all day long? Oh, I want to be a dermatologist when I grow up."

"Fuck you, Ladmo," Ida shot back with the familiarity of people who have known each other for a long time.

"Enough," Paul quietly commanded. "I want to hear this."

On the screen, Paula, radiating almost too much respect, was handing off to her on-the-scene reporter Moira Weyland in Southampton. Then a good-looking young woman appeared in front of a mansion garishly lit with police lights and barricaded with yellow ribbons.

"Thank you, Paula, and yes, TVNews is the first to report official confirmation from the FBI"—Moira was eager, her voice excited—"that one of the missing pieces stolen from the Gardner Museum has indeed been found here in this historic house behind me."

The image of *Storm on the Sea of Galilee* again filled the screen as she continued, "It is also confirmed that the owner of this mansion, an art dealer named Raphael Sharder, was killed here, apparently shot sometime last night."

Paul Marin turned off the set and sipped his drink.

"You look worried." Ida was watching him with concern.

"No," Paul smirked, "I never get worried. Everything will be fine."

Ladimir leaned forward and refilled their glasses.

Ida's fingers played pensively with the pretty blue gemstone of her necklace.

"Paulie," she said quietly, using a name that told him she really needed his attention.

He looked up at her and waited.

"Please don't hurt my sister," she said simply.

Paul's lavender eyes flashed for a second before he smiled at her and said, "Lucille is not as fragile as you or anyone thinks."

"I know, but—" she started.

Paul cut her off, "And Lucille is cosmically important to me and to the class."

There was something about this pronouncement that made any further protest impossible. Ida obediently nodded her acceptance.

Ladimir, his odd mismatched eyes watching them both carefully, finished off the rest of his drink and poured another.

"You know, Paul," he said, "sometimes I think you really believe your own bullshit."

Paul, not offended, smiled and murmured, "I always think there's a band, kid."

"Huh…?" Ladimir looked confused.

Paul shrugged and added, "It's just a line from an old movie."

Chapter Two

Saturday, February 29th

The fog had cleared overnight. The morning was sunny but very cold in New York. Detectives Drew Sweeney and Jerome Clayton Collins walked into a mid-century apartment building on East 65th Street, off Park Avenue. They found the Superintendent, who was a small, neat, middle-aged man in a jacket and tie. He took them up to an apartment on the twenty-first floor.

"Mr. Sharder was the salt of the earth," the Super was saying, his Brooklyn accent pronounced, as he unlocked the door and let them in. "I just can't believe anyone would kill him."

"How long was he here?" Drew asked as she and Clayton looked around the place.

"Lord, I'm not sure." The Super scratched his pale, balding head and shrugged. "Before I was here, that's for certain. I'm thinking maybe thirty years. I'll take a look downstairs and be able to say better."

"That would be about when he opened the 64th Street Gallery." Clayton nodded to Drew.

The apartment was a study in simplicity: wallpapered in grays, highlighted with mahogany wood trim, and devoid of decorations of any kind.

The furniture was modern, expensive, and equally understated. The bedroom off the main room had an upholstered bed and a small antique writing desk. On the desk was a pen set and a blotter and in the drawers nothing except a blank pad of writing paper. The closet had three designer suits, three white dress shirts, some ties, and a pair of shoes.

"Doesn't seem like he lived here much?" Drew turned to the Super, who was waiting respectfully by the front door.

"No, Mr. Sharder spent most of his time out in Southampton," he answered.

"Anybody come here regularly?" Clayton was squatting looking under the sofa. "Seems really clean."

"Sure," the Super nodded, "a maid comes in once a week. She does a lot of the apartments here. I'll give you her name and number."

"Thanks." Drew said. "Anyone else? Friends, relatives?"

"Well," the man looked at the tall, strong woman in front of him, and was uncertain, "you know… I respect the privacy of my tenants."

Drew smiled. "Raphael Sharder is dead. He won't mind."

The Super thought for a moment and then nodded. "I do want to help. It's pretty well known here, and you'd find out anyway. You know how people love to gossip—"

Clayton cut him off, "Of course, you're right. So, what's the mystery?"

"No mystery," the little neat man was quick to assure them. "There's a woman, a friend of his, who comes in to make sure that everything is all right. Mr. Sharder signed a release allowing her full access. She has a set of keys. Sometimes she would stay here—"

"With Sharder?" Drew asked.

"No, when he was away. Her name is Roxie Lee. She told me once that she works in television. But I try not to get too involved in what people do here. None of my business, really," he added too sincerely.

"Right." Drew nodded as Clayton made notes. "Roxie Lee. What does she look like?"

"Oh, a very nice-looking Black girl, always dresses, you know, classy," the Super smiled for the first time. "I mean, you gotta notice a woman like that coming through your lobby. And she's always polite to the staff."

"You think they were ever an item?" Clayton asked, keeping it friendly.

"Nah, I don't think so." The man smiled wide, almost laughing. He turned to the woman detective. "I mean, Mr. Sharder... Well, I don't think he went for the girls too much, you get me?"

"So"—Drew took this—"more like a father and daughter thing?"

"No, he was more like her grandfather. I mean, this is a young woman in her thirties. And Mr. Sharder, he was what, like, eighty...?"

"Yeah, like that," Drew confirmed.

"But listen," the Super added quickly, "he was a good guy. I think he was just helping her out. I think he maybe knew her from his gallery or something. I'm not really sure...."

Drew looked disappointed. She shifted her powerful shoulders and let out a short sigh. The Super thought for a second and offered a bit more:

"You know, that Roxie Lee is the kind of woman that makes a man happy when the weather gets hot," he said and waited.

Clayton knew that it would be a long time before his boss took the bait, so he jumped in. "And why is that?"

"Because the woman likes to wear a real low-cut top," he answered like a comedian. "And she has the rack for it, if you get what I'm saying."

Drew nodded, having had enough of this guy. But the Super had one more thing to offer.

"And she always wears the same red stone necklace. Always. One big rock on a silver chain. Looked really good on her. Stood out sweet on her black skin." Suddenly, the little man realized he might have said too much. He looked at Clayton and added, "No offense, I hope."

Clayton, who was used to every kind of person by now, just smiled and said, "Nah, whatcha gonna do. A pretty woman is what she is, right?"

"Exactly!" The Super grinned in relief.

"So, when was the last time Roxie Lee was here?" Clayton asked.

"I'm not sure. Maybe a couple of days ago. We can check the lobby desk. We record everything."

*   *   *

In Southampton, some ninety miles to the east, the morning sky was covered with clouds. Outside the big glass doors of Raphael Sharder's gallery on Main Street, Artemis and Mak stood behind Ray Gaines, who was holding up his FBI Special Agent badge and ID. The man inside nodded his understanding, unlocked the door, and let them in.

"I've been expecting you, gentlemen," the polite Japanese man began as he locked the gallery door behind them. "We're closed, of course, things being as they are. My name is Taki Fukuda." And he bowed. "How can I help you?"

Taki Fukuda was in his early sixties but nicely preserved, having had judicious work done from time to time to keep his eyes looking young and his chin from sagging. He had a full head of carefully arranged curly blond hair that almost looked natural. He was a little short and a little chubby. He was dressed in a button-down pink shirt, posh plaid sports coat with a pink pocket square, light blue dress slacks, and brown suede shoes. His manner was patient, respectful, and professional.

"I am sorry it's so dark in here," Taki said softly. He switched on two antique Murano crystal chandeliers that lit up the large gallery of fine paintings, vases, and cases of jewelry.

Ray introduced himself and then Artemis.

"I've heard of you, Dr. Bookbinder." Taki nodded in a self-important way. "It's nice to meet you."

Artemis smiled and said, "I like your shop."

"Oh, not my shop," Taki gently corrected him. "Mr. Sharder's shop. I'm the manager here. At least, I was." He swallowed hard and looked worried. "Honestly, I don't know what will happen now."

"And this is Agent Makani Kim," Ray said.

Taki's smile became more forced as he took in the young, fit man. "You're Korean?"

Mak felt the wave of disapproval but let it go. "Yes, by descent, and Hawaiian too," he answered simply and took out his notepad.

"Are these by local artists?" Artemis asked after a moment, looking around the gallery.

"Yes." Taki turned backed to Artemis. "Some are. Mr. Sharder always tried to support the new people coming up. Of course, there are far too many seascapes and boats here." Taki shrugged and wistfully looked around at the paintings. "But it's a beach town, and people seem to expect it. Our sister gallery in New York handles more modern pieces."

"And do you ever work there?" Artemis asked.

"Oh, no," Taki answered. "I like Southampton, where everything is so lovely. You know, it doesn't seem possible that such a terrible thing could have happened here."

Taki's eyes teared up, and he pulled out his handkerchief. "Excuse me," he murmured, "it's just too much."

"I understand," Ray said tactfully. "You and Raphael Sharder go back a long way, I'm guessing."

"Yes. Let's see. More than thirty years," Taki said softly as he collected himself. "God, weren't we all so young once."

"And you've been to his house a lot?" Ray asked.

"Well, for press parties from time to time. Not really a lot," Taki answered carefully. "And I'd hardly call The Arethusa just a house. That's one of the grand old Dames of the Hamptons."

"Did Raphael Sharder ever show you his Rembrandt?" Ray looked him in the eyes.

"No, never." Taki's voice got a little louder and more emphatic. "I don't know anything about that. And for the record, I can't believe that Mr. Sharder ever had anything to do with a stolen painting."

Ray nodded slowly. "And I have to ask, where were you on Thursday night?"

Taki held his breath, taking in what Ray was asking. Then he answered carefully, "I was here working in the gallery until very late. I'm not sure what time exactly. Then I walked home, I live just south of town. I ate a little something and went to bed."

Mak Kim wrote in his notepad.

"Mr. Fukuda," Artemis started.

"Taki, please. Everyone calls me Taki."

"Right, Taki." Artemis smiled. "I'm sorry to ask a personal question, but were you and Raphael Sharder ever lovers?"

They watched carefully as Taki took this in. After a moment he looked at Artemis and shook his head sadly.

"I wish." He smiled. "He was so lovely and so very rich. Can you imagine what a life that would have been…?"

Artemis nodded.

"But he was always wonderful to me. Paid me well. Listened when I had ideas for the gallery. He was always kind. He was cut from a different cloth." His voice had grown soft as he remembered. "A very old-world gentleman."

Ray asked if there were any other employees, and Taki told him there weren't any. Ray said that they'd like to have information on the gallery's artists, clients, and sales. Seeming eager to assist, Taki agreed but said that he'd need a little time.

Ray smiled, the wrinkles around his eyes deepening. "Thank you, Taki. Let's say by tomorrow morning."

Taki nodded and added, "Mr. Sharder's lawyer lives here in town, just down the street, toward the beach. She's a very nice woman named Barbara Borsa." He went to a laptop, found her details, and wrote it out for them on a card.

"So, what will you do now?" Artemis asked kindly.

"I don't really know." Taki looked truly puzzled. "It's still just sinking in. Usually by now we would be making plans to fix up the shop after the winter and be getting ready for Memorial Day, when the tourist season really kicks in. But, now…? Now the world has changed."

Taki looked out the front windows. A light rain had begun to fall.

"Ah," he murmured sadly, "that's fitting somehow."

The address that Taki had given them was a large, well-weathered Hampton-style house. It had two entrances on the front: the main door, and off to the side, a simpler professional-looking entrance. A brass plaque there displayed: Barbara Borsa, Attorney-at-Law. They rang the bell, tried the door but found it locked. So, they stepped quickly through the rain to the main door on the covered porch and tried the bell there. The door opened, and a frail-looking woman took in Artemis, Mak, and Ray, shaking off the wet.

"Can I help you?" she asked cautiously.

Ray showed his ID, again handled the introductions, and asked if they could speak with Barbara Borsa. The woman identified herself as Sally Borsa, the lawyer's sister, and said that Barbara was away for the weekend. Ray said that they would return on Monday.

* * *

By lunchtime, the rain had stopped, and a pale sun was fighting through breaks in the clouds. The Primrose Restaurant on Main Street, Southampton, was busy, and the pleasant aromas of soups and muffins filled the air. Ray Gaines led Mak and Artemis in, quietly wincing as he pulled off his wet trench coat. Artemis took this in before he turned his attention to the place.

The long wooden bar was full of shopkeepers and other locals. The bartender was a slim, energetic woman in her late fifties. She said something funny, and all the people at the bar laughed. One of those was a man in a bright plaid sports coat. Taki Fukuda looked up and saw them. He made a quick decision, got up, grabbed his overcoat, waved to the bartender, and happily led her over to them.

"Gentlemen, this is Madeline Griffin, better known as Maddy Griff. She's the owner of this wonderful place and is known and loved for her generous pour," Taki enthused.

"And for my good looks," she added with a self-deprecating shrug, wiping a loose wisp of blonde silver hair back off her forehead.

Taki laughed and half bowed to her. "Yes, you are absolutely right there."

Dropping his voice to a discreet level, Taki leaned close to her and explained, "These men are with the FBI, and they are investigating Mr. Sharder's death and that business with the painting."

"Ahh," Maddy Griff murmured as she sized them up.

"And we're here for lunch," Ray said pleasantly. "What smells so good?"

Maddy Griff smiled. "That would be our lunch special: Irish stew and hot soda bread."

"I will leave you then," Taki said politely, turning to Ray. "I'm going back to the gallery to gather up the information you asked me for. I hope you have a pleasant lunch here."

He gave Maddy Griff a light kiss on the cheek, draped his coat over his shoulders, and left.

"He hides it well," she said, watching him go, "but Taki is really broken up about Raphael's death. We all are. Come on, guys, let's find you a seat."

With that, she led them to a comfortable booth by a big window looking out on Main Street.

"You know, Raphael was one of the good ones," she said quietly as she handed them menus. "Did he really steal that painting?"

Ray looked up at her. "We're pretty early on in our investigations. But would it really surprise you if I said yes?"

"It would shock me. It's wild." She shook her head in disbelief.

"You knew him well, then." Ray nodded with understanding.

Maddy Griff took a second to think about that. "Yes, I guess I did. I would help out from time to time at his house when he was hosting events. And he came in here a lot, especially in the quieter winter months. You know, before all the tourists descend on the place. He was one of those rare people who actually listened. I loved that about him. I'm gonna miss that old man."

Artemis looked at the woman in front of them, bowing her head to collect herself. She was tall, thin, dressed in faded jeans and a neat white button shirt. She seemed young, not in age but in spirit. She was smiling to herself, remembering.

Very gently, Artemis asked, "Did he ever bring people here?"

She took a breath and answered, "Not so much, but everybody here knew him. He and Morty Singer would have lunch together sometimes. Morty owns that antique jewelry store over there." She pointed through the window to the far corner of Main Street. "And sometimes they'd sit together, have lunch, and have a laugh or two. See, Morty is as old as Raphael. Well, as Raphael was. I still can't believe it."

She focused on Ray and asked, "I heard on the news that he was shot. Is that true?"

"Yes," Ray answered. "We think by someone who knew him well."

"My God." She dropped her head again, and some strands of her hair fell into her face.

"Hey, Maddy Griff! The well's run dry," a businessman at the bar yelled across the room to her, displaying his empty glass and getting a loud laugh from his friends.

"Simmer down, Little Teapot," she answered with a smile.

She turned back. "Sorry, fellas, duty calls. You know what you'd like for lunch?"

Ray and Mak ordered the Irish stew. Maddy Griff nodded her approval. Artemis ordered a turkey club with no pickles, no onions, and no dressing.

Maddy Griff looked at him for a second, considering. "Allergies? To what, alliums?"

"Exactly." Artemis smiled, impressed.

"I get all kinds in here." She seemed pleased with herself as she walked away.

"I wonder what will happen to this place…," Artemis said quietly as he watched her return to the bar. "Restaurants will close. Theaters, too, probably."

Mak took this in for a second before he said, "I don't know. They're saying it's just like the flu. I think the press is making too much of it."

"As usual," Ray agreed.

"I hope you're right," Artemis answered softly, and his eyes grew alive with cool fire.

Ray watched him. He knew that when Artemis was following his mind's inner pathways, it was always best to give him time.

Artemis looked down, and, bothered by the disorder in front of him, began to meticulously arrange his silverware, napkin, and the salt and pepper shakers.

Mak, not aware that Artemis was only half with them, asked, "So, what happens if you eat garlic or onions?"

Artemis answered, but his voice was soft and distant. "Depends on how much they've been cooked and if they come from organic soil, but it can be bad, starting from getting sleepy, grumpy, to feeling sick, breaking out in big red bumps, and might even make me pass out." He trailed off.

Mak looked from Artemis to Ray. Ray smiled and indicated they should just wait. Then with a short sigh, Artemis returned fully to himself and looked up.

"How's it doing, son?" Ray asked. "Anything we should know?"

"If Taki Fukuda is lying," Artemis said softly, "he's in danger."

The silence that followed was broken by Mak, who asked, "Lying about not being Sharder's lover or not knowing about the Rembrandt?"

Artemis looked at Mak and smiled. "Both."

Ray nodded once to Artemis and said, "I'll get on it."

"So, how long have you two known each other?" Mak asked.

Ray smiled. "God, let's see." He looked to Artemis, searching. "A long damn time... I guess about a quarter century."

Mak looked puzzled. He knew that Ray was old enough to be considering retirement from the service, but Artemis was in his mid-thirties.

"Ray worked with my father, on the Gardner Museum robbery," Artemis explained. "I was twelve when my parents were killed...."

"Nate was killed in the line of duty," Ray said with great respect, looking at Artemis. "God bless both your parents."

Artemis nodded once to Ray and continued, "After, I stayed with my uncle, Matt Sweeney, who was an NYPD captain, and Drew, my cousin, who was by then a cop. By the time I got to choosing colleges, it was a toss-up for me, whether I should study criminology or art history."

"He studied both," Ray said, sounding like a proud father.

"Either way," Artemis said grimly, "I've always had a need to know about the Gardner case."

"It's been a long time, but there will be justice," Ray said softly.

"Emily, my wife, says I'm obsessed," Artemis said to Mak. "But I think she understands."

"Of course, she does. She's a cop's wife," Ray said.

"No, not anymore," Artemis said truthfully. "I'm an art historian providing consultation on a case."

"Okay, if you say so." Ray smiled kindly. "But you're one of the best investigators I've ever worked with. It's good to be on the hunt with you again."

"Thanks, Ray, me too," Artemis said with a smile.

Ray smiled back. "When Artemis was still a boy, he'd call me from time to time with some new idea he'd have about the Gardner case, and we'd talk it over. He always had something good to offer." Then he looked to Mak and added, "That was kinda informal, back then, so that's just between us, okay?"

The young agent nodded that he understood.

"So, by the time Artemis became an NYPD detective, we'd already been working unofficially together for years," Ray summed up as lunch arrived.

By mutual agreement, they let the case go for a while and ate. Fortified, and with the clouds overhead beginning to lift, they headed out to investigate the store across the street.

*　*　*

It was one of the oldest buildings on Main Street, with large, curved glass windows filled with sparkling gems, antique jewelry, and fine watches. Ray pushed the doorbell. They heard the snap of the lock releasing and went in.

The large shop was full of rows of tall glass cases. The cases were themselves fine antiques, and each one displayed a particular theme: some of emeralds, some rubies, some aquamarine, and some of watches, pens, and the like.

In the center of the shop an old man was sitting hunched over a vintage glass desk, looking through a loupe at a dozen pieces of jewelry. He was heavy and filled out his wooden chair from arm to arm. His hair was thin and white. And in front of the desk, a defeated-looking middle-aged man in a tired suit stood waiting for the old man's appraisal.

"Welcome," the old man said as he looked up, his shrewd eyes making a quick assessment of the newcomers. "I'll be with you shortly. Feel free to look around," he said and dropped his head back down to study the jewelry.

Artemis looked up and saw the expensive pin-point lighting and the security cameras.

"I'm sorry, Eli, I just can't do it today." The old man shook his head. "None of these are for me."

"You're killing me," the man answered sadly and put the pieces back into his worn briefcase.

"I always need more after Memorial Day. Come see me then," the old man added, his voice gruff but not unkind.

"Thanks, Morty, I'll see you soon." The man shook his hand, snapped his case closed, and left.

"Mr. Morty Singer...?" Ray asked as he and Mak pulled out their identifications.

"Yes." The old man nodded carefully.

"I'm FBI Special Agent Ray Gaines, this is Agent Makani Kim, and Dr. Artemis Bookbinder."

Artemis, as always, inwardly winced to hear his title.

"Okay. So, what can I do for you?" Morty's eyes focused, and he sat back in his chair.

"We're investigating the murder of Raphael Sharder. We'd like to ask you a few questions," Ray said.

"Ah, I see...." Morty sighed and sagged a little, his large hand rubbed the back of his neck. "Poor Raphael," he said sadly. "I'll miss him. Please, sit down if you like."

Ray and Artemis pulled up a couple of bentwood chairs and sat in front of his desk. Mak remained standing and pulled out his notepad.

Ray said, "You two knew each other a long time then?"

"What's a long time?" Morty mused. "Yes, I guess I did. Let me think… maybe about thirty years. Yes, that seems right. I've been here in the shop for over forty years… God, I can't believe that even when I say it."

"You have great stuff here," Artemis said truthfully.

"Thanks." Morty smiled proudly. "It's from estate sales, mostly in Europe. I still get there during the winter months." He reached over to a side table piled with pieces waiting to be sorted and priced and lifted up a heavy gold necklace with large red gems.

"Rubies, on 18 carat gold, over two hundred years old, I think. I just picked this up in Croatia."

"That's impressive." Ray nodded.

"I don't know, it's a little gaudy, but it will sell." Morty smiled and put the necklace down.

"So, you were in Croatia?" Artemis asked.

"Yes, for a couple of weeks in November. Been going there forever. Wonderful place. I've always had good luck finding things there. But I'm getting too old for it, you know." He shook his head. "Travel has become such a pain in the ass. I miss the old days. Used to be so classy. Now it's like a cafeteria for prisoners, all the searching, the lines, documents, X-rays, security guards… it's enough. So, I've got someone helping me now. Nice college girl, smart. Her name is Ginger Hayes. She's from here, from Montauk. Her family has been buying my stuff for years."

"Is she here?" Ray asked, looking toward the rear of the large shop.

"No," Morty answered, "she's on the road, buying. And she's getting pretty good at it too. She's probably in Czechoslovakia by now. I don't expect to see her back here for at least a month."

"Okay"—Ray nodded—"we'll need her information so we can be in touch."

Morty looked at Ray. "Look, Agent, is that really necessary? Ginger is just a kid. She didn't know Raphael at all."

"Don't worry"—Ray smiled easily—"it's just routine."

Morty looked at the senior agent and nodded. He opened a drawer, took out a handwritten address book, found her information, and copied it out on a scrap of paper.

"I just feel protective of her," he said as he handed Ray the paper. "She's a good kid. She's not involved with anything."

Ray smiled, and the lines around his eyes deepened. "Involved in anything? Like what?"

"Come on"—Morty shook his head at him—"it's all over the news, and everyone here is busting a gut talking about it. The man was shot in his own home, and you guys found a stolen painting from the Gardner."

"Right," Ray said. "Anything you care to say about that?"

Morty looked at Ray for a second and then said, "Fenway Court. You know what that is?"

"That was what the museum was called when Isabella Gardner was still living there," Artemis answered simply.

Morty turned to him, interested. "That's correct. See, I'm old. Old enough to remember lots of things." He turned back to Ray. "I never knew anything about that stolen painting. Nobody did. I have no idea who killed Raphael. He was a kind, gentle man. And my friend."

"Did you ever sell paintings in this shop?" Artemis asked.

Morty jerked his head toward Artemis, and for a second, he looked angry. Then he took a long breath and answered, speaking very clearly, "Why would you ask me that?"

Mak Kim quietly joined in, "Because you knew Raphael Sharder for over thirty years, and you probably have a long list of faithful wealthy customers who like fine art."

"Think of it,"—Morty looked up at the young agent, intrigued by the idea but now sounding more patronizing—"you pay what, say millions for a stolen painting that no one can ever see but you. What's the point? Who would do that?"

"Raphael Sharder, your friend, did just that," Ray said evenly.

Morty rubbed the back of his neck and sighed.

"Look," he said, choosing his words, "I liked Raphael a lot. He was good to talk to about art, or just gossip about the townies, you know, like old men do. But no, gentlemen, I never knew anything about stolen paintings, or jewelry, or anything, ever. My reputation is my life. People buy from me because I am trustworthy. And that's everything."

The sound of Mak's pen scratching was all that was heard for a while.

"Anything else?" Morty asked.

"Yes." Artemis smiled. "Did Raphael Sharder ever own a boat?"

Morty smiled a little and nodded. He rested his heavy body back in his chair. "That takes me back. Yeah, he did. Was proud of it. A big, old yacht. But it's long gone. It rotted or burned up or something, I don't remember. I'm not too nautical myself."

"Where did he dock it?" Artemis's eyes glinted.

"It's been too long. I really haven't a clue."

"Thank you," Artemis said sincerely.

"Glad to help," Morty answered but sounded puzzled.

"What about Raphael Sharder's other friends, besides you?" Ray asked.

Morty shrugged. "I don't really know. I guess the guy who runs his gallery. His name is Taki Fukuda."

"Anyone else?"

"You know, when you live long enough you get choosy about who you want to spend time with. He was old, like me." He smiled at Ray. "And like you, too. It happens before you know it."

Ray made no reaction.

The doorbell rang, and Morty reached under his desk, hit a button, and the front door opened. A couple of well-dressed people came in, and Morty said in the same business-like way as before:

"Welcome, I'll be with you shortly. Feel free to look around."

The couple went to look at something in the aquamarine case toward the back.

Morty opened his desk, pulled out a business card. "This is me, and how to reach me." And as he wrote on the back, he said, "And this is where I live. It's a nice little place about two blocks that way." He pointed.

"My housekeeper is there right now. Feel free to go and check it out. I can call her and let her know that you're coming, if you want."

Ray said, "I'd appreciate that."

Morty lifted the phone on his desk, punched in a number, and waited.

"Sadie," he started, and then spoke louder, "Sadie. It's Morty." He rolled his eyes and sighed. He continued, almost shouting, "Some men are coming by to see the house. Let them in and be nice to them... No, we're not moving. Just let them in, okay?... Okay.... Yes, I'll see you later."

He hung up and smiled at them. "Deaf as a politician, but she's been with me for years. What can you do?"

They thanked him for his time and left. Outside on the street, Ray sent Mak off to get search warrants for Morty Singer's shop and both of Raphael Sharder's galleries. Then Ray and Artemis walked to Morty's house.

"Makani seems like a good hire," Artemis said.

"Yes, he is." Ray nodded.

"You picked him? Or was he assigned?" Artemis asked.

"I picked him," the older man answered.

"And are there many Hawaiian-Koreans in the agency?"

"Not so much," Ray admitted. "He worked his ass off and was ready for promotion but wasn't getting a second look. The kid deserved a break."

Artemis smiled. They arrived outside Morty's house, a charming single-story stone cottage, like something from a Cotswold village. "Curious that he volunteered to let us come look around his house."

"Yep," Ray said. "So, we're sure not to find anything here."

"Not at his shop either, of course," Artemis added.

"I know," Ray said. "And we're not going to find anything at the galleries or in Sharder's house. We're just doing the job."

As they walked through the small gated front yard, they could see where the long winter had sagged a drain pipe and chipped some paint. The door opened and Sadie, an ancient white-haired housekeeper, gave them a suspicious look and a nod and let them in. She followed them from room to room as they performed a cursory look through. They found nothing of note. When they finished, they thanked Sadie, very loudly, and left.

*　*　*

In the peaceful New Jersey suburban town of Halesburgh, daylight was fading, and it was growing cold. Emily pulled her car into their driveway, got out, and breathed deeply. She loved her job, as head of a small school in town for special needs children, but she missed having more time to herself. She opened the back of the SUV, lifted out a couple of large bags of groceries, and headed up the steps of the back porch.

"I saw you coming," her aunt Delia said as she opened the door, reaching out her strong arms to help. Emily smiled her thanks, and as she handed off one of the bags, she noticed a folded piece of paper tucked under the corner of the outside doormat. Emily took the paper in with them.

74

"Oh no," Emily whispered softly, and Delia came close to read the note over her shoulder. It was printed in a standard black font:

Artemis Bookbinder, what happened to your father and mother was so sad. And you have such a nice little family.

Emily closed her eyes and leaned into Delia's supportive hug. It had all seemed so safe here. All the nice houses with pretty gardens and strong stone walls. Emily shivered. Everything had changed.

Chapter Three

Sunday, March 1st

The midday sun was bright, but the wind was up, and the air still cold. On the desk of the front room Artemis used as his home office were neat piles of old reports and folders and his laptop opened to a news report about the murder in Southampton. A square framed corkboard on the wall held color-coded notes perfectly arranged in rows, and pinned in the exact center was a small printout of the recovered Rembrandt painting.

"Let's talk in here," Artemis said as he led them in and shut the door. Emily and Artemis sat on the sofa. Ray Gaines unbuttoned his suit jacket, and he and Bert Rocca settled into chairs.

"You still make a nice cup of coffee." Ray smiled at Emily as he put his mug down.

"Not me, Ray," Emily said. "Aunt Delia makes the coffee now."

"Well, it's good. And it's nice that you have someone to help out."

"I think she's pretty upset about the death threat," Emily added. "Though you'd never know it. She's a tough old girl."

"So"—Ray was watching her—"how you doing with all this?"

Emily looked kindly at Ray. Through Artemis she had known the older man for a long time. "I've been better." She smiled a little. "But what can I do? I'm a cop's wife."

Something in the removed sound of her words made Artemis wince. He said quietly, "No, Emily. You're not. I'm off the case."

She took his hand but spoke to Ray, "So, what can you tell us about that note?"

"Nothing yet," Ray answered, "but we're on it. I've set up round-the-clock protection for you all. The team is already in place." Ray nodded out the window to the cars stationed beyond the hedges in front of the house. "Special Agent Rocca will be in charge," Ray said, indicating the senior agent.

"It's Bert, right?" Emily turned to him.

"Yes," he nodded.

"I'm Emily. And we appreciate your being here."

Bert smiled. "It's a privilege," he said, his Boston accent strong.

Emily asked, "So, will you both stay for dinner? Drew Sweeney will be here, and I'm sure you all will have lots to talk about."

"Emily," Artemis broke in, "didn't you hear me? I'm off the case."

Emily looked at him for a long moment before she answered quietly, "I heard you. And I believe you. But I don't think you should give this up."

"I…." Artemis looked confused. "We are here, in this house, because we decided to live in a safer world. And I promised you—"

"Yes, I know all that," she stopped him. "And I love you for getting us here. I love this house and what we have. But," she spoke very clearly, "I think there will be no place safe for us until you get this thing settled. And I don't want you to give up or run away because you're trying to do the right thing for me. Or Silas. Our brilliant misfit. Trying to find his way. I think he needs to see his father stand up to bad things, not try to hide from them."

"But"—Artemis shook his head—"I cannot handle…"—he swallowed and started again—"…I cannot live in a world without you."

Emily looked at his troubled eyes and nodded.

"It will be all right," she said.

Artemis turned and looked at the piles of his father's old folders on his desk, a wealth of information, a frustration of unsolved leads. His father's last work had become a legacy of searching and a need for justice. Artemis needed a way to heal the image that was burned into his heart: his parents lying dead and bloodied on a New York City sidewalk. His father was killed because he was getting too close. His mother was an innocent bystander. Artemis was only twelve years old.

"Silas is twelve." Artemis turned back to Emily.

"And today he wants to join the track team," she answered. "His school's having tryouts in a couple of days."

Artemis took that in and smiled. Emily smiled back. Silas was still small for his age. He was a genius and always the last boy chosen for any team.

"Life goes on," she said simply.

Artemis looked to his old friend Ray. "What do you think?"

Ray took a second and then said, "I agree with Emily. She always had more sense than you."

Artemis smiled. "That's so true."

"And I need you," Ray continued. "Look, we both go back a long way on this, and I'm getting too old."

Artemis looked as if he might argue, but Ray waved him off. "Don't worry, I'm not done yet. I just mean, I think that Nate and Sarah would want this."

Artemis breathed in. It was strange hearing his parent's names.

"You are uniquely positioned to help us here," Ray went on, "what with your background and how you know everything there is to know about the Gardner museum, the art pieces, the investigations."

"Obsessed." Artemis looked pointedly to Emily. "I think I've heard that somewhere before."

She smiled.

"Okay, but I get that," Ray said forcefully. "Those fuckers killed your parents; you should be obsessed. Sorry for my language, Emily."

"No problem, Ray," she said. "I agree with you."

"So finally, a miracle happens." Ray shook his head and smiled. "An old guy gets feeling guilty, and we recover a painting from the Gardner."

"And then he gets dead," Artemis said evenly.

"Yes"—Ray nodded—"And now there are nervous people out there. So, you get that note stuck on your back porch. We've shaken the cage, and all the critters are getting worried. This is the time when things start to happen."

"And that note does prove one thing"—Artemis's eyes grew darker—"by referencing my parents' death, they're announcing loud and clear that they are *the same people* from back then."

"I agree," Ray said.

Artemis looked to Emily. "Are you sure?"

"Yes," she answered.

Artemis turned to Bert Rocca. "You will protect my family twenty-four hours a day, every day." It was a demand.

"Absolutely. All the time," the agent assured him.

"Like a guardian angel," Emily murmured softly.

Bert smiled at her, his voice gruff. "Well, not so holy. But we'll be there."

"I've known Bert a long time. He's the best of the best," Ray said.

Artemis took Emily's hand.

"Okay," Artemis said.

"That's good, son." Ray smiled.

"So, stay for dinner?" Emily asked again. "Delia's going all out with a special lamb dish she learned in Greece."

"No, thanks. It sounds great, but we're still on the clock," Ray said.

Bert Rocca then took over, explaining how his team would coordinate with them, providing security wherever Emily, Silas, and Delia would go.

"Even to track team tryouts," Bert told them.

Life would continue for them, as normal as possible.

*   *   *

"They're pros." Drew nodded with approval as she looked out the window. It was getting dark, and she couldn't see the FBI agents sitting inside the cars parked on the street, but she knew they were there. She turned to look at her cousin. "You okay?"

Artemis nodded. "Yeah, I think so."

"You don't sound so sure." Drew watched him.

"There's some ninety thousand COVID cases overseas," Artemis said softly. "Italy, Iran, South Korea have all closed their borders. And today we have our first case in New York City."

"I know." Drew sighed. "We've been prepping our asses off."

"Are we ready for this thing?"

"No," Drew said truthfully, "not at all. Seems like people just don't want to believe that it could happen here."

Artemis turned away and looked out the window. The streetlights across the road had come on, casting the FBI cars in a strange cool light.

Drew moved closer to him but was careful not to touch him.

"You gonna be alright with all this?" she almost whispered. She had been there before, when Artemis was twelve and his fears of germs and contact had kept him prisoner in his own room.

"I…hope so," Artemis managed.

"I'm counting on you, Artie," she said.

Artemis started to chuckle. "I fucking hate it when you call me that."

"I know." Drew smiled back.

"Hey," Delia's loud voice called out, "dinner time!"

Drew nodded, and Artemis led her into the dining room, where the long wooden table was set with blue and white plates, glasses, and napkins.

"Colors of the Greek flag," Artemis explained to Drew. "Delia's doing something special for us."

"Well, it smells amazing," Drew said as she took a seat.

"Souvlaki!" Delia announced proudly as she and Emily came in with two steaming platters. "Silas!" Delia called out loudly. "Now!"

From upstairs they heard running feet, then down the steps. Silas stopped at the doorway to the dining room. He looked curiously at the festive table, the chopped salad with chunks of feta cheese, roasted potatoes, pita bread, and little bowls of olive oil.

"Hi, Drew." He smiled as he took the chair next to her.

"Hey, kid"—Drew threw her large arm around Silas's shoulders—"I hear you're trying out for track and field."

"Yep." Silas pushed his glasses back up into place.

"I think that's great," Drew enthused.

"We all do." Delia smiled warmly at Silas as she handed out very full plates. Emily looked across the table to Artemis and smiled. They had gotten used to the way that her aunt Delia would take charge.

"This is really wonderful," Artemis said with a hint of mischief. "Thank you, Big Dee."

Delia gave him a sharp look. "My pleasure, and knock off that Big Dee stuff. Unless you're happy with me calling you Artie?"

Drew coughed out a laugh, and Artemis smiled and raised his hands as a way of offering a truce.

"Besides," Delia sighed, "I wouldn't want anyone to think you call me that 'cause I'm getting too fat."

Emily caught Artemis's eyes with a quiet appeal.

"Everything really is wonderful, Delia," Artemis said sincerely. "Thanks for going to all this effort."

"Well, I planned this to celebrate the good work that you and Drew have done, finding that stolen painting." Delia had forgiven him and was looking at them proudly. "But with that note and those FBI boys outside, I wasn't sure I should…?"

"Nothing to do but to carry on," Emily answered firmly. "And this is helping so much."

Delia reached out her strong hand and patted Emily's arm.

"I thought so, too," she agreed.

"And the lamb is perfect," Drew said, her mouth full of souvlaki.

Delia smiled at the compliment. "It's from New Zealand, not Greece. But I'm pretty pleased with it. And you know about my Bookbinder boys: no garlic, no onions. But I'm getting to like the challenge." She smiled kindly at young Silas, who was eating steadily, stopping from time to time as he chewed to study the flavors.

"Oregano… and rosemary," Silas announced quietly.

Delia beamed at him. "Right! It's not traditional, but when in Rome—"

"New Jersey, Auntie." Silas looked up at her and laughed. It was a rare sound for him. Delia laughed with him and reached across to give him more potatoes.

Artemis watched the way Delia had with Silas and was grateful. The woman had been living with them for only a few years, but he couldn't imagine what their lives would be now without her steadying force. She cooked most of the meals, she cleaned the house. And for her part, she was grateful to have a place to be in the world. For many years Delia had lived in Greece. But when her husband died, she'd written to her only living relative, her niece Emily, and asked if she could come and stay for a while. At first it was a rough arrangement, especially for Artemis, who wasn't sure he wanted this bossy stranger living with them. But soon it became clear how well Delia fit, and they invited her to stay with them as long as she wanted.

"These plates and glasses are from Delia's home in Greece," Emily was explaining to Drew.

"Ah." Drew nodded as the last of the meal was disappearing from their plates. "Where in Greece?"

"On an island called Kimolos." Delia smiled wistfully. "It's a wild, beautiful place, with white cliffs looking out over the bluest waters of the Aegean."

"That's one of the Cycladic Islands." Silas looked up interested.

"Trust you." Delia nodded at him proudly.

"Do you miss Greece?" Drew asked as she helped herself to seconds.

"Well," Delia answered, "in truth, it was getting a little hard to make ends meet once Stavi died." She nodded gratefully to Emily and went on. "But every day with him was a wonderful adventure."

"He worked as a sailor?" Drew asked.

"Yes, when we first met. But he gave up the sea so we could be together. He knew how hard it was on me, especially at first, being away from home, and all the trouble with my parents, God rest their souls." She took a sip of water before going on. "I'm sorry Emily, I know you've heard all this too many times."

"Don't know what you mean," Emily quipped, and Delia laughed. "No, I love it when you speak about Greece, I really do," Emily reassured her.

"And your parents, did you ever make it up with them?" Artemis asked.

"Sadly, no." Her eyes clouded over. "They never forgave me. I came back to the States once years ago to try and win them over, but it was quite hopeless. They were so set in their ways."

"I remember you from that trip. You came to stay with us"—Emily smiled—"I was just a kid."

"Oh, yes." Delia nodded.

"I remember how kind you were to me and how sad you seemed. But not much else," Emily said.

"Well, I went back to Greece, and my folks died not long after that. We never got another chance." Delia was quiet for a moment. Then she thumped the table with her open hand and loudly announced:

"But why waste time on all that when there is so much good all around us?" Her smile had returned. "Spring is not far off, famous cases are being solved, we're alive, and the world is full of promise. Now, for God's sake, that's enough about me, let someone else do the talking."

The rest of the meal passed pleasantly, with Drew telling how well her father Mathew was doing in Florida and how pleased he was about the recovery of the painting. Over dessert, a tasty lemon cake proudly served by Aunt Delia, the conversation turned to Emily's job as a school administrator in town and how Delia was going to replant the beds in front of the house.

"I'm going to see what I can find out about Raphael Sharder online," Silas announced to Artemis as he got up and went upstairs.

Artemis watched him go and smiled until he saw Emily staring at him across the table.

"He has a need to know, what are we going to do?" Artemis shrugged.

Emily thought about it for a moment, then without a word, got up and started to clear the table.

"I got this," Artemis said. "You guys cook, I clean."

Drew laughed. "You know we have to let him. He really does like it."

Delia put together a plate of sliced cakes. "What's the agent's name?" she asked Emily.

"Bert Rocca."

"Well, let's go feed the troops. Those boys must be hungry out there."

Drew got up. "I'll come, too."

"We'll be alright," Delia assured her.

"Ok." Drew nodded, accepting this. "I'll go up and see what Silas is working on."

"Thanks, Drew." Emily smiled as she and Delia grabbed their coats and headed out.

"They'll be okay," Drew said quietly to Artemis and went upstairs.

With a long sigh, Artemis stacked up the dishes, cleared the table, and focused on cleaning. By the time Emily and Delia came back in, he had the dishwasher running. By the time Drew found him, he was just finishing wiping down the kitchen counters with vinegar spray.

"Just like when you were a kid." Drew smiled at him. "You must really like it."

"Yeah, I suppose," Artemis said as he dried his hands. "But it has to add up to more than this. How about a single malt?"

"Absolutely," Drew said and followed him to his study.

"I love that you have those." Drew grinned.

"What?" Artemis asked as he poured two neat drinks.

"Books." Drew laughed as she settled into a big leather chair.

"I know, I know." Artemis smiled. He sat on the sofa, kicked off his shoes, and put his feet up on a pad of paper set in the exact center of the coffee table. Drew watched him kindly.

"So, what's with that *it has to add up to more than this* shit…? You and Emily okay?" Drew asked quietly.

"Yes," Artemis said truthfully, "we're great."

"Good. Otherwise I'd have to kill you." She smiled. "And that note? It's not every day you get your life threatened. Is she dealing?"

"Yes," Artemis answered, "I think she is. She told me to stay on the case, anyway."

"Good for her." Drew smiled a little. "So, what is it? Is Delia driving you crazy again?"

"No, we're all fine." He shook his head. "I'm even getting to like the way she irons my shirts."

Drew barked out a laugh. "You let Delia iron your shirts? Who are you? And what have you done with Artemis?"

"I know"—he shrugged—"but the cuffs and collars are perfect."

"Okay, that's nice." Drew put down her drink. "Look. We just recovered a stolen Rembrandt, and that should make you happy. Very fucking happy."

"It does. Makes me feel like I'm finally doing something important. It's just that…," Artemis trailed off. Drew watched him and waited.

"So, I'm a consultant on the case," Artemis spoke carefully. "And in the fall, I'll still have my life teaching…."

"You miss being a cop," Drew said, understanding. "But if you come back to the NYPD…"

Artemis nodded. "Emily will—"

"So fucking kill you," Drew finished for him.

Artemis took a slow sip of scotch and shook his head. "Ray's guys are working on the note, but they're not going to find anything."

"You sure?" Drew watched as Artemis's blue eyes grew distant with thought.

"Yes, I'm sure," Artemis answered softly. "They're pros... been doing this a long time."

Artemis could still see his parents, Nathaniel and Sarah, lying dead on a dark sidewalk outside their New York City home.

And you have such a nice little family.

"It's the same people. And they're here." The dire words brought Artemis back from the past. He looked up at his cousin.

"What to do, hmm?" Drew mused quietly. "You know that you can't just show up and be a detective again. Strings would have to be pulled. My dad, of course, would give a kidney to help. And me, too. So, it could be done. If you want it."

Artemis thought about Emily, Silas, and that old bully Delia. He breathed out slowly and shook his head.

"Thank you, Drew, but no. For now, I'm just a consultant."

Drew watched him for a moment, then slowly raised her glass:

"To your mother and father."

"Amen," Artemis answered, and they drank together.

Emily stood in the doorway of Silas's bedroom, watching him work at his three laptops. In sharp, quiet movements, he was turning from one screen to the other, gathering information and comparing notes. From time to time he would sit absolutely still, thinking. Then, after a moment, turn back to the streaming lists of information. Sometimes she felt as if she'd given birth to an alien. An alien that she loved and deeply wanted to protect from the ordinary world outside.

She ran her fingers slowly through her long hair, sighed softly, went in, and sat on the edge of his bed. Without looking away from his work, Silas addressed her:

"This one's interesting." He lightly tapped one of the screens, and pushed his forever sliding eyeglasses back up into place. "It's a Google walk-through of Raphael Sharder's gallery in Southampton."

Emily looked at it, impressed at what her son had found. "Nice. Lots of beach landscapes," she offered gently.

Silas turned in his chair to another laptop. "And expensive. Look at these prices."

Emily saw a list flash by of recent past sales. "Well, it's the location. It's to be expected."

She watched him working, so focused and involved. She felt removed, but impressed. Sometimes she felt this way about Artemis, too.

"Thought you could do with this," the commanding voice of Aunt Delia announced as she came in carrying two mugs of herbal tea. Emily thanked her. Delia sat next to her on the bed. And together they sipped their tea in silence and watched Silas. But he no longer knew they were even in the room.

Delia's cell phone rang; she saw the number and looked apologetically at Emily. Emily smiled and nodded. She was used to calls coming at this time of night from *friends of Bill W.* Delia was a sponsor for some of the newer AA members.

"Hi"—Delia got up and headed off to her room—"Where are you calling from? ...Good. I'm glad you called me...."

*   *   *

The place was in the Two Bridges district of lower Manhattan. Five women and one man stood in silence outside a nondescript doorway that was protected by a rusted roll-down metal gate. The street around them was deserted. The ancient buildings were dark, and the few Chinese trinket stores and nail salons were shut tight.

It was Sunday. And so, at five minutes before midnight, the metal gate was lifted from inside by a large man with strange mismatched eyes. Ladimir Karlovic looked at each of their faces, nodded once, and let them pass in. Once the solid inner door was shut, he stepped out onto the street, pulled down the metal gate, and sat watchfully on a stone step nearby. After a moment, a large fat man came out of the shadows of an adjacent storefront.

With a grunt, Fat Nicky eased himself down next to Ladimir, pulled out a cigarette, and lit it. They sat for a while in silence, blue smoke floating around their shoulders.

The building they were guarding had once been a speakeasy. The cavern-like basement was still intact. Inside, the six people made their way down the uneven stone steps and without a word sat down on gold-colored folding chairs. The curved, vaulted ceiling was lit by six dark bronze standing candelabras, each with six lower flames and one center flame higher than the rest.

Before them, a large metal-framed leather chair was a set on a low wooden platform. Next to it was a simple table that held a metal chalice. Behind this stage was a door, and behind that door stood Dr. Paul Marin. He opened his dark blue robe and unbuttoned his white shirt so that his pendant necklace could be clearly seen on his muscular chest. His tanned skin set off the large, clear diamond hanging on a silver chain. He slowly ran his fingers across his temples and through his short curly hair.

Here I can be myself.

He went through the door and sat on the throne-like chair. The group sat up, watching and waiting. Paul slowly lifted his eyes and stared up high and to his right, listening, for a moment. Then he took a long breath in, nodded gently, and lowered his strangely beautiful lavender eyes and looked at them. In response, each in turn opened their shirts to reveal their own gem pendants.

Roxie Lee, so fucking sexy with that ruby. Paula DeVong, my media star is rose quartz. Cute little Deni Diaz is pink sapphire. Ida Orsina, my always loyal comrade with blue tourmaline. And next to her, her sister Lucille, so hot and so needy.

Paul smiled at her, and Lucille seemed uncertain what to do. She didn't yet have a stone like the others. She undid a few buttons, showing him the tops of her pale breasts and how much she wanted to be included.

Paul looked at Greg Schaefer, the only other man in the group. Greg, too, had no stone pendant. With a smile, Greg simply bowed his head to Paul.

Paul looked up to the right again and started to speak in a low, even voice.

"The Voices said that the key to understanding ourselves is found in our dreams." He dropped his eyes down and looked at them as he continued. "Our days are filled with the many things we do: our jobs, chores, cleaning, shopping. Lots of shopping for some of you here, I think." He smiled kindly at Paula DeVong. She smiled back and nodded in agreement.

"There's no trouble there unless we forget that it's all just the weight, the weight we're carrying from generations of survival training and conditioning." He reached out his right hand for the chalice and took a sip. The taste of dry Mediterranean wine in his mouth relaxed him and reminded him of where he came from. He set down his drink and felt the way the flickering candle light heightened his proud features and enjoyed it.

He smiled knowingly and went on, "But in our dreams, if we listen, we reveal ourselves. There we can find the person we were meant to be before we were interrupted by circumstances."

"Lucille"—he turned his full attention on her—"The Voices said I should ask you first. Would you like to say anything about your dreams?"

Lucille was frightened to be called on but thrilled that Paul and his Voices had spoken to her. She folded her delicate hands together so tightly that her fingers went white. After a moment she spoke in a soft, reedy whisper,

"Yes, I can." She looked up at his eyes and seemed to draw strength from them. "But… I don't know how to start."

"The beginning," Paul said kindly. "Do you remember dreaming as a child?"

"Well, I must have done. We grew up in New Jersey and all we did was dream about getting the hell out of there."

Ida chuckled a little and nodded, encouraging her sister to say more. Lucille pushed a strand of hair off her face and continued.

"Then I had some troubles… for a long time, and there were no dreams."

"Nothing?" Paul pushed her gently.

"Well, I guess I remember some jumbled-up pieces"—her hands had started to tremble—"like me running from something or falling or trying to fight back." She stopped and took a breath.

"Okay." Paul nodded. "So, what about now?"

"Yes, I am starting to dream again. Because now everything feels better, more hopeful." She smiled at Paul, and he smiled back.

God, she's so eager to please me.

"Very good, Lucille," Paul said and looked up quickly to hear something his Voices said. "Please tell us more about what you are dreaming now."

"Well." Lucille looked over to Ida, who nodded again in support.

"I have this dream. The same one"—Lucille turned to Paul—"It's night, in a burnt-out city, like after a war. It's wet and foggy. I can't see much. So, I start to climb up a tower, trying to get above so I can see where I am. And then there's a bright beam of light. It comes through the clouds, and I realize that it's not really night. And I want to keep climbing. But I feel so tired. And then I wake up."

Paul looked up again and listened. In a reverent whisper he asked, "And what color is the beam of light, Lucille?"

"Blue, a strange dark blue coming from the sky, like it was looking for me." Her gentle voice was trembling. She looked up at Paul, waiting to see if he would approve.

Paul, still looking up at his Voices, smiled and nodded.

"Good, Lucille, that is so very good," he said benevolently as he looked into her eyes again. Lucille blushed with pleasure.

"The Voices said that it is time. Blue is exactly right, and a strange, wonderful blue it is, too. Just like you saw in your dream." With that, Paul opened a drawer in the table at his right hand and lifted out a delicate necklace: a small dark blue gem on a silver chain. Lucille found it hard to breathe.

Paul stood up and said, "Come to me, Lucille."

Lucille stood up on shaky knees and stepped to the front of the platform. The group around watched in respectful silence. Ida bit her lip.

Paul leaned down, reached around her, and fastened the pendant around her neck. He saw the way the blue stone lay between her perfect little breasts. He smiled.

Last night he had so enjoyed dominating her, fucking her. And after, when she was lying in his arms, how she had told him all about her dream and the blue light that called to her.

It really is too easy.

Lucille looked down at the dark blue gem on her chest. "It's so beautiful," she whispered.

"Yes, it is." Paul touched her cheek, and she looked up at him.

"It's called azurite," he explained kindly. "And it is an angel force for people who don't give up easily. It comes from a metal, from copper. Through millennia it changes. First it decays into a green mossy substance, which sometimes becomes a hard matrix. That's called malachite, and it's a pretty enough stone but too common for you."

Lucille's cheeks flushed pink again.

"But sometimes, that malachite stone isn't finished, and it changes again. And over time it turns dark blue. The hard stone is gone, and it is again fragile. That takes courage. That we can learn from and give honor to the mineral kingdom. But the transformation of the stone can go further still. If there is enough time, pressure, and patience, it crystallizes again and becomes its highest and best self."

Paul leaned forward and gently kissed Lucille's forehead. Then speaking louder, he announced to her and the class:

"This clear, perfect blue gem is called azurite. Outside of class you are Lucille. But here, inside these protected walls, you are called *Azurite*." Then Paul looked at her again and asked quietly, "Is that all right with you?"

"Oh yes, it is!" She was almost laughing with relief. Paul smiled widely at her and looked to the group.

"Welcome then, *Azurite!*" Paul pronounced happily, and the other women got up, and each in turn hugged her. Only Greg remained sitting, but he smiled in support.

"It's a beautiful gem, and you look so happy, *Azurite*," Ida said as she hugged her sister tightly.

"Thank you," Lucille whispered, "I owe you so much."

Lucille turned to find Paul, but he was on the stage having a private conversation with Roxie or as she was called here in class, *Ruby*. Something in the relaxed way they were relating to each other bothered Lucille.

Paul called the class back to order, and Lucille watched Roxie's sexy body as she sat down again.

On the stage, Paul sat and took a drink of wine. Lucille watched him. Her lips tightened, and a strange look of recognition came into her eyes.

As he set the chalice down, Paul saw her staring at him. She looked so different all of a sudden.

Chapter Four

Monday, March 2nd

The early morning air was warmer, and hundreds of New Yorkers jogged around Central Park's reservoir. Just outside the park, on a sidewalk of Fifth Avenue, Lucille stood hidden behind a large coffee cart watching the entrance of Paul Marin's apartment building. Through the glass front doors, she saw the elevator open and Paul and a beautiful woman come out together. It was Roxie Lee. The doorman discreetly turned his back, and Paul and Roxie pressed against each other and kissed deeply.

Across the street, Lucille found it hard to breath. She watched as Roxie pulled back laughing and wiped her lipstick off Paul's mouth. He whispered something into her ear, and she smiled wickedly back at him. Then they separated, straightened their clothes, and Paul sauntered out the lobby and walked away quickly down Fifth Avenue. After a moment Roxie came out, and with the doorman's help, got into a waiting cab, and was gone.

Lucille dropped her head and wiped her wet face with her hand.

God damn me, don't cry… it's my fault. Ida warned me.

But tears were rolling freely down her cheeks as she tightened her delicate fingers around the azurite gem on her chest. Slowly she turned and wandered away into the park, where people were walking dogs and young mothers pushed baby carriages.

I'm so fucking stupid. Have I learned nothing by now?

* * *

In Southampton, high, thin clouds drifted across the sky, and the air smelled of sea salt.

"Raphael Sharder did have a yacht out here somewhere," Mak Kim was saying as they got out of the car. "But it was a long time ago. I'm still working on it."

Artemis nodded to him as he and Mak followed Ray Gaines to the door.

The door was opened by a woman, about forty-five years old, wearing a fitted plaid shirt and jeans that showed off her slim, healthy figure. Her gray-blond hair was neatly pulled back. Her sharp eyes took them in for a second before she greeted them with a friendly smile.

"I'm Barbara Borsa. And you must be the law."

Ray smiled and introduced them. As she let them in, Artemis asked, "It's an unusual name, Borsa. Is it Greek?"

"Yes," she answered easily as she led them into her comfortable home office. As they sat down, she added, "There are lots of people here in the Hamptons of Greek descent. My family has been here for generations now."

"Here in this house?" Ray looked around with an approving smile. The room had a nice old-world feel with high wood wainscoting and French doors looking out onto a private garden in the back.

"Yes. Only my sister Sal and I live here now. But we love it. I can work from home, and I get to run on the beach in the mornings."

Ray turned the conversation to Raphael Sharder. Barbara told them that he had, in fact, been her client. She told them that her father had been Sharder's estate lawyer before her. And when her father died, some ten years ago, she had updated all of Sharder's documents.

"But Raphael would make revisions from time to time. His last revision was about three months ago," Barbara said.

"Do you have a copy of his will here?" Ray asked.

"I do," she answered carefully. "But I can't show it to you."

Ray just sighed and waited.

"Look"—Barbara Borsa smiled—"you're not family, and as far as I know he had none. And we all know that because of the stolen Rembrandt found at The Arethusa, the will is going to be contested. So, there's just no room for me to do anything until all the dust settles, all right?"

Ray still said nothing. After a moment Barbara continued in a professional tone.

"I assume you don't have a court order with you?"

"No," Ray said flatly. "I hoped we wouldn't need it."

"Sorry to say, Special Agent Gaines, but you will. Let me know when you get that, and I'll be happy to cooperate with you."

Ray nodded. "Fair enough." He got up to go, and Artemis and Mak got up with him.

At the door, Artemis turned back and said, "I've heard that Raphael Sharder loved boats, that he had a big yacht somewhere around here?"

"Yes." She looked at him a moment considering and then added, "She was a beautiful old thing, too, but long gone now. He liked to have big parties out on that boat."

"You ever get to go to those parties?"

"Yes, maybe once or twice. Raphael was friends with my father."

"Do you remember where he had it docked?"

"God, it was a long time ago… twenty years at least." Her brow wrinkled as she thought. "Well, it might have been the marina just west of town, past the bridge."

Artemis smiled. "And I'm guessing that Raphael didn't captain his own ship?"

"No, you're right there." She smiled back. "He was a lovely old man but never the physical type. He would have hired someone to take care of that."

"Thank you, Barbara, that helps," Artemis said truthfully, and they left.

* * *

Despite the warmer day, the carousel in Central Park was still shuttered and fenced. Lucille had always liked this place. On hot summer days, garish circus music played, and crowds of children would line up to ride the fantastically painted horses and chariots. She wondered, with all the news, if the carousel would open in the spring. She turned away and walked along the path around the barren softball fields. A sudden breeze made her shiver. She sat down on a bench and buttoned her coat.

After a moment, she took out her cell and slowly scrolled through her few contacts. She stared at a name for a while. She took a long breath and hit the number.

"TVNews, where can I direct your call?" a voice said.

"Calvin Prons, please." Lucille sounded unsure.

"One moment," the voice answered. Lucille thought about hanging up.

"Mr. Prons's office, may I help you?" a secretary said.

"Yes, is Calvin in?"

"Who may I say is calling?"

"It's Lucille. His wife." Her hand started to shake a little.

After a short pause, she heard, "One moment please, Mrs. Prons, I'll see if he's in."

She hugged herself and waited. Then his angry voice broke in, harsh and loud:

"Fuck you, Lucille. You are not my wife. We are not married anymore. You fucking need to stop saying that." In his large, sleek office on the executive floor of TVNews, Calvin Prons was in a meeting with Jock Willinger. Calvin rolled his eyes and waved Jock away with the back of his hand. Jock nodded once, obediently got up, and left the office, closing the door behind him.

Calvin Prons, head of the TVNews Network, enjoyed power. He was a good-looking, well-dressed man, with wide shoulders, a square jaw, and dark eyes. He could look dangerous when he got angry. Which was often. He had once been a Marine Captain and served in combat. Before that, he was a newsworthy college quarterback as two gold trophies prominently displayed in his office attested. But that was more that twenty-five years ago. Now his blond hair was thinning, and his belly had grown big, which not even his expensive dark suits could hide.

Calvin put his feet up on his massive metal desk with a thump loud enough for Lucille to hear and looked with disgust at Columbus Avenue far below.

"All right, Lucille. I'm fucking too busy for this shit. What do you need now?" he growled.

"Nothing, Cal," Lucille whispered, "I just needed to talk to you."

"What?" he answered loudly, "You're killing my day, at least you could fuckin' talk loud enough for me to hear."

Lucille closed her eyes and spoke louder, her voice raspy. "Sorry, Cal. Is this better?"

"I can hear you, but it is never going to be better." Calvin Prons was known for his winning smile, but he wasn't smiling now. "Okay, okay. So how much do you need this time?"

"I…" Lucille shook her head. It was hopeless. "I don't need any money. I just wanted to talk to you."

"Right," Calvin smirked. "You know, I'm actually trying to make a living here. What the fuck do I have to do to get you to stop calling me?"

Lucille's eyes welled up with tears, and she hung her head. "I'm sorry Cal, I just thought—"

"No, fuck, no," he cut her off, "you didn't think. You never do. It's always all about you. What you need. How much you can get. You know what… Don't call me again."

"Oh, please Cal…" The words stopped in her throat.

"Look, I'm glad you got yourself straightened out. But you and I are done. If you need to talk, you can call my lawyer." Calvin hung up and yelled for his secretary.

A very attractive, scared-looking young woman opened his office door.

"Never put through a call from that fucking psycho. Ever again. You understand me?" he commanded.

"Yes, Mr. Prons, I understand." She wondered if she was about to be fired.

Calvin looked at his secretary and saw her fear. She was new here. He smiled forgivingly. "I'm sorry, Bess."

The young woman smiled back, and her shoulders relaxed. "You have an eleven o'clock with Roxie Lee. Shall I ask her to come up?"

"Yeah, thanks, kid. And you can call me Calvin." He smiled.

Lucille had her arms wrapped tightly around herself. She looked at the field of mud and yellow grass before her and felt helpless. Drawn against her will, she looked again at her cell. She slowly scrolled to her sister Ida's number. But she knew that Ida would be at work by now and wouldn't answer.

Then she found Paul Marin's numbers: his cell, his office. She shook her head, disgusted with herself, and pressed the number for his office.

"Dr. Marin's office, may I help you?" a pleasant, efficient woman said.

"Yes, hello… This is Lucille, and I'd like to make an appointment."

"Certainly, Mrs. Prons, what day are you looking for…?"

"Actually"—Lucille took a breath to steady her voice, came to a decision, and spoke clearly—"I'm not using Prons anymore. It's my own name now, Lucille Orsina."

"Oh, of course, I understand. I'll make sure your file is updated. So, what day do you have in mind?"

"Does Paul have anything open tomorrow?"

There was a short pause, and then she heard, "Oh yes, you're in luck. He has a cancelation. Could you do noon?"

"Yes, I can."

"Very good, Ms. Orsina. You're all set for tomorrow."

Lucille thanked her and hung up. The park was strangely quiet all around her. She got up and started to walk. Then, hating herself, she hit another number on her phone, Paul's cell.

A machine voice invited her to leave a message. She tried to sound happy:

"Hi Paul, I missed seeing you after class last night... But I know how busy you are. Anyway, I just made an appointment at your office for tomorrow. Unless you want to see me tonight first...? I would love that. I really would...."

She stopped. She felt sick and needy. She focused on sounding normal. "So, call me if you want to get together. Or just call me. Bye."

She hung up and started to walk slowly. By the time she got back to the carousel, a totally new thought had occurred to her. Something that felt less like crawling and more like... justice.

She looked at her short contact list again. She scrolled to a name she hadn't thought about for a long time: Professor Artemis Bookbinder. Her finger moved to his cell number. It would be so easy to call him.

But what would happen if I did? What could I say?

Lucille heard some voices and saw a group of rowdy boys heading her way. She felt suddenly vulnerable. She put her cell in her pocket and walked quickly away. As she got to the busy sidewalk of Central Park South, she breathed out. Then an ambulance sped past, sirens screaming, and she winced. She felt ashamed to be so fragile.

* * *

"I found this note over here. She's gone for sure." Mrs. Luciano was in her late sixties and out of shape. The walk up four flights had winded her, and her round face was shiny with sweat. She held out the note that Beth Schaefer had left on the little kitchen table, and the younger cop, a handsome Black man, took it.

"You own this building?" Detective Clayton Collins asked as he passed the note to Drew Sweeney.

"Yeah, I inherited it from my father. And I've lived here all my life," she said proudly, in her strong Brooklyn accent. "I've always rented out this top floor. Helps to make ends meet. I'm going to miss that girl."

The note was simple:

Dear Nora, I have to go. Anything left here is yours to keep. Thank you for everything, Beth.

"You were friends, then?" Drew asked, her voice friendly.

"Yeah. She was good company. I'd cook a nice meal sometimes for us. We'd sit and chat." Mrs. Luciano went over to the sink, found a clean glass, and filled it with cold tap water. "Lately though, I hadn't seen as much of her. She was busier at work, I suppose." She took a drink.

"Did she talk about work much?" Drew asked.

"Not much. I know she managed some kind of art shop in Manhattan." The older woman shrugged.

"And how long did she live here?" Clayton asked as he looked around.

"Oh, just under four years, I guess. Time goes quick, no?" Mrs. Luciano's breathing was becoming easier.

The studio around them was simple, pleasant, and softly lit by cloudy skies above a large garret window. Everywhere, there was evidence of Beth Schaefer's hurried departure: drawers left open, dirty dishes in the sink, paint and brushes left behind.

Something caught Drew's eye. She walked over to the easel and studied the watercolor painting there. It was a gentle seascape.

"Who is Khloe?" Drew asked.

"Who?" Mrs. Luciano said as she came to look at the painting. "My, she really is good, isn't she?"

"Have you seen this before?" Drew nodded.

"No, it's getting too hard for me to make all those steps, so I had to wait for Beth to bring down whatever she was working on. But it's sweet, no?"

"Yeah. It's nice. But I mean this"—Drew pointed to the blue letters in the lower corner of the painting—"Did she usually sign herself as Khloe?"

"Uh, no…" Mrs. Luciano bent close to see. "She wouldn't sign anything at all. Though I was always telling her that she should. But she said she wasn't good enough. Made her feel pretentious or something. Kids, right…?"

"Would it be all right with you if we borrowed this for a while? I want to show it to someone"—Drew smiled at her—"I'll make sure you get it back once we're done with it."

"I guess that would be all right." She nodded.

Drew and Clayton spent some time looking around. In the closet they found a shoebox filled with receipts: for paint supplies mostly. Mixed in with these were three handwritten receipts for doctor visits earlier in the year. They saw that she'd paid with cash, the doctor was expensive, his office was on the Upper East Side, and that his name was Paul Marin.

"I guess she had no insurance then?" Clayton shook his head. "I wouldn't have guessed it to look at her."

Mrs. Luciano looked up at him curiously.

"I met her a few days ago at the gallery," he explained simply.

Drew asked if they could hold onto the box of receipts, too.

"Why not?" Mrs. Luciano shrugged her shoulders.

*　*　*

At day's end, Artemis and Mak had come to the Southampton Marina to get information about Raphael Sharder's boat. But it seemed that Barbara Borsa had been wrong.

"That boat would have been way too big for this place," a harried young woman named Sheila, in the marina office, told them. But Sheila was sure that it had been docked in nearby Sag Harbor, that she'd been at parties on the boat, and that she could tell them who had been the captain.

"You seem kinda young. I mean, that boat's been gone a long time now," Mak said, thinking that Sheila couldn't be more than thirty.

"Thanks." She smiled at him but spoke sharply. "But I'm talking about my grandfather, so I guess I know. Toby Brown was always captain of old man Sharder's yacht."

"Is your grandfather still around?" Artemis asked carefully as Mak took notes.

"Oh yeah," Sheila said proudly. "He'll work till he drops. He runs a fancy day boat out of Sag Harbor, makes lots on the rich and the lazy, when in season. Just ask around the marina next to Long Wharf. Everybody knows Toby Brown."

"Do you remember the name of Sharder's boat?" Artemis asked as he sized her up.

"Nah, agent… um"—she looked to Mak—"agent… whatever-his-name was right. I was just a kid then."

Mak looked up sharply, but it didn't seem like Sheila was trying to insult him. "Kim," he said simply, "Agent Makani Kim."

"Right. Look, things are really busy," she said apologetically. "Everybody needs everything right now." She nodded to the busy marina outside her window. "I gotta get back to work. Give Toby my love when you see him, okay…?"

It was a clear dismissal. Artemis and Mak left the office.

Mak got a text on his cell. "The coroner has made it official. Death occurred Thursday night around seven," he reported.

Artemis nodded once. They sat down together on a bench that looked out across the wooden docks to the wide waters of Shinnecock Bay. At least the weather was getting better. Before them, a thin ribbon of bright red sunset was glowing below drifting clouds.

"Do you smoke?" Mak offered, holding out an open pack.

"Nope, never have," Artemis said factually, his blue eyes looking far away.

"Yeah. I've been quitting for years now." Mak smiled as he shoved the cigarettes back into his jacket.

It was the end of a long, frustrating day. Armed with warrants, FBI agents had spent the day searching through both of Sharder's art galleries and his home: The Arethusa. Agents searched Taki Fukuda's home in Southampton and Morty Singer's jewelry shop on Main Street. They found nothing.

"It's enough for one day," Artemis said softly. "We'll go find this Toby Brown tomorrow."

Artemis felt tired and worried. They were out there still. The people who killed his parents, who left the note threatening his family. He felt overwhelmed by the knowledge that after so many years of searching, nothing had ever been found. Until now.

He looked out at the day's last light, a sharp crimson band shining across the sea, and shivered.

It looks like a ribbon of blood.

Chapter Five

Tuesday, March 3rd

The overnight rain had cleared, and the early sun breaking through the clouds promised another warm day in Sag Harbor. The marina next to Long Wharf was open, and a few people were already working on their boats. Standing at the entrance to the docks, Artemis thanked a couple of old men with fishing gear, who headed off. It seemed that it was true, everyone here did know where to find Captain Toby Brown.

"Morning." Mak Kim walked up. "Here, I got you a coffee."

Artemis looked at the paper cup in Mak's hand and wondered if it was safe to touch. The news this morning reported that the coronavirus had killed more than three thousand people globally. The United States had six dead. And last night, in North Carolina, over ten thousand people attended the President's rally.

Artemis took the cup, peeled back the plastic lid, and took a sip.

I will not surrender to fear.

"Thanks," Artemis said. "Toby Brown's out there, working on his boat."

They made their way along the wooden docks, the water dark around them, the smell of the sea air keen and sharp.

"Sleep okay?" Mak asked.

"I never do away from home." Artemis shrugged.

"Hate hotels?"

"No, I just miss Emily," he answered truthfully.

"There's my problem," Mak said. "I'm too used to being on my own. I like living on the road."

"So, you're well suited to what you do."

Further out, where the larger boats docked, they arrived next to a sleek white yacht named *Lady Sheila*. On board, a thin teenage boy was busy unpacking a box of cleaning supplies. Leaning out from the pilot house, a hard-looking old man watched him.

Artemis and Mak stood nearby on the dock, sipping their coffees, taking in the scene: the expensive boat, the smell of resin and varnish, and the harbor wide and peaceful around them. And, as Artemis had learned to do, he looked to see if anything odd jumped out at him. Artemis smiled. There was something that didn't seem to fit here. It was the older man, who had to be Toby Brown. He was short and chubby, with lots of wrinkles around his close-set, mischievous eyes. His head was small and topped with a full growth of bristly white hair, making him look like an old badger. Or maybe a long-ago retired rugby player. He just didn't look like a sailor.

"Oy, son, go get me a tea, would ya," the older man called out in a harsh nasal voice, his British accent clear. "And not too much milk this time."

The boy, clearly intimidated, nodded once and without a word climbed off the boat, passing Mak and Artemis.

"Manchester…?" Mak quietly guessed.

"No, Liverpool," Artemis answered definitively.

"You sure?" Mak looked at him, unconvinced.

Artemis shrugged and called out to the old man. "Excuse me, we're looking for Toby Brown."

"It's your lucky day then." The man's little chin stuck out proudly. "I'm the one and only. Come on board and tell me your business. You guys looking for a charter?"

Artemis and Mak stepped over the watery gap onto a beautiful teak deck that opened to a salon with fine white leather seats and shining silver fittings. Toby Brown came down a few steps and joined them.

"No, but we bring a hello from your granddaughter, Sheila." Artemis smiled.

"Ah, well she's a great girl." Toby was smiling but cautious.

"My name is Artemis Bookbinder, and this is FBI Agent Makani Kim." Mak held up his identification.

"And we're investigating the death of Raphael Sharder," Artemis explained. "We met your granddaughter yesterday, and she told us that you once captained a boat for him?"

Toby Brown squinted at them for a moment before he nodded and answered, "Yep. I was his skipper back when. Years ago, though."

"This is some beautiful boat," Mak said as he took out his notepad. "Had her long?"

"Thanks." Toby jerked his head up proudly, his accent suddenly sounding thicker. "Yep, she's a wonder. She's just three years old. My last boat got too well used."

"I'm thinking she moves like the wind?" Artemis said appreciatively.

"She'll make forty knots." Toby smiled, revealing his tiny yellow teeth.

"And she's what, seventy feet?" Mak asked.

"She's seventy-four," Toby started talking louder. "She's fitted with the latest navigation, fish finder, and communication gear. She's got three en suite cabins and these fully adjustable helm chairs. So, I can handle fishing charters, day trips, and longer, too."

"She looks all set to go"—Artemis smiled—"but isn't March kinda early to be going out?"

"Yeah, but opportunity knocked." Toby's little eyes gleamed with greed. "I got a wealthy couple coming from New York. Said they wanna get out while they still can. They seem to think that it won't be long before everything gets shut down." He barked out a short laugh.

"Well, it might happen," Artemis said.

"Bullshit." Toby shook his head. "Bunch of wankers afraid of gettin' the flu. Comes from trusting all the crap news on the telly."

"Don't mind my asking"—Mak shot a quick look to Artemis—"but you're from Manchester, I'm guessing?"

"Then you're guessing wrong, son. Manchester? Fuck you, I'm from Liverpool!" Though he was still smiling, Toby aggressively poked his stubby finger into Mak's chest to make his point.

Artemis hid his smile by sipping his coffee, then added, "But I'm hearing a touch of Boston there, too."

Toby turned to look at Artemis. "Damn! That's pretty good. What are you anyway? A cop?"

"Art historian, actually," Artemis answered.

"Okay," Toby spoke more quietly, taking this in. "Because of that painting they found, right?"

"Exactly." Artemis nodded.

"Well, it's true," Toby said carefully. "I lived in Boston after I left England. But I've lived in Sag Harbor a long time now."

"More than twenty years?" Artemis asked, watching him carefully.

"Don't know how you did that, but yes, something like that." Toby stopped talking, waiting for Artemis to explain himself.

"Raphael Sharder's boat," Artemis obliged. "You were his skipper, and we keep hearing that was some twenty years ago."

"Ah!" Toby smiled and nodded in understanding. "Back then, it was before I had my own boat. I would job out for some of the local gentry. It paid well. Helped me get started."

"Your granddaughter said that Sharder kept his boat here?" Mak asked.

"Yep," he answered carefully. "He needed a big dock. That boat was well over a hundred feet, you know, and a very lovely thing she was. Powerful. Moved like a great gray ghost."

"Was she American built?" Artemis asked. Mak looked up from his notes.

"No, she was from somewhere in Europe, I seem to recall"—Toby's forehead wrinkled as he remembered—"She was maybe German or Italian. I'm not sure. She was built before the Second World War and was completely refit as a pleasure craft. Sorry, it's too long ago...."

"Did Raphael Sharder ever drive her?" Artemis asked.

"That's a funny question." Toby frowned.

"Just wondered." Artemis shrugged.

"Well, sure. Once you're out of the harbor, it's safe enough. It was his boat. He could do as he liked, right?"

"Of course," Artemis said. "And when was the last time you sailed her?"

"Like you said to me, maybe twenty years ago."

"And Raphael Sharder? When was the last time you saw him?" Artemis continued.

"I've not seen him in as many years." Toby shook his head. "I never really knew him that well. But he was a good man, paid well, knew how to have a good time."

"We've heard he had great parties on that boat." Artemis smiled in agreement.

Toby chuckled a little, "Fuckin' great parties. Fun times, indeed. Anybody who was anybody wanted to be out with us then."

"Like who?" Artemis asked.

"Oh, I don't know who they all were." Toby shook his head. "Not really my thing, the rich and famous. I was just a hired hand, you know."

"So, where's the boat now?" Mak asked.

"She's gone." Toby looked sad, and his Liverpool accent got heavier again. "She was stolen one night. From this marina. They never found out who did it. There were rumors that she exploded. Some say there was a fire, that she burned and sank out at sea. But I never knew. Like I said, after twenty years… I do remember that Mr. Sharder was terrible broken up about it."

In the silence that followed, Mak made notes.

Artemis turned away and looked out across the harbor. The morning sun was higher, and the calm water was glistening.

"Why did you leave Liverpool?" Artemis asked as he turned back. "You must miss it."

Toby nodded. "I was just out of school, and there was no work. I had to do something or starve. I had a friend in America that needed help at a marina. So, I went."

"A marina in Boston?" Mak added.

Toby's beady eyes flashed for a second at the young agent before he answered calmly, "Yes."

Toby looked down the dock and saw his teenage worker returning.

"Look, fellas, I've still got lots to do. So, if there's nothing else I can help you with…?"

Artemis and Mak thanked him and stepped off the boat as the teenager went on board and gave Toby Brown his cup of tea.

"Ah, thanks, lad. Cheers!" Toby uncapped his cup and took a quick gulp.

"Shite! That's fuckin' hot!" he cried out, and the boy quickly returned to work.

From the dock, Artemis called out, "Oh, Captain Brown, I forgot to ask you. What was the boat called?"

"Mother of balls," Toby muttered as he wiped his mouth. "What's that?"

"Sharder's boat. What did he call her?"

Caught unaware, Toby answered quickly, "Khloe. Spelled with a K."

"Was that someone he knew?" Artemis called.

"Fucked if I know. Good day and good luck, boys!" And with that Toby Brown turned his white helmet of hair away from them and climbed back into his pilot house.

Artemis and Mak walked away back along the docks.

"Funny that…" Artemis mused as he tossed his cup into a trash bin.

"What?" Mak asked.

"If Raphael Sharder's boat exploded, burnt, and sank at sea… Then how did her steering wheel end up on the wall of his pool house in Southampton?"

"You really think that wheel came from his boat?" Mak asked as he finished off his coffee.

"Yes."

"Okay. I'll see what I can find out about a boat named *Khloe* and if she really was stolen and lost at sea."

*   *   *

Taki Fukuda was always fastidious in his dress, ever since his boyhood in Tokyo. And that was a long time ago. He finished brushing his curly blond hair and looked at himself in the vanity mirror. He was pleased; his weave took years off him. He pulled a stylish denim sports jacket over his light blue gingham dress shirt and finished his ensemble by fluffing a sky blue silk hanky and arranging it just so in his top pocket.

His home was on the top floor of an old, completely renovated, three-story mansion, a few blocks south of Main Street, Southampton. It was a small modern condo with one bed and one bath. But it was elite, and he owned it outright. He had filled it with designer furniture and choice pieces of art. In the back, French doors opened onto a little balcony, where he could catch a peek of the ocean through rows of low houses and trees.

With a sigh, Taki looked around his home and shook his head at the disarray. Yesterday three FBI agents, armed with a warrant, had searched the place. It had been a humiliating experience. He had protested, of course, but they looked everywhere: his closets, bed, and drawers. The nerve! As if there was stolen art in his underwear drawer. Worse, they had taken away his laptop and his cell phone.

The kettle on the stove whistled, and Taki poured water over the ground beans in his French press and left it to steep. As he had been doing all morning, he went to the front windows and looked down. They were still there, two FBI agents inside a parked car. One of them noticed him and looked up.

Oh Raphael, I'm so sorry it has come to this.

Taki frowned at the agent, went back to the kitchen, got his coffee and a couple of donuts on a plate, and went out to the balcony in the back. He sat down at the little glass table, and almost at once a seagull appeared overhead, calling and flying in a low circle. Taki smiled. Gulls never forgot where the food was. As he had done on so many nice mornings before, he broke off a piece of donut and tossed it high in the air. The gull turned in flight, swooped lower, caught it, and flew away. Then two more gulls appeared. The ritual was repeated until no more food was left.

Taki smiled wistfully. It was always the little things that made us happy. Not someone's money or secrets....

He looked down at the wood trellis that ran along the side of the house to the back gardens. Taki sighed. He was definitely not young anymore. But he remembered a night, just a few years ago, when he'd forgotten his keys and, truth be told, had had a few too many peach martinis. That night, he'd actually managed to climb up the trellis, hop up over the balcony rail, and get in. Now all he had to do was reverse that process. He finished his coffee, went inside, got his wallet, his car keys, but nothing else. With a sad last look at his pretty white home, he closed the door, carefully climbed over the rail, and made his way down the trellis.

It surprised him that he could still manage it. He was a little over sixty, though he never admitted that to anyone. Only to Raphael. And now he was gone.

Feeling proud of himself, he arrived safely on the ground. He quickly made his way past the burlap-wrapped bushes and out the back gate. He had parked his green Mini Cooper a block away on a back street. Taki was feeling very clever to have so easily escaped the FBI guys out front until he was brought up short by the sight of the large, threatening form of a man leaning on his car, smoking a cigarette. The man turned his head and looked at him with his strange mismatched eyes.

Ladimir Karlovic smiled at him, and Taki suddenly found it very hard to breathe.

*　*　*

The building had a prestigious Fifth Avenue address across the street from the Metropolitan Museum. But the glass door Lucille went through was around the corner on the side street. Inside was a marble foyer, with one stainless steel door and an intercom box. She pushed the button and identified herself. The door buzzed, and she walked into the reception area of Dr. Paul Marin's office.

"Hello, Ms. Orsina, it's nice to see you again," a professional-looking older woman greeted her. "The doctor is running just a few minutes late. Please have a seat."

Lucille nodded, hung up her coat, and sat down gently on the cream-colored leather sofa. The space around her was done in *Upper Eastside tasteful*, with pin spot lighting, frosted glass floating panels, and large black-and-white photographs of flowers, depicted in extreme close-up.

Lucille felt intimidated here. She wondered if that was what Paul wanted people to feel.

She looked at the closed mahogany door to his office. And she wondered if her classmate, *Ruby*, was inside.

"I don't suppose Roxie Lee's in there with him?" She couldn't help herself.

The receptionist looked up from her work and studied Lucille for a moment. Then she smiled in a patronizing way, making it clear that she would not answer, and returned to her typing.

Lucille looked away, embarrassed. She folded her hands tightly on her lap. And waited.

After ten minutes the door opened, and to her great relief, it wasn't Roxie who came out. But it was someone she knew. Well, at least a little. It was Greg Schaefer, that sweet man who sat so quietly to the side in Paul's classes.

He smiled at her and gave her a friendly nod. She half-waved to him and watched as he set up his next appointment with the receptionist. The older woman waited until Greg had gathered his things and left the office before she told Lucille she could go in.

Lucille went into the inner office, closing the solid door behind her. Paul, dressed in a stylish sports jacket and black T-shirt, was sitting at his large wooden desk, writing some notes. Without looking up, he lifted a finger, and she stopped in the middle of the floor and waited.

Paul's office was both modern and old-world. The furniture was well designed and expensive, but the wood paneled walls gave the room a feeling of the last century. The large window that looked out to Fifth Avenue was covered by sheer drapes and framed with heavy brocade curtains. It was hard to feel comfortable here. She wondered again if Paul had made it that way on purpose.

He looked up and smiled at her. And once again she felt the pull of his beautiful face, his proud features, and his intense eyes. He watched her, and she felt the overwhelming need to say something, to please him. But she could think of nothing and was quietly starting to panic. Paul seemed to sense it and finally spoke. "It looks so great on you," he said, his voice purring.

"What does?" She struggled to clear the confusion in her mind.

"Your azurite necklace, of course. Did you forget it so soon?" Paul smiled as he chided her.

"Oh, no." She reached up and touched the dark blue stone with her fingertips. She looked at it, trying to find some courage. "No, I just thought..." She sighed.

Fuck me, just tell him the truth.

She looked up and spoke clearly, "No, Paul, I will never forget."

"I'm so glad," Paul said softly.

"But will you forget me?" She could not keep the tremor out of her voice.

He looked at her standing halfway across the room like a lost child.

After a time, he said, "No, of course not. Come, sit down."

She did as he directed and sat down on the sleek sofa near his desk. She folded her hands to keep them from trembling and said, "Did you get my message yesterday?"

"Yes, I did," he answered, watching her.

"But you couldn't call me back?" she asked gently.

"My dear Lucille"—he smiled kindly and leaned forward in his desk chair—"I have many obligations, causes, patients, and I can't just turn my back on them because I get a phone call."

She frowned, and he added, "Much as I might like to."

"I know many people need you," she said slowly. Then she took a breath and looked into his eyes.

"I just thought I mattered more than the others," she added.

There was something in the way she'd said it, something in the stillness of her body, that worried Paul. He said nothing but watched her.

After a while, she began to fidget. Then he spoke,

"Is this going to be a problem, Lucille?" His voice was dangerously quiet.

She swallowed before she could manage to answer, "No, Paul, absolutely not."

Paul leaned back in his chair, parted the sheer curtains with his hand, and looked out the window at the busy entrance to the vast museum across the street. So very many people on the steps, taking selfies, buying souvenirs, hailing cabs, going about their busy touristy day.

He had always known how to handle people. What to say, how to look to get them to do what he wanted. He looked back curiously at Lucille.

This one is going to be a challenge.

He got up, came over, and sat beside her on the sofa.

"You know, you might be right," he said in a tone of soft confession. "I do get too tied up in my own stuff, and I lose track of where I'm needed most. Of what's important. And of *who* is important."

Lucille relaxed, her eyes grew bigger, and she smiled a little. Paul leaned forward and lightly kissed her lips.

"I apologize." His words sounded like an ancient ritual. "Most humbly, and sincerely. I ask you to forgive me."

Lucille's eyes grew moist, and she whispered, "Yes, Paul, with all my heart."

He took her hands and said, "Let me make this up to you. I could see you tonight. You said that you wanted me to see your place. I could be there around seven, if you'd like."

She smiled and nodded yes.

"Good." He leaned in and kissed her neck just below her ear. She felt his warm breath and giggled softly.

"We can even break the rules a little," he murmured. "I'll bring some champagne."

"Are you sure I should...?" she whispered, uncertain.

He leaned back, lifted her chin, and said simply, "Yes, I'm sure."

"Okay. Thank you," she managed.

"Great." He smiled.

Lucille again wondered why she was so willing to do whatever this man asked her to do.

"So, you're here for a session, right?"—he switched gears pleasantly—"Why don't we do a little work in the time that remains."

"All right, Paul." She smiled at him.

"So, you were telling me about your time at Columbia University"—Paul got up and retrieved a notebook from his desk—"You had some success there, you said?"

"And some failures, too." She shook her head at herself. "It was a really confusing time for me."

"But you spoke about someone who helped you there," he said finding the page in his notes and sitting at his desk. "A professor named Bookbinder. Can you say anything more about him?"

*   *   *

Sarah Johnson had been the nurse at the Halesburgh School for a long time, and Emily trusted her and often asked for her input.

"I think that went well," Emily said as they walked together down the hallway. School was done for the day, and Emily had kept her staff behind for a short meeting to discuss the COVID-19 situation.

"Yes, they all seem to be on board"—the older Black woman sighed—"but it's confusing. The state is telling us one thing, and the White House is saying just the opposite."

"I know." Emily stopped outside her office. "So, it's up to us."

"I just want our kids to be protected," Sarah said earnestly.

"Me, too." Emily smiled. "I'll see you tomorrow."

Sarah left, and Emily went into her office and sat at her desk. The building was quiet, now that everyone was gone. It was a small school for special needs children between the ages of eight and fourteen. When Emily was hired as principal, some five years ago, it cemented their decision to move out of New York City and into the quiet little town of Halesburgh. And she loved the way things had worked out. Until now.

She looked out the window and across the street. There she saw Special Agent Bert Rocca sitting in his parked car. His window was cracked open, and he was smoking. He noticed her looking his way and nodded to her.

Emily sighed. She picked up her phone and called her aunt Delia.

"I'm heading home, do we need anything?" Emily asked.

"They look stupid," Silas said, loud enough to be heard through the phone.

"What's up?" Emily asked.

Delia sighed. "He's put on his new sneakers, you know, for the tryout."

"Running shoes," Silas muttered.

Delia turned to him. "Well, whatever they're called, they look perfect. And you do, too."

Silas smiled a little.

"Good." She nodded. "Now, go get ready."

Silas looked uncertain as he left.

"I don't know about this track thing," Emily said having heard the exchange.

"No, Em, he needs this. It'll get him out of the house and away from his damn computers," Delia answered. "And it means a great deal to him that you'll be there today."

"I know"—Emily sighed—"but, I mean that we don't know about the coronavirus. Maybe there won't be any more track. Maybe all the schools will have to close."

"That may be so," Delia said after a moment. "But until then, we should *keep calm and carry on.* Churchill said that, you know."

Emily thought about it and then said, "Thanks, Dee."

Delia opened the fridge and said that they could use some eggs. Emily signed off and gathered her things. Her cell phone sounded; she checked it and answered.

"Hi." Emily smiled. "I missed you last night."

"Me, too," Artemis said.

With Mak at the wheel, Artemis was in a car heading back from Sag Harbor to Southampton.

"Everything okay?" Artemis asked.

"Yes," Emily said. "Bert Rocca and team are on the job. And I'm heading home to take Silas to track and field tryouts."

"Kinda late in the day, isn't it?" Artemis sounded puzzled.

"No, they use the gym, and it's not free until school's done."

"Oh." Artemis considered his son's chances. "I don't remember him ever liking running much, do you?"

"Never," Emily chuckled. "But I think this is really important to him."

"Well, good for Silas." Artemis smiled.

Emily ran her fingers through her long hair. "So, will you be home tonight?"

"Definitely." Artemis looked up as they arrived in front of Barbara Borsa's house. Ray Gaines was parked outside, waiting for them. "We're just meeting up with Ray. I've gotta go."

"I'll see you tonight," she said with a smile.

It was midafternoon in Southampton, and the gathering clouds and moist air promised a foggy evening ahead. Ray saw them, got out of his car, and smiled as he held up a folded warrant for them to see.

Barbara Borsa greeted them at the door and led them into her home office. She carefully read the court order, nodded once, unlocked her desk drawer, and took out Raphael Sharder's estate documents.

"I think you'll be most interested in the dispositions?" she asked.

"Yes," Ray said, and Mak took out his notepad.

Barbara opened the will and read:

"To my friend, Taki Fukuda, I give the sum of twelve million dollars and sole ownership of my Southampton Gallery, inventory and contents therein."

They took that in for a moment before Ray murmured quietly, "That's substantial."

"Indeed." The lawyer nodded and went on:

"To the manager of my 64th Street Gallery in New York, Beth Schaefer, the sum of ten thousand dollars. To my longtime housekeeper, Patty Figgins, the sum of thirty thousand dollars. To my friend, Madeline Griffin, the sum of thirty thousand dollars."

Barbara looked up and added, "She owns the Primrose Restaurant in town."

"Yes, we've met her." Artemis nodded once.

"As to the remainder of his estate," Barbara continued, "his home, The Arethusa, along with everything else, is to be sold and all proceeds given to Oak Bluffs Village."

In response to their questioning looks, she explained, "It's a home for recovering drug addicts, in New London, Connecticut."

"And what was Sharder's connection?" Ray asked.

"I really have no idea." Barbara shook her head.

"Yesterday," Artemis said softly, "you said that Raphael Sharder revised his will from time to time and made his last revision three months ago?"

"Yes, I did," Barbara answered carefully. "Give or take a few days. He usually made some small increase in the gifted amounts every year or so."

"Ah…" Artemis watched her. "And always given to these same people and Oak Bluffs Village?"

"Yes, always the same." Barbara shifted a little in her seat. Then she added, "Well, since I've been handling his estate, anyway."

"And that's been ten years, since you took over from your father," Artemis stated.

"Yes," she said.

"Did he have a healthcare proxy?" Ray picked it up.

"Yes." Barbara nodded as she opened the document and reported, "Taki Fukuda was his healthcare agent."

"I see," Ray said.

"So, Special Agent Gaines"—she sighed—"What happens now? I'm thinking I can't have a reading of the will anytime soon."

"No, I think not," Ray answered factually. "It'll be up to a judge to decide. There's obvious criminal activity. We're just beginning our investigation of the stolen Rembrandt and how much of Sharder's wealth came from ill-gotten gains."

"It's so hard to believe." Barbara smiled sadly.

"I'll need a copy of these documents," Ray said as he got up.

"I thought you would." Barbara nodded and handed him a large envelope from the same desk drawer. "I had this made up for you."

With that, they thanked her and left. Out on the quiet street, Ray suggested to Mak and Artemis that they walk the few blocks into town and head for the Primrose Restaurant.

"We'll start with Maddy Griff," he said.

The Primrose was still quiet in the lull between lunch and dinner. At the counter, having a coffee and going over paperwork was a healthy-looking, middle-aged woman, neatly dressed in jeans and a button-down shirt. She saw them come in, smiled, and came over to greet them.

"Nice to see you again, fellas," Maddy said. "You here for lunch?"

"Just some coffee, thanks, for all of us." Ray smiled back. She led them to a large booth, grabbed a coffee pot, and poured out three cups as they sat.

"Actually"—Ray looked up at her—"if you could spare a few minutes, we would really like to talk to you."

Maddy saw the serious look in the older man's eyes.

"Of course." She nodded, grabbed her coffee from the counter, and sat down with them. "So, how's your investigation going?"

Mak opened his notepad.

"Progressing," Ray said evenly. "We've come here to tell you that we've heard the terms of Raphael Sharder's will, and he left you some money."

She smiled softly and looked down. "Did he?"

Artemis took in her reaction and nodded once to himself.

"He left you thirty thousand dollars," Ray said, watching her.

Maddy shook her head. "Thank you, Raphael," she whispered quietly.

"Does that surprise you?" Ray asked.

"Yes, and no." She smiled but didn't explain further.

"I'm afraid his estate will be contested and tied up for a long time. You may never see that cash," Ray added.

"Oh, that's okay. I'm doing fine here, anyway." She shrugged.

"Any idea why he left you the money?" Artemis asked.

"He had a kind heart," she said simply.

"Yes, but why you?" Ray stayed after her.

Maddy took a sip of coffee and nodded. "Yeah, I know what you're asking. See, I knew him a long time. Since my husband and I first opened this place some eighteen, nineteen years ago… Raphael was a regular here from the first. He knew what it cost us to get here and how hard we tried. I mean, this place was a dream for Mick and me." She smiled sadly and brushed a loose hair back off her forehead.

"We worked so well together. Mick cooked, and I ran the bar, did the books…" She took a long breath and went on, "My husband died of lung cancer eight years ago, and I was really in a bad way. I hired a chef, so the place was still okay, but I sure wasn't. Though I kept pretending I was."

"Sorry," Artemis offered quietly. She smiled back.

"Anyway, Raphael would come in when it was quiet, and we'd sit and talk. He just let me go on and on. Never seemed to mind." Her voice caught, and she breathed in again to steady herself.

"Raphael was one of those rare people, you know. He just wanted to help. He started hiring me to cater his parties… Anyway, I found my footing again. So, no, I didn't know anything about him leaving me money. But it doesn't really surprise me."

"You know," Artemis said, "we hear from everyone the same thing. That he was a kind, decent man."

She nodded sadly.

"So, it was good to hear that he had someone to share his life with." Artemis looked down and stirred his coffee. "But who was luckier, Taki or Raphael?"

Maddy laughed softly. "I know, right? I think it was a good match both ways."

Artemis nodded. Ray sipped his coffee. Mak looked out the window at Main Street, Southampton.

"They were always so protective of their relationship. Nobody really knew about them"—she looked curiously at Artemis—"Who told you that?"

"Sorry"—Artemis looked up at her and shrugged—"I really can't say. But we did wonder about it. I mean, Raphael was twenty years older than Taki, right?"

"I think that was what made it work," Maddy relaxed and explained, "Taki is a lovely, lonely soul, and Raphael was a natural patron, right. When Taki first came over from Japan, he was studying art in New York City. They met, Raphael liked him, and hired him to work here." She turned her head to indicate the closed gallery across the street.

"They were lovers right away, then." Artemis nodded knowingly.

"Yes," she confirmed, "I think so. Not that anyone would know it. They had their own places. Taki's is just a few blocks away." She pointed off toward the ocean.

"Yes"—Ray smiled—"we've been there."

She looked at him. "I see."

"Do you think Taki knew anything about the stolen Rembrandt?" Ray asked.

Maddy took a moment before she answered, "That's a good question. I really don't know."

"Do you know if Taki owns a gun?" The kind voice of Mak Kim seemed to surprise her, and she answered quickly, "I haven't a clue, but I can't imagine he does. He's not the type." Then she added pointedly, "They really cared for each other, Raphael and Taki."

"We've heard a lot about those parties at The Arethusa," Artemis picked it up. "Taki would show up at those, right?"

"Sure, of course. Everyone would come"—she smiled remembering—"That was a time. They were really big gala events. I'd hire a half dozen girls, and a hundred people would come. There'd be press, and security… But as Raphael got older, he scaled them back."

"Until it was just you and Patty Figgins taking care of…? How many people came to the last one?" Artemis asked.

"Let's see… That was in the spring, right before Memorial Day. Maybe only a dozen people came."

"Remember who?"

"Well, Taki, like you said, and a few of Raphael's old friends: shop owners like Morty Singer, and his lawyer Barbara Borsa, and her sister Sally," she reported.

"Toby Brown?" Artemis asked.

"Who?" Maddy shook her head. "I don't think I know who that is."

Artemis nodded once at her.

"Any younger people there?" Ray asked.

"Well, Beth Schaefer was there. She's the manager of Raphael's gallery in New York."

"Right. And people from the media?"

"Yes, Roxie Lee," Maddy offered.

"Who's she?" Ray asked.

"Someone you really can't miss." Maddy sounded impressed. "She's a tall, beautiful girl, with very dark black skin. When she's in a room, everyone notices her. I think she works in television, in New York."

"Did Beth Schaefer or Roxie Lee ever bring someone along?" Mak asked, referring back to his notes.

"Not Beth, as I remember, but yeah, Roxie brought a real good-looking guy to that last one. I'm not sure who he was though."

"Remember anything special about him?" Mak asked.

"Well," Maddy turned and smiled at Artemis. "He had powerful eyes, like yours."

Artemis shifted self-consciously. "Anything else?"

"He had short, curly hair, a really strong body, and a nice face." Maddy grinned. "Not that I noticed him or anything. They made a sweet-looking couple."

Some people came into the restaurant, and Maddy waved to them.

"I gotta go; they'll be coming in now." She looked to Ray.

"Thank you, Maddy. You've helped a lot," he told her.

Maddy nodded, got up, and went off to greet her customers.

Ray knocked back his coffee and said, "Let's go talk to Taki."

Artemis, Mak, and Ray walked easily down Main Street, past where the stores ended, and onto a side street. Taki lived here in a condo, on the top floor of a fully renovated, gleaming white, historic mansion.

Ray looked to his two FBI agents across the street, leaning on their dark car. One of them nodded to let Ray know that Taki Fukuda was still upstairs.

Ray sighed and led Artemis and Mak up the three flights. At the door, Ray took a moment to catch his breath. Mak threw a look to Artemis, but both said nothing.

Ray pushed the bell. And after a while, pushed it again. Then he knocked. And knocked louder. He tried the handle of the door, and to his surprise, it turned, and the door opened.

"Mr. Fukuda? Are you home? It's Ray Gaines, are you here?"

There was no answer. Ray nodded, and they went in and quickly looked through the rooms. Artemis went out onto the balcony, looked at the trellis, and called to Ray. Taki Fukuda was gone.

"Get those two guys up here now," Ray growled to Mak, who turned and ran down the stairs.

Ray looked down to the garden and the quiet, empty streets beyond.

"God damn me," he muttered darkly.

* * *

"Silas, it's time to go," Aunt Delia called as she put the new carton of eggs in the fridge. She and Emily looked up as he rounded the corner into the kitchen and stopped. He looked worried.

"All set?" Emily asked.

"I guess so." Silas shrugged.

"You're gonna do great," Delia said proudly as she handed him his coat. "And I can't wait to see those new sneakers get all dirtied up."

"Running shoes," he sighed.

"All right, off you go." Delia ushered him to the back door. "And remember to lift your knees as high as you can," she added as he went out to the car.

Emily shook her head. "Well, at least he'll make the team."

"That's the spirit." Delia grinned at her.

"I mean, they take everybody who tries out." Emily smiled.

"Oh"—Delia laughed—"well, that's good, too. Now go have a good time. And by the time you get back, the house will be as clean as a whistle."

Emily thanked her, grabbed her coat, and went out to join Silas. As she got into her car, she looked down the driveway to the street, where Bert Rocca was standing with two other FBI agents. He saw her and gave a friendly wave. She looked at her son sitting next to her and told him to buckle his seatbelt.

Bert turned to one agent and told her to take the lead. The woman got into her car and pulled out onto the side of the quiet suburban street and waited. He told the other agent to stay by the house and keep watch on Delia. The agent nodded and walked away to his own parked vehicle.

Then Bert got into the third car, started the engine, and watched as Emily slowly drove down the length of the driveway to the street. Following the procedure, as she had been instructed to do, she lined up behind the first car on the street, and Bert pulled up behind her.

Bert pushed the microphone clipped to his lapel and told the lead agent to go. In this formation, they started off.

From the bedroom window, up on the second floor of the old house, Delia watched this curious parade and sighed. She turned away, plugged in the vacuum, and started to clean.

But only a few blocks away, Emily put on her signal and pulled over. The agent in the lead car pulled over. Bert parked behind Emily and walked easily up to her window.

Emily rolled down the glass and looked up sheepishly. "I'm so sorry, Bert, but I've got to go back. I forgot something."

Bert smiled kindly at her. "Not the slightest problem. We can all turn around here and head back." Then he leaned down and took in Silas. The boy looked worried.

"Running is the greatest sport, kid. You're gonna love it." He smiled like a proud grandfather. Silas looked up, unsure how to respond, pushed his thick glasses back up on his nose, and nodded a little.

As he walked back to the car, Bert spoke into his microphone and told the lead agent that they were heading back. In a similar three-point formation, the three cars all swung left, backed up, and reversed their course. In a few minutes, Emily and Silas were safely delivered back into their driveway. On the street, Bert and the agent turned their cars around to wait for their departure.

Emily wondered how long they would have to put up with all this.

"Come in with me," she instructed Silas. Obediently, he followed her to the back door and into the kitchen. There she told him to wait, and she ran lightly up the stairs.

At the entrance to the master bedroom, she had to step across the vacuum. She headed to the big walk-in closet where Delia was up on a step stool, cleaning with a long-handled duster.

"Oh!" Delia jumped a little as she saw her.

"Hi, I came back for a sweater. It's getting cold," Emily said as she got a pullover from a shelf near Delia. Looking up at her hardworking aunt, she added, "Honest to God, I don't know who's worse, you or Artemis. Nobody cleans like you two, it's not human."

Delia barked out a short laugh. "It's not a competition, you know. Though, I have to tell you, it's what I do best!"

Emily smiled and pulled on her sweater.

Delia returned to dusting the top shelf. "So, what's in all these boxes? Rare treasures or just lots of junk?"

"Probably both," Emily said as she moved to a mirror and straightened herself out. "That green box has old photographs."

"I remember photographs, how quaint," Delia quipped as she dusted the shoebox.

"I know. Don't tell Silas, he'll disown me," Emily said.

Delia picked up the old green box, shook it lightly, and turned to her. "Can I see some of these pictures? It would be great to fill in what I've missed in your life, all the years I was away."

"Absolutely. Maybe this weekend. You know, I think there's even a couple of you from way back when."

"Oh, that's a scary thought. Don't grow old, my dear," Delia said in mock-seriousness as she put the box back and climbed off the step stool.

"You look very fine in that." Delia smiled approvingly at her.

"Thank you," Emily said.

"I admire you, you know, the way you've been carrying on after that threatening note," Delia said as a wave of concern passed across her face.

Emily came over and touched her arm. "You, too. But like you said, what else can we do? Run away?"

"No, of course not." Delia sniffed in a short breath and straightened her strong shoulders. "That would be the worst thing for Silas to see."

Emily looked at her aunt and smiled. "I agree. We'll see you later."

Emily headed off down the stairs, collected Silas, and headed back to the car. As they got in, she nodded to Bert down the driveway. She sighed quietly and started the engine. As before, they followed the same procedure, and the three cars headed off.

*　*　*

"So, her story checked out," Mak Kim said as they pulled up and parked in front of a row of attached townhouses in Hampton Bays.

"Patty Figgins did go see her sister," he continued, "who is an Alzheimer's patient and lives in a home in Amagansett. And after, she did spend the night here with her friend Salvatore Molina, the owner of the Antlers Bar."

"I never doubted that," Artemis murmured as he studied the cedar shingled structure. There were twelve matching two-story condos in a long curving row, each with a small balcony above the parking lot, with a view beyond of the grassy dunes and the wide waters of Shinnecock Bay.

"This is pretty nice," he added quietly.

"Yeah." Mak sounded tired but still willing. This was their last stop at the end of another long day. "So, what are we looking for?"

"She was Sharder's maid for a long time," Artemis answered. "So, she knows things."

Mak sighed and nodded in agreement. "Well, she sure did seem guilty about something when we questioned her."

"Exactly."

They got out of the car and walked toward the last unit in the row. The late winter days were still short, the last light was fading, and the landward winds felt cold and fresh.

"That helps." Mak smiled and pushed the bell.

Almost immediately, the door was opened by Patty Figgins.

"Oh, just you two?" She frowned, making the wrinkles on her worn face multiply.

Artemis smiled. "We're not enough?"

"Well, last time it was like an inquisition. So, when you called, I just didn't know what to expect." She nervously straightened her simple house-dress. "Well, come in."

They followed her through a small, neat living room into the kitchen, where she washed her hands at the sink.

"You have a really nice place here"—Artemis smiled at her—"And you can see the water; that's great."

"Well, from upstairs I can." She wiped her hands quickly on a dish towel. "How about some coffee? I just made it fresh." Her Irish ancestry was again unmistakable in her speech.

They thanked her and sat at the small blue linoleum table.

"This is in great shape." Artemis ran his hand across the stain-less-steel trim.

Patty turned from pouring coffee and smiled. "Thanks, I got that table years ago in an antique store in Southampton."

"1950s… maybe '51," Artemis mused. "You've taken good care of it, too."

Patty seemed pleased at the compliment. She set down three coffees and sat across the table from them.

"There's milk and sugar, if you need, on the counter." She took a short breath and continued, "So, what else can I tell you, other than what I've done already?"

"Good coffee." Mak smiled at her and pulled his notepad out of his field jacket pocket.

She nodded at him and turned to Artemis with an appeal, "Because I have to go out soon. You know, I see my sister Mary in the home—"

"Yes, I remember." Artemis was smiling. "Biddy Socks."

Patty looked at him for a second and then laughed. It was a simple, happy sound. "I forgot you saw that. Mary's always called me that."

Artemis smiled, picked up his cup, and went over to the granite counter where she had put out a small porcelain set, with milk and sugar.

"I need a spoon," Artemis said casually as he opened a drawer and lifted one out. Patty's head spun around quickly, and she looked alarmed. She started to say something but then changed her mind.

Artemis smiled as he came back and sat across from her. He slowly stirred his coffee with the spoon.

"Um, you didn't put in any sugar?" Patty looked confused.

"No, I don't like sugar." Artemis lifted his cup and took a sip, watching her over the rim. "You really do make a proper coffee."

"Thanks," she said very softly.

Mak watched this performance and nodded once. Then he said,

"Ms. Figgins, we're here to tell you that we've heard the provisions of Raphael Sharder's will and that he left you thirty thousand dollars."

She gulped and tried to speak but couldn't. Her eyes got wet, and she pulled out a handkerchief from the pocket of her housedress.

"He was so very kind," she managed to whisper.

"But I'm afraid that you may never see that money," Mak continued. "Because of what we might find in our investigations."

As his words got through, she looked up startled. "But Mr. Sharder was a wealthy man. Very wealthy."

"Yes, but we have yet to determine if his money came from honest means," Mak explained patiently.

"It's that Goddamn painting," she spoke bitterly, the lilt in her speech sounding stronger.

"The money might someday come through," Artemis said, watching her.

"Well, I could sure use it." Patty shook her head in disgust.

Mak said, "But, you worked for Mr. Sharder for so many years, and he must have paid well."

"Yes, that's true enough." She shrugged. "But I don't know what I'll do now. I'm almost sixty-five, and jobs don't just fall off the trees, you know."

Mak took a sip of coffee.

Patty folded and unfolded her hands and said, "Well, if there's nothing else I can help you with…?"

"Well, you could tell us who installed the mechanism that hid the stolen painting above the fireplace," Mak said calmly.

Patty looked at him astonished. "No, for the love of God, I surely can't tell you that because I haven't the slightest idea what you're talking about." The fight in her voice was growing.

Artemis picked up his spoon and slowly stirred his coffee. The quiet sound of the metal circling the bottom of the cup became the only sound in the room. Patty focused on what he was doing.

"Nice weight, this," he murmured appreciatively. "It's old. 1820s maybe. British. Sterling silver."

Patty held her breath and watched him. Artemis lifted the spoon up, so it was eye level with her.

"Do you do a lot of entertaining here?" he asked.

"No, why?" she whispered.

"Because I saw that you have enough silverware in the drawer to host dinner for eight," he said.

"I…"—Patty began to cry—"I only did it once, I swear it. And Mr. Sharder would never have missed them. He had three sets of silverware; he didn't even know he had them. They were just in a box in the back of a closet."

She breathed in short, ragged gasps. Her face flushed red.

135

"So," Artemis said not unkindly, "I'm thinking you took this silver to sell because it's so expensive keeping your sister in that home."

Patty opened her eyes wide and nodded. "Yes, that's exactly it. Mary's room and board are paid for by the government, God bless them. But she has nothing else except what I can provide. And she needs things, simple things, like socks or a warmer blanket and a supply of proper teas."

"So, why is this still here in your home?" Artemis asked, slowly turning the spoon in his fingers.

"I haven't had time to try and sell them yet," she said. "I took them about a week ago, and before I could do anything, Mr. Sharder was killed, and everything just went to hell."

"You said this was the only time you stole from Mr. Sharder?" Mak asked, sounding doubtful.

"Well, I took a gold ashtray once, a few years ago. But just that, and this silverware. And that's all. I swear it."

Mak looked to Artemis as if they would have to do something about this felony.

Artemis focused on the spoon. "Oh, there's the maker's mark. I was right, 1820." He looked up at Patty. "Well, there are a few things we've learned about, that you could confirm for us."

Patty understood. "All right, what do you want to know?"

"We've been told that Taki Fukuda and Raphael Sharder were lovers," Artemis reported.

She thought for a moment and nodded. "Yes, they were. They didn't want people to know."

"And they were together for a long time?" Mak asked.

"Yes, for as long as I can remember. Mr. Fukuda was always ever so kind to Mr. Sharder, especially as he got older. It was nice to see, you know."

"Why didn't you tell us this before?" Mak asked.

"I just thought it was what Mr. Sharder would have wanted"—she shrugged—"And, well, I never have trusted cops. No offense."

"None taken. I'm FBI," Mak said.

"And I teach art history." Artemis smiled, and Patty relaxed a little.

"We've heard a lot about big parties at The Arethusa," Mak continued. "That guests there included a woman named Roxie Lee."

"Yes, and not just at the parties. Mr. Sharder would have her over from time to time."

"How did they know each other?" Artemis asked.

"I don't know, they were just friends," she answered. "In nice weather they'd sit out by the pool, have lunch maybe." Then she laughed a little.

"What?" Artemis smiled.

"Just the thought of them. Him, so old, and you know, out of shape. And her, so very good-looking. It could be hot as blazes, and Mr. Sharder would be covered from head to toe, in his robe and towels. But that woman loved the sun. She'd be out there lounging around with nothing on but a little string of a suit. God, what the girls think is proper today!" she said with disapproval.

"And her boyfriend," Mak asked, referring to his notes, "did he ever come to the house with her?"

"Yes." Patty wrinkled her forehead remembering. "Maybe once or twice."

"Know his name?" Mak asked.

"Um, no. I don't think I ever heard it. Nice looking man, though. He didn't wear too much out by the pool either." She chuckled.

Artemis smiled. "Anything else about him?"

She considered for a moment and said, "I seem to remember hearing that he was a doctor. And that he had a house out here somewhere. But that's about it."

Mak pulled out his cell and typed in *Roxie Lee, Producer, TVNews*. A picture of a good-looking Black woman came up, almost at once. He showed it to Patty, who confirmed that it was the same woman. Mak saved the link.

After a few more questions, they thanked Patty for her time and got up to go.

"Be good now," Artemis said quietly as he handed her the silver spoon.

"I will," she answered sincerely.

Leaving her clutching her prize, they went outside, where the early night sky was dark with clouds. Mak and Artemis got in their car and drove off to Southampton, where a waiting FBI chopper would take them back to New York City.

* * *

Paul Marin stood at the counter in the renovated kitchen, pouring two glasses of champagne. Behind him, Lucille nervously undid the top button of her blouse to reveal the dark blue stone lying above her breasts. It was night in New York, and Paul could easily see her reflection in the dark glass of the windows. He stirred one of the drinks with his finger.

"Are you sure I should be having that?" she asked quietly.

"Yes, I am." He turned and handed her a glass. "To you, Lucille. I'm so proud of how hard you've been working." He clinked her glass.

Still uncertain, she took a little taste.

"Oh, that's nice"—she smiled at him—"And I have been so very good."

"So," he chuckled, "give me the tour."

"Of course." She relaxed, took his hand, and led him down a long hallway to the living room, where the large windows looked out over a row of brownstones on West End Avenue.

"It's a Candela building," Lucille said as if Paul would know who Candela was. When she realized that he didn't, she explained in a rush that Rosario Candela was the best designer of the 1920s. That he built all over the city but especially here on the Upper West Side. That the way he laid out rooms was again being valued for their grace and privacy. And that buildings like this one were being renovated, turned into condos, and sold for large profits.

"How big is this place?" Paul sounded impressed as they wandered into her bedroom.

"Classic six," Lucille spoke softly, watching to see his reactions. "It's too big for just me, of course, but Calvin insisted. It was part of the settlement."

"So, you're feeling grateful to him?" Paul smiled, but he was testing her. Her ex-husband Calvin Prons had been much discussed in their sessions.

"No, he betrayed me and slept with everyone in a skirt"—for the first time she sounded a little angry—"especially if they were cute, stupid, and told him how great he was."

"To Calvin Prons, TV guy, and head asshole," he toasted lightly in agreement and took a sip.

She laughed gently and said, "My God, it's so nice to have someone on my side."

Paul smiled and looked around. The lights were out in the bedroom, but the bright city around them glowed through the windows, creating angular shadows across the walls and her large linen-covered bed.

"I like it," Paul pronounced softly.

Lucille smiled, "You do?"

"Yes, it's romantic," Paul purred and kissed her.

"I'm so glad you're here," she whispered. Then a sudden, piercing siren of an ambulance far below made her jump. The wave of red and blue lights passing across the ceiling made Paul's eyes flash strangely as he watched her.

"We'll have to help you get better with that," he said softly.

"I know." She shrugged and took a sip of champagne.

Paul walked easily over to the windows and looked down at the busy street, nine floors below them. The night was getting cold, but everywhere people were walking dogs, heading to dinner, riding in cabs. A delivery boy on a bike dodged in and out of the moving rows of cars and trucks. His radio loudly played a song in Spanish, a horn sounded, someone shouted. He rode away along a flashing line of yellow lights, which marked the edge of a utility trench that had been left open for months.

Paul turned back to her room and studied the empty walls and simple furnishings. On the dresser was a single object: a framed photo of a distinctive looking woman.

"Ida has always been good to me, like an angel," Lucille said and watched as he lifted up the picture of her sister. "I'd probably be dead by now without her help. She got me to you."

"Yes, she did." Paul nodded as he carefully put the picture down and continued to explore the room. He opened the door to a walk-in closet and switched on the light. It was bare except for a few things on hangers, four pairs of shoes, and a half dozen file boxes on the shelves above.

"Nice big closet," he said.

"Yes." She nodded.

"But, there's not much in here? Are you doing okay?"

"Yes, I am," she reassured him. "Calvin is a prick, but I did okay in the divorce. And I have money of my own. It's just that"—she came up close to him and leaned into his back—"I haven't really had much interest in buying new stuff for a while."

"Well, it's time to fix that," he said kindly and put his arm around her. "We have to start taking better care of Lucille."

"Can I ask you something?" she began timidly.

"Of course," he said, looking at the labels on the boxes.

"Why don't you call me *Azurite*?" Her fingers touched the stone on her pendant. "I know that we don't talk about each other outside of class," she spoke quickly before he could stop her. "But when you've talked about them, you've called them by their class names... like *Ruby*, not Roxie Lee?" Her voice trembled just a little. She hoped that he hadn't noticed.

"Ah, well." He turned to face her and considered for a moment. Then he said gently, "Because you are special. You, Lucille, are precious to me."

She smiled and whispered, "Thank you, Paul. I feel that way about you, too."

He looked at her for a moment, then said, "I see that one of these boxes is from your art history class?"

"Yes." She looked a little unsure.

"I'm curious," he explained. "Only today you said that going back to Columbia after your divorce saved you from... How did you put it?"

"My slide into hell." She nodded. "Only, it didn't take. I think because I knew that Calvin was paying for everything, I just couldn't see it through."

"But at college," Paul said quietly as he went and sat on the edge of her bed, "there was Professor Bookbinder. He helped you?"

Lucille looked at Paul sitting on her bed, his handsome face so powerful and mysterious in the angles of shadow and soft light. She so wanted to feel him inside of her.

"Sometimes I think there's just too much therapy in the world, don't you?" she said with a smile as she started to undo the buttons of her blouse.

"I know a lot about him, you know," Paul said, and her hands froze.

"Who?" she asked.

"Doctor Bookbinder. Artemis. I know him." Paul's face was half-lit, half-dark. "And I'm wondering if, after all you've said about him, I should be jealous."

Lucille stared at him, stunned for a moment. And then she laughed. "No, Paul, no." She came and sat next to him. "He was just my teacher. I had a crush on him. He was kind to me, that's all."

"But, in a master's program, aren't there always private meetings with your professor?" he asked quietly.

"Yes, I suppose, eventually, but I never got that far," she answered. "I dropped out, remember?"

"I remember everything, Lucille," he said darkly.

"Paul," she spoke with quiet urgency, "I was destroyed by the divorce and was desperate for anybody to care about me. Anybody. And the drugs were getting out of hand. And anyway, that was almost five years ago. He doesn't even know who I am by now."

Paul sat still and watched her.

"Paul...?" she trailed off, uncertain.

Then he smiled at her.

"Good, Lucille, very good."

She opened her mouth to say something, but nothing came out.

"I just wanted to make sure that you were over your fixation for the man," he explained, sounding professional but kind. "After all you've told me, about the files you kept, how jealous you were of his wife, the diary you wrote... I mean, I had to be sure."

"Oh"—she nodded, understanding—"I guess you're right. I must have sounded nuts."

"Not nuts." He smiled freely at her. "That's not a term we professionals use."

She laughed, despite her confusion in the moment; she couldn't help herself.

"Oh, Paul, whatever the proper term is, I don't know. But you drive me crazy."

He kissed her lips and smiled.

"I'm glad you've closed the book on that dark chapter," he said reassuringly. He finished his champagne and put the glass down on the bedside table.

In turn, she finished off her drink and seemed to come to a decision. She got up and went to the closet.

"This is all I've kept from that time," she said, pulling down a large file box.

She put the box on the bed, opened it, pulled out a leather-bound dairy, and gave it to Paul. As she sat back down, he read through some of the entries. He shook his head.

"You poor thing," he murmured, "you really were going through some dark times."

In the diary, he found entries of how much she wanted to sleep with her professor, Artemis Bookbinder, but he never noticed her. Of how she was too shy to approach him. Of how angry she was when she read in the news that he had a wife named Emily. Paul lifted out a small online photo of a pretty looking woman with long dark hair.

"This is Emily Bookbinder, his wife?" he asked.

Lucille, embarrassed, simply nodded her head and looked away out the window.

Paul then found the entry that Lucille had told him about in their sessions. It was a strange, almost incoherent drug-rant about how she wanted to erase Emily Bookbinder from the world and help her husband start over. And that Artemis deserved someone who shared his interest in art....

After that, the entries got more confused: odd bits of poetry, strange song lyrics trailing off into nothing but blank pages.

Paul took a breath and said, "It's a lot, this."

She nodded again but still couldn't say anything.

"How did you get past it?" he wondered softly.

Lucille still looked away out the window, at the lit-up buildings and the ever-glowing sky above.

"Their son," she said sadly. "I read that they had a little boy, named Silas. It kinda woke me up, and I felt ashamed. After that, I just stopped thinking about Artemis."

She stifled a small yawn and added, "And then I dropped out of Columbia, and you know the rest."

Paul watched her and said, "I think it's a good thing to be able to let off steam in a safe environment. I know you would never have done anything bad to Emily Bookbinder."

"No, never." She tried to focus. "That's why I kept the diary. So I could read it later and see how much I sounded like a child."

"So, no one has ever seen this"—he held up the diary—"not even your sister?"

"Not even Ida," Lucille confirmed, smiling. "I'm too embarrassed by what she knows about me already."

She yawned again.

"I'm so sorry, Paul, I don't know why, but I'm so tired right now."

"Doesn't surprise me," he said kindly. "Going back over stuff like this can take a toll. Would you like to lie down for a while?"

"Yes, if you lie with me." She was frustrated that her romantic evening was dissolving, but she felt so heavy.

He cleared the box away and pulled her down onto the bed. She rested her head on his muscular shoulder.

"So… sorry…," she managed to whisper as she fell soundly asleep.

Paul looked up at the moving patterns on the ceiling, created from the passing headlights far below. As he listened to her breathing, he smiled.

It really is too fucking easy.

Chapter Six

Wednesday, March 4th

The fog had cleared, and the early morning sun was warm with the first hint of spring days ahead. And as always, New Yorkers, eager to forget the harsh winter, were out in force. Outside the 19th Precinct, the streets were jammed with traffic, and sirens from cop cars, fire engines, and ambulances were almost continuously heard.

Upstairs, in the fourth-floor conference room, where the sounds were more muted, Detective Clayton Collins was the last to arrive. He closed the door behind him and sat at the long table between Ray Gaines and Mak Kim and fired up his tablet.

By the large windows, Drew Sweeny was pouring a couple of coffees, her movements, as always, suggesting military precision. Fresh from a morning workout and swim, her cheeks and strong neck were still slightly flushed pink and her short, neat hair was still damp.

"How many laps?" Artemis asked pleasantly.

"Um, I guess about fifty lengths." Drew shrugged.

"I'm so scared of you," Artemis joked.

"So, tell me the truth, you missed this place, right?" Drew smiled as she eased her large frame gracefully into the chair next to Artemis and set a coffee down in front of him.

"Yes," Artemis said truthfully. "But I don't miss the paperwork."

"Amen to that." Clayton smiled.

Drew looked at Artemis, dressed so neatly in his vest and tie, so focused as he arranged his coffee cup, notepad, and pen just so. Drew smiled. "Well, I missed you, cousin. Welcome back."

"Me, too," Clayton said, adding, "It's good to be working with you again."

"Thanks." Artemis nodded to both.

"Ray, this is your show," Drew said respectfully to the older agent.

"First of all, the people at the Gardner Museum send their thanks." Ray smiled and looked at each person sitting at the table: Makani, Clayton, Drew, and Artemis. "They are, of course, very grateful that we've recovered the Rembrandt."

"So, I have a question," Clayton began. "How come it took this long to recover one of these paintings?"

Ray turned to him. "It wasn't for lack of trying. The FBI followed every lead, dug up backyards, searched old warehouses, and the Gardner offered millions for information. But nothing has ever turned up."

"Till now." Artemis smiled at Ray. "And some of us have been there since the beginning."

Ray nodded grimly and explained, "We were centered in Boston then, me and Bert Rocca. Late night, after St. Paddy's Day, 1990, two guys dressed as Boston cops showed up, tied up the guards, and then had a leisurely wander around the museum."

"Wait," Clayton interrupted, "wasn't there a security system?"

Ray shrugged. "Sure there was, but it was pretty simple stuff. You gotta remember that it was really just Isabella Gardner's mansion that became a museum when she died."

"On July 17, 1924," Artemis murmured to himself.

Drew caught Ray's eye. Ray smiled back at her and continued, "There were motion sensors but no live connection to the outside world. So, the two guys wandered around, cutting certain paintings out of their frames."

"And what they take is confusing," Artemis said. "Some great master-pieces, some minor things, some objects. Thirteen pieces in all."

"And the two guys?" Clayton asked.

"Dead a long time now," Ray answered. "But we know they had ties to the Frenelli crime family in Boston."

"And to the Croatian mob in Cleveland," Drew said, "and several groups in New York. That connection was how my father and Artemis's father got involved working with Ray and the FBI."

"At such a heavy cost." Ray looked to Artemis, inviting him to continue.

Artemis nodded. He explained to Clayton: "In 1994, my parents were shot on the steps of our brownstone here in Manhattan. I was twelve. I lived with Drew and her family in Brooklyn after that." He turned to Drew, who responded with a smile.

Artemis took a sip of coffee and, speaking very quietly, continued, "I started learning all I could about what had happened. Then Richard Frenelli, the head of his family, was arrested, not for murder or robbery, but for tax evasion. It took some arguing, but I got permission, and Drew took me to see him in prison."

Drew added, "I was on the force by then."

Artemis's eyes grew dark. "Frenelli was in maximum security. He was a sick old man. I sat face to face with him and asked him if he had ordered the death of my parents. He said no."

"You impressed him," Drew said. "You were just a kid, but you had balls."

"I guess." Artemis shrugged. "Then I asked him if he knew who had killed them. And he hesitated. He knew something. He smiled at me but said nothing."

Drew nodded, and she added, "Three days later, Richard Frenelli was found dead in his cell. Killed by persons unknown."

"Same as now"—Ray watched Artemis carefully—"Frenelli was old and knew that he was dying. Maybe he was considering giving up some information. Then he got himself dead. And now, Raphael Sharder wanted to give back that painting, and he's shot point blank."

"By someone we think he knew and trusted," Mak added.

Artemis felt a sudden wave of worry, like a darkness in his chest. He picked up his pen and started to draw a series of perfectly square, interlocking boxes.

"Anything yet on the 9mm bullet?" he asked quietly.

"Not yet," Mak answered.

"Right." Ray looked at Drew. "So, what are we working on?"

"Clayton and I went looking for Beth Schaefer, the 64th Street Gallery manager," Drew reported. "She's got a clean record. But she's gone. She left her place in Brooklyn in a hurry."

"She left everything behind, including a box of receipts," Clayton added. "She'd been seeing an expensive psychiatrist near here on Fifth."

"And we found this"—Drew got up and picked up a small square canvas that had been turned away and leaned against the wall—"The girl was a part time painter. I thought you should see this." She put the painting down on the table in front of Artemis.

Artemis studied it for a moment and then smiled. "She has talent."

"And?" Drew asked as she sat down again.

Artemis began slowly: "What do we know about Beth Schaefer? She was Raphael Sharder's friend; he left her ten thousand dollars. He liked being a patron to the young. She was an artist. She showed up at his parties…."

"And she was really upset when he was killed," Clayton offered sympathetically. Drew looked up curiously at the young detective.

"I liked her." Clayton shrugged.

"Okay." Drew turned back to Artemis and the painting. "But what about this?" She pointed to the blue signature in the lower corner. "Her name is Beth. Why'd she sign as *Khloe*?"

"It's a message," Artemis said simply. "And she was afraid. Look, the picture is a watercolor, but this"—he ran his fingertips gently across the blue letters—"is in oil. She wanted us to find out about *Khloe*. And we have." He looked to Mak.

"It's the name of Sharder's boat." Mak nodded. "The boat is no longer around, but the guy Sharder hired to be his captain told us it was called the *Khloe*. Spelled with a K."

"Did you find anything more?" Artemis asked.

"Police records are mysteriously missing," Mak sighed and flipped open his notepad. "But we've dug up a couple of local newspaper articles. Twenty years ago, the *Khloe* was stolen from the marina in Sag Harbor and never seen since."

"I think Captain Toby Brown was right," Artemis spoke softly, his mind following another path. "That boat was most certainly burned out at sea and sunk."

They watched him in silence, waiting.

Still absorbed in his own thoughts, Artemis murmured, "And what about the name? Any idea who Khloe is?"

"No," Mak answered. "But we still can't find much on Raphael Sharder before forty-nine years ago."

The time frame was so specific, it caught Artemis's full attention. He looked up.

"We've been through his phone records, computers, and paper files," Mak said. "And there's nothing there, just current business stuff. We haven't even found a bill of sale for anything further back than two years ago."

"That's a guy who didn't worry about being audited by the IRS," Clayton said as he ran his hand across his close-cropped hair.

"The mob never does." Ray shook his head.

Mak continued, "But credit card records show that Raphael Sharder turned up in New York City forty-nine years ago."

"He went there to study painting, I think," Artemis said, almost to himself. But Mak heard him.

"Yes," Mak sounded impressed as he confirmed, "in 1971 he was enrolled at the Arts Students League."

"He would have been thirty-three years old," Ray said, doing the math.

"Right." Mak nodded. "And records show that ten years after that he opened a small art shop in the village. Nine years later, he opened the 64th Street Gallery and bought a nice apartment a few blocks away from here."

"Yeah, on 65th just off Park," Drew confirmed. "We were there on Saturday."

"And just a couple of years after that, in 1992, he buys his mansion, The Arethusa, and opens the gallery in Southampton," Mak finished.

"Seems the man suddenly came into a shitload of cash," Clayton said.

"Yes." Artemis nodded. "And not long after the Gardner Museum robbery. So, it's likely that Raphael Sharder was the fence."

"It's good work, Makani." Ray smiled.

"Thank you, sir." Mak nodded.

Clayton got up to top off his coffee and said, "So, I'm guessing we haven't found any connections between Sharder and organized crime in Boston?"

"No, nothing," Ray sighed. "But I'm not surprised. We never even heard of this guy until last Thursday. So, what did you find in Sharder's apartment?"

"Nothing," Clayton said as he returned to the conference table.

"And it was weird, way too clean." Drew sounded frustrated. "No pictures on the walls, nothing personal anywhere, except a change of clothes."

Mak pulled out his cigarettes.

"Sorry, man," Drew said in a friendly way, "but there's no smoking in the building."

"I know"—Mak smiled sheepishly—"but I'm trying to quit, so it helps if…" He put a cigarette between his lips and left it there unlit.

"Knock yourself out," Drew chuckled.

"Okay." Ray brought them back to the business at hand. "Let's talk about the people Sharder left money to."

"Taki Fukuda stood to get a fortune," Mak said, his cigarette bobbing. "His alibi for Thursday night was pretty weak. And he has disappeared."

"And his phone and computer are clean. Too clean," Ray growled.

"Taki was Raphael's longtime friend and lover. They were kind to each other." Artemis listed what they knew. "But the security system at The Arethusa was coded off at the front gate. So, the killer was probably someone Raphael trusted."

"And someone who knew that he was planning on returning the painting," Ray added, with emphasis.

"Exactly…," Artemis started but had to wait as a series of loud car horns sounded from the street below. When the traffic returned to its normal hum, he sighed and went on:

"We should talk about Roxie Lee, Sharder's friend who went to parties at his house and hung out at his pool with a good-looking boyfriend."

"Roxie Lee had a key to Sharder's apartment here in the city," Drew announced.

They turned to her.

"Apparently, she'd go by from time to time, to check up on things." She shrugged her large shoulders. "At least that's what the Super told us."

Clayton scrolled his tablet and reported from his notes: "Roxie Lee is a television producer in town. She works on Paula DeVong's TVNews show. They shoot at Columbus and 64th street. And Roxie Lee has an apartment within walking distance, over by the river."

Clayton swiped the screen and found a press photo of Roxie Lee. At the same time, Mak pulled up the picture of her that he'd found on his cell phone. He caught Artemis's eye and smiled.

"Good," Ray said to both men, pleased, "but I have a question." Ray looked at the photo. "This Roxie is a beautiful woman. She has her own apartment on the West Side. And she also has a key to Sharder's apartment, over here on this side of town. So, were they fooling around?"

"Nah, I don't think so," Clayton sounded convinced. "The Super said that they were just friends, and that Sharder was like her grandfather."

"That patron thing again?" Ray looked to Artemis. "I wonder," he trailed off and took a sip of cold coffee.

"Hell, that's pretty bad." He winced.

"It's NYPD's finest," Drew quipped.

"Okay," Ray said. "Mak, why don't you and Artemis go find this Roxie Lee."

Artemis nodded to Mak, who answered, "Yes, sir."

"At that studio you should find Greg Schaefer," Clayton added, checking his notes. "He works there at TVNews. He's Beth Schaefer's brother. He called her on Friday morning to tell her that Sharder had been killed."

Mak made notes and nodded.

As Artemis considered this new information his eyes again grew soft and distant.

"So, Drew," Ray said to the senior officer across the table. "Could your people stay after locating Beth Schaefer?"

"We are"—Drew nodded—"and Detective Collins will be seeing her psychiatrist…?" She looked over to Clayton.

"I'm seeing him this afternoon," he confirmed.

"And we're working on the client lists from the 64th Street Gallery," Drew added. "But like Agent Kim said, those records only go back a couple of years."

"Thank you." Ray nodded. "And my top priority is finding what the hell happened to Taki Fukuda."

Ray got up with a soft grunt and said, "Okay, let's get to it."

*   *   *

It was too dark to see, but all around, and too close, she could hear the ragged breathing of hundreds of The Hungry. Desperate, she began to climb, cutting her hands and bare feet on broken bricks and rusted girders. As she reached the top of the wreckage, the growling below became louder, frenzied. She was trapped. Gasping for air she looked up to the ever-black sky, and tried to scream, but no sound came out.

Then a miracle happened. The clouds opened, and a beam of strange blue light broke through, spotlighting her, naked and shivering on top of the rubble. The hungry voices below whimpered in fear and went silent. She stood up and gratefully opened her arms wide to feel the warmth from above.

The blue beam of light grew hot. Then hotter still, and it started to hurt her. She looked at her arms and watched in horror as her flesh burned blue and fell from her bones.

With a cry, Lucille snapped awake. She sat up quickly, still in a panic from her dream, and looked around. She was in her own bed, in her own apartment. Outside her windows, the morning sun was bright, the old buildings of the Upper West Side were still there, and from the street below, she heard the usual sound of traffic and horns.

A dull ache, like a hangover, pounded slowly at the back of her head. As she pulled away the covers, she realized she was naked. Then she realized she was alone.

"Paul," she called out. There was no answer. She sighed. There was no need to call again. She knew he was gone.

She rubbed her neck with her delicate fingers and leaned back against the pillows. She tried to remember what happened last night. She remembered Paul holding her. She was sleepy, and they were lying together, dressed, on top of the covers. But there was nothing after that.

Something felt wrong. She reached down to touch the blue azurite stone that hung on her chest. It was gone.

Lucille rolled over and knelt on the bed, frantically searching for her pendant. She looked on the bed tables, in the drawers, under the bed, but couldn't find it. She sat on the floor, wrapped her arms around her chest, and rocked back and forth, trying not to give in to her rising panic.

She forced herself to focus. The door to her closet was still open. The box of her Columbia University things was on the floor near the bed. She crawled over, looking for her diary. Like her necklace, it was gone.

Lucille, still naked, knelt on the floor and looked up to the blue sky through the large windows. She had never done much praying, but something new was waking up in her. Something dark and dangerous.

I will do it. If I have to. I will.

*   *   *

Mak and Artemis stepped out of the sleek elevator on the eighth floor of TVNews headquarters. A young, athletic looking Hispanic woman saw them, opened the door of the glass wall that separated the lobby from the offices, and greeted them.

"My name is Deni Diaz," she spoke quietly, but her voice was charged with an energetic, happy professionalism. She looked at the printout on her clipboard and continued, "And you must be Agent Makani Kim."

Mak smiled, showed his identification, and said, "Yes, and this is Dr. Artemis Bookbinder."

Deni nodded. "Roxie is expecting you, gentlemen. Please follow me."

She led them past reception, a coffee station, and through a maze of open work stations clustered with energized staff preparing for the show that would go out live that night. At the far corner of the open space, they came to a large glass-enclosed office. They followed Deni up a few steps, where she knocked once on the door and took them in.

Roxie Lee was standing by the large corner windows that looked out at the always busy Columbus Avenue. Her strikingly dark skin and sensual features were highlighted by the bright late morning sun. She finished her call and came over. Deni introduced them.

Artemis was struck by her intense eyes, her judicious use of some exotic fragrance, and her silver pendant necklace. Though she was dressed professionally in a dark jacket, her white dress shirt was unbuttoned enough to show a single, large, flawless red ruby dangling enticingly just above her breasts.

"Thank you, Deni." Roxie smiled at her, dismissing her.

Deni nodded and headed for the door.

"Close the door, please," Roxie added. "But stay nearby. We'll need you in a bit."

Deni accepted the order without question and closed the door. Through the glass wall they watched as she sat at a nearby desk and started work on a computer.

"So, what can I do for you, gentlemen?" Roxie asked pleasantly as she settled her shapely body into her desk chair. "Please, have a seat." She gestured. "I can't give you a lot of time; I have an appointment across town in a bit."

"Thank you for seeing us," Mak answered easily and took out his notepad. "We'd like to talk with you about Raphael Sharder."

Roxie let out a long sigh. "I'm going to miss that old man. He was always a good friend to me. How can I help you?"

"Well," Mak began, "how long did you know him?"

"Jesus… you know"—she smiled and shook her head—"it feels like I knew him forever. But, let's see." She leaned back in her chair and considered. "I guess it was about eight or nine years ago. Raphael was having a big press thing at his gallery…."

"The one here in town or in Southampton?" Mak asked.

"Here, the 64th Street Gallery," she answered. "He had acquired some great surrealistic pieces and wanted to make a fuss over them. I brought a crew and covered the opening."

"Are you into art?" Mak asked.

"Yes." Roxie smiled. "And I collect a bit."

"That's interesting." Artemis sounded pleased. "Did Raphael Sharder find things for you?"

Roxie looked at the thin, handsome man sitting across the desk and his curious dark blue eyes. She considered for a moment before she asked, "So, are you with the FBI, Dr. Bookbinder?"

"Artemis, please." He smiled freely. "No, I teach art history at Columbia University. The Bureau hired me to consult on this case because of the Gardner Museum piece that was recovered."

"I see." Roxie was smiling but sounded careful. After a second, she nodded and volunteered: "Raphael did help me acquire one really fine canvas a few years ago. It's by Max Ernst."

"I love Ernst," Artemis said truthfully. "What's it called?"

"*Earthquake*," she answered and waited to see what he would make of it.

Artemis smiled at her, liking the challenge. "He made more than one with that title. What year is it?"

"1925," she answered.

"I think I know that piece." Artemis's eyes glowed happily. "It's a large canvas in dark blue and brown: above, the spheres of the golden sun, and below, the disturbance of the earthquake, which he created by *grattage*."

Roxie shook her head in disbelief and let out a laugh. "Jesus, am I afraid of you or what?" she said softly.

"What's *grattage*?" Mak wondered aloud.

"Ernst scraped paint over the canvas to show imprints of objects underneath," Roxie answered. "It's a technique he discovered that year, in 1925. The result is incredible."

Artemis smiled at her. "I should be pretty afraid of you, too," he said pleasantly. "That's pretty good."

"Thank you, Doctor."

"Ouch." He winced. "Just Artemis, please. And I would love to see that canvas sometime."

She smiled. "So, do you know everything, about every painting that has ever been made?"

"I wish." Artemis shook his head at himself. "But do I remember that one. Did you know it has another name? Ernst called it *Earthquake or The Drowning of the Sun*."

"Yes." She nodded slowly. "... I guess I forgot that."

"That piece was sold to a private buyer, in a London auction, five or six years ago," he continued. "So... I'm guessing that Raphael Sharder was that buyer?"

"That makes sense"—she shrugged—"because it was in his gallery about then."

"And it set something of a record, for a Max Ernst piece of that era; it went for somewhere around eight hundred thousand," Artemis said, watching her.

"That seems about right," she said cautiously.

Mak picked it up: "We don't have any records of Raphael Sharder's purchases and sales that far back. Do you have a receipt? That would help us a lot."

"I'm afraid not," Roxie answered smoothly. "It was a gift."

"Oh, from Raphael Sharder?" Mak followed.

"No," Roxie answered a little too quickly. "Though Raphael helped me pick it out. Told me all about it. But that's all."

"I see," Mak said. "So…who gave you this gift?"

Roxie shook her head and smiled. "Just a friend."

"A friend who hung out with you at Raphael Sharder's pool in Southampton?" Artemis asked quietly.

"My, my… somebody's been gossiping about me," she scoffed. "Probably the maid, Something Friggins."

"*Figgins*," Mak corrected her gently.

"Okay." She started to sound annoyed. "So, who did she say I was hanging out with?"

"She didn't. That's why I'm asking you," Mak said.

"Just a friend. Someone who values his privacy, okay?" she answered firmly, closing the topic.

Artemis looked away through the glass walls, to the large, busy office beyond.

"Look, fellas," Roxie said politely, "like I said, I've an appointment to keep. We need to wrap this up."

"Not a problem"—Mak nodded—"just a couple more things."

"Like?" she said, with a show of being patient.

"Like, where were you this past Thursday night at seven?" Mak answered.

Roxie nodded. "The night Raphael was killed. I was here, working. The show is on every weekday night at nine, live, for an hour. And after we wrap, we have a series of meetings to set up the next day. I left here around midnight, maybe. Lots of people can verify that."

"And you went home after?"

"Yes," she answered. "I have an apartment on the river not far from here."

"Is that where you keep the Ernst?" Artemis joined in.

"Yes"—she looked surprised—"where else?"

"Don't know," he answered. "You spent a lot of time with Sharder out in Southampton. I wondered if you have a place out there?"

"No," she said, "just my apartment here."

Mak spoke in a non-confrontational way: "And you have a key to Sharder's apartment over on the East Side, right?"

"Yes. And…?" she challenged. "I went there once in a while to make sure everything was okay. You know, it's what friends do."

"That's true." Artemis sounded soothing.

"Is there anything you can tell us about the stolen Rembrandt painting found at Sharder's mansion?" Mak asked.

"Nothing." She shook her head. "I learned about that, like everyone else, when the FBI told us about it on Friday afternoon. And honestly, it seems incredible to me even now. Raphael was a good man. He cared about people. I can't believe that he could be involved with anything dangerous or dishonest."

"Just a last question," Mak said, "you must know Beth Schaefer…?"

"Um, sure, yes," she answered carefully. "She runs the gallery on 64th Street. We've met a few times. But I don't know her all that well."

"Did you know that she's gone?" Artemis said.

"What?" Roxie seemed worried for a second before she recovered. "Gone where?"

"Nobody knows. But she left her apartment in Brooklyn in a hurry."

"Well, that's news to me." Roxie shrugged.

"We understand that her brother works here," Mak stated.

"Yes, Greg," Roxie confirmed.

"Can we speak with him?"

"Sure," Roxie said as she got up, pulled on her jacket, picked up her bag, and led them out of the office. She called Deni Diaz over.

"I have to go now, but Deni here will help you find Greg Schaefer," she said, nodding to the young woman. "And if I can help you with anything else, just give a call, and we'll set up another meeting." She turned to go.

"That's a beautiful ruby," Artemis said, and she stopped. "Did that come from that friend, too?"

Roxie touched the stone with her fingers, looked at Artemis, and smiled widely. "You really are too clever, Artemis. It's been nice meeting you."

She spun away and was soon out the glass doors and into the elevator.

"I think Greg is down on the studio floor," Deni said pleasantly. "This way."

She walked them back through the workplace, which was growing louder as the day went on.

On the opposite corner from Roxie's office was a matching glass-enclosed space. From the door of this office, an oddly out-of-place figure emerged. She was a frumpy, olive-skinned, middle-aged woman with thinning, oily-black hair. She looked across the room, saw the strangers with Deni, and openly scowled at them before she marched off in a superior way to her own little office and slammed the door.

"Who is that?" Mak asked puzzled.

"That's Anna Canneli." Deni rolled her eyes.

"Uh… Cannoli…?" Mak looked surprised.

Deni laughed. "No, *Canneli*, and there's really no explaining her. Officially, she's Paula DeVong's assistant. But really"—she lowered her voice to a tone of friendly conspiracy—"she's Paula's ass-kisser. And she's very good at that."

Mak chuckled, "There's one in every office, right?"

"I wouldn't know." She smiled and walked them to the large, open stairwell. "But one of her here is enough for me." She started down the steps, but Artemis stopped her with a question:

"So, what's on the upper floor?"

"Oh, right." Deni smiled apologetically. "I forgot you guys haven't been here before. Up there are the bosses: Calvin Prons, Head of Network. And Jock Willinger, our Executive Producer."

"I thought Roxie Lee was the Producer." Mak looked confused.

"Welcome to television, where *everybody* is a producer." She was starting to like Mak. "Jock Willinger answers to the Network, but Roxie Lee, as *Supervising* Producer, makes sure that the show gets on the air. Paula has a producing title, too."

"Okay." Mak nodded, assembling this information.

"And you like working for Roxie?" Artemis asked in a friendly way.

"Oh, yes," Deni enthused. "She's a great boss. Paula, on the other hand…" She stopped herself and laughed. "Sorry, it's my first time talking to the FBI. I just don't know when to shut up. Come on." She headed them off down the steps again to a landing and through a heavy metal door.

"This is our studio, which takes up half of the entire seventh floor of the building," she continued. "The other half is where they shoot the ten o'clock show that follows us."

They descended a long, open staircase, past a ceiling full of hanging lights, down to the open area where the show was shot. Here, around the news set, large cameras on rolling pedestals were being cleaned and checked by crew members. Deni led them through a soundproof door to the control room. There, sitting in front of a wall of monitors, they found a delicately handsome, nicely groomed young man.

"Hi, these people are here to see you," Deni announced in a friendly way.

"Oh?" Greg Schaefer looked up surprised, from his sheets of notes.

Mak pulled out his credentials and introduced them.

"Well"—Deni looked curiously at Greg—"I'll leave you to it, then." She went out, closing the door behind her.

"What can I do for you?" Greg asked politely.

"We're investigating the death of Raphael Sharder and have a few questions," Mak began.

"Sure." Greg nodded uncertainly.

"Your sister Beth worked for him, ran his gallery across town."

"Yes," Greg confirmed quietly.

"She told us that you called her on Friday morning to let her know that Sharder had been killed," Mak said as he watched him.

"Yes," Greg answered. "He wasn't just her boss, they were friends. And I thought she should know as soon as possible."

Artemis's eyes suddenly had that strange faraway look. "What time did you call your sister?" he asked softly.

"Um," Greg considered, "I guess around nine. She hadn't opened the gallery yet. And after she heard the news, she decided that she wouldn't. She was pretty upset."

"And who told *you* the news?" Artemis asked.

"Roxie Lee did."

"And where did she hear it?" Mak asked.

"I couldn't say." Greg turned to him. "But we're in the news business here, you know. We all have sources that tell us when stuff happens."

In the silence that followed, Greg started to gather up his papers.

"We know you're busy, but there's one more thing," Mak said. "Have you heard from your sister since you spoke with her on Friday morning?"

"Uh, no," Greg became very still. "Why?"

"She's missing," Mak reported evenly. "And her apartment in Brooklyn shows signs of a very hasty exit. We can't locate her."

"I haven't heard from her," Greg looked worried. "Hang on," he added as he pulled out his phone and punched in a number.

He listened and then shook his head. He left a message:

"Beth, it's me. I'm worried about you. Call me." He hung up and let out a long breath.

"She's a good kid, and smart. She'll be okay," he said softly as if he was convincing himself.

"Any ideas where she might have gone? A friend somewhere? A favorite place to go for vacations?" Mak asked, noticing that Artemis was still off somewhere deep in thought.

"Um, no, not really." Greg looked apologetic. "See, we've always pretty much kept to ourselves. You know, her world out there in the wilds of Brooklyn, and mine here in Manhattan. I've always liked that about her. But this…" he trailed off.

"You'll let us know if you hear from her," Mak said as he handed him his card. "And if we find out anything, we'll let you know right away," he added kindly.

"Thank you," the young man said sincerely.

Then Mak took down Greg's contact details and asked if he could show them the way out.

Out on Columbus Avenue the lunchtime crowds were everywhere, but Artemis didn't seem to notice them. Mak studied him as they slowly made their way against the current.

"I feel like a salmon swimming upstream," Artemis murmured softly as he was returning to the real world around him.

"Where've you been?" Mak smiled curiously at him.

"I've been thinking about time," Artemis answered, sounding worried, "and the *Drowning of the Sun.*"

Nine floors above, a reedy man, wearing a thin tie and a dark blue suit, watched as Artemis and Mak walked away up the avenue. He adjusted his thick rimmed glasses to focus on Mak's FBI field jacket.

Executive Producer Jock Willinger ran his hand across his carefully arranged thinning hair and pulled repeatedly on his earlobe. It was something he did when he was nervous.

He knew that they had been talking to Roxie Lee, behind closed doors.

*   *   *

Across town, Lucille Orsina was coming out of a little shop on Third Avenue. The painted name on the dirty awning above the door said: *News & Stationery*. But nowadays, these last surviving shops also sold beer, cigarettes, candy, magazines, and lotto tickets. But Lucille hadn't come here to buy any of these things.

She slipped the small bag into her purse and looked up. Above the tall buildings, the midday sun was bright. It made her feel exposed, thin, and shallow.

She looked at the crowds of people surging past her on the sidewalk, some just barely missing her. As if she wasn't even there. She flinched as the aggressive horns blaring from the jammed-up traffic in the street were drowned out by jackhammers breaking concrete a half-block away. There were just too many people, too packed together, in this always too noisy world.

She used to love this city. She felt so alive and connected here. But it had all gone wrong. Now she felt threatened and on guard all the time. And so alone.

Suddenly, the consequence of what she planned to do was overwhelming. She breathed slowly in.

I need to be sure.

She nodded to herself and slowly started walking west, heading toward Fifth Avenue.

*   *   *

"I'm sorry Detective, but I just can't tell you anything else about Beth Schaefer," Dr. Paul Marin said. "You have these receipts, so I can confirm that she is, in fact, one of my patients. But to say anything else would be a clear violation of doctor-patient confidentiality."

He handed the paper receipts back to the young man sitting across the desk from him.

"I'm sorry," Paul added with a smile.

"That's too bad, but I understand." Clayton Collins nodded.

"Well, if there's not anything else, I'm actually done for the day here," Paul said in friendly dismissal.

Clayton stood up, buttoned his jacket, and took in the room. The wood paneled walls, the expensive furniture, the large window looking out at the Metropolitan Museum across the street; it all reeked of privilege to him.

"That's lucky for you, doc," he said respectfully but making a point. "Wish I could work half-days and get by."

Paul laughed, not offended. "Well, usually I'm full up. Today is just a rare thing."

Clayton nodded, thanked him for his time, and left through the reception area.

Paul looked at his Rolex and smiled. He turned off his laptop, buttoned his sport coat, wrapped a cashmere scarf loosely around his neck, and checked himself in a mirror by the door. He roughly brushed his hands through his short, curly hair and grinned, pleased with himself. He went out, past his receptionist.

"I hope you have a good afternoon, Paul," the older woman said as she smiled discreetly.

"Thanks." He smiled back, his eyes flashing mischievously. "No calls, okay?"

"Yes, doctor." She nodded efficiently.

Paul went out into the little marble foyer and through the large glass door that opened directly onto the sidewalk.

Across the street, by the museum, Lucille saw him and ducked back behind a kiosk of postcards. She watched as Paul headed to the near corner of Fifth Avenue and turned north. He stayed on the east side of the avenue, avoiding the crowds of tourists by the museum. Being careful to be unobserved, Lucille stayed on the west side of the street and followed him.

She knew where he was headed. Just a couple of blocks north, Paul approached the entrance of his apartment building on Fifth. Lucille again kept herself hidden, standing behind a utility truck parked across the street. She watched as Paul greeted the doorman and asked something. She was too far away, and there was too much traffic, for her to hear anything. But she could see by the doorman's reaction that whoever Paul was looking for hadn't arrived yet. Paul checked his watch. The doorman discreetly walked back inside the lobby. And Paul scanned the traffic coming from the north.

Lucille waited. And all too soon a cab pulled up. Paul bent to see who the passenger was. He smiled, opened the door, and reached out his hand. A beautiful hand reached out for him. Paul helped Roxie Lee out of the cab and kissed her hard on her mouth. She responded by pushing her sexy body into him.

Lucille was blinded by tears. She wiped them away quickly.

The cab went, and Paul whispered something in Roxie's ear. She threw her head back and laughed. Paul wrapped his arm around her, and they went into the lobby. Through the glass doors, Lucille could see them kissing by the elevator. Paul's hands were under Roxie's jacket. The elevator doors opened, they got on and were gone.

Lucille felt dizzy. She turned away and started walking.

A couple of blocks south, she turned back and looked up toward Paul's penthouse. It was set back and too high to see. But she knew what it looked like, how it felt. She had been there with him. And now....

She wrapped her arms around herself and slowly walked back toward the Metropolitan Museum. As always, a long line of taxis and tour buses were parked, like a wall along the sidewalk, in front of the massive, blocks-long structure. Above the temple-like entrance, a long row of unforgiving stone faces looked down at the swarms of people coming and going.

Lucille focused on finding a path through the madness. Just past the museum, the sidewalk was a little easier to navigate. Here were vendors selling posters and postcards, and by the curb, a couple of food carts.

Lucille bought a large cup of coffee. She looked around, wondering where she could be alone. At the south corner of the building, she turned and followed the paved walkway into the park.

She passed some tourists, noisily posing for selfies by three curiously realistic bronze statues of bears. She came to a small play area, intended for toddlers. Here, a few strollers were parked, and young mothers with their tiny children were exploring the small slide, climbing area, and swings. A small wading pool stood empty, waiting for the hot days of summer. Lucille watched the children play, and she felt so sad.

She heard horns honking, and looking up above the trees, at the wall of windows across Fifth Avenue, she felt still too close to the crowds here.

She made her way past the museum and deeper into the park. She carefully crossed the East Drive, closed now to cars but crowded still with speeding bikers. She turned and followed a wide path lined with leafless trees. Here, dozens of joggers passed her in both directions, their earbuds in place, their eyes distant and fixed forever forward.

Then, up ahead, she saw a familiar site: a tall obelisk appearing above the branches. She entered into a protective circle of wooden benches that surrounded the ancient Egyptian artifact. Miraculously, there was no one else here.

Lucille used to love coming to this place. Cleopatra's Needle, as it was called, was a strange remnant from a forgotten time. Made of rose quartz and nearly seventy feet tall, it was covered with weathered hieroglyphs that described the achievements of a once great pharaoh. Now, over three thousand years later, it stood here in a lonely corner of the park, growing old.

In the wrong place, at the wrong time. Just like me.

Lucille sat down on a bench, opened her purse, and took out the small bag. Inside was a phone. An off-the-shelf, untraceable, disposable burner phone. She pulled it out of its plastic wrap.

She sat still, listening. She could hear traffic, but it was distant and muted. She could hear children somewhere through the trees, playing on the Great Lawn. But they seemed far away, too. Lucille looked up at the old stone pillar before her.

There must be justice.

She reached into her purse, pulled out her own cell phone, and scrolled through her contacts. There, she found a number for Artemis Bookbinder. Carefully, she punched in his number on the burner phone.

Mak and Artemis came out of the Broadway Diner, where they'd stopped for lunch.

"That building?" Mak asked as he pointed to a grand old Beaux-Arts building a few blocks north.

"Yep," Artemis confirmed, "we have a condo on the top floor there. When we moved to Jersey, we rented it out."

His cell rang.

"Hello," Artemis answered.

"Hi. This is Lucille," a gentle voice said softly.

Artemis signaled to Mak, and they stepped into a doorway and out of the flow of sidewalk traffic. He put his hand over his ear and said, "Sorry, who? I can't hear you very well."

"Lucille," she said a little louder, her voice trembling. "Do you remember me, Professor Bookbinder?"

Artemis shook his head. He hated not being able to find a name. Especially a student's. "I'm sorry," he said apologetically, "I don't."

"That's so sad," she murmured and took a long breath before she went on. "I was so pleased to hear that you'd found a Rembrandt from the Gardner Museum. I remember how much that meant to you."

Artemis's eyes flashed with interest. "Yes, it's been in the news a lot."

He signaled to Mak that he should listen in.

"So, Lucille, do we know each other from Columbia?"

Lucille closed her eyes. The sound of Artemis saying her name was warm and reassuring. She knew then that this was the right thing to do.

"Got a pencil, Professor? You're going to want to write this down."

Mak pulled out his notepad and nodded to Artemis.

"Go ahead," Artemis said, controlling the excitement in his voice.

"There is another Gardner Museum piece waiting to be found," Lucille spoke slowly and clearly. She gave them an address, on the edge of Chinatown, in the Two Bridges district.

"It's called *The School*," she added with a soft laugh. "That should appeal to you, Professor Bookbinder. And you should bring your FBI friends along."

Then Lucille hung up. She opened the lid of her cup and carefully submerged the burner phone into the coffee. She put the lid back on, gathered her things, got up, and walked calmly away from the Obelisk. Back on the path, she dumped her coffee cup in a trash can. She took out a pair of dark sunglasses and put them on. She felt stronger than she had in a very long time.

She started walking. She headed through the park, back toward her apartment on the West Side.

* * *

Silas Bookbinder sat at the kitchen table, staring out the window at the still barren trees in their backyard. Behind his big glasses, his brown eyes were far away as his mind journeyed considering the seasons, the rebirth of nature every spring, and what determined the size and number of leaves.

Aunt Delia stood at the counter, drying her hands, watching him.

So much like his father.

She heard Emily coming downstairs and into the kitchen. After the threatening note, she had started coming home for lunch.

"There's still some coffee left, if you want?" Delia offered.

"No, thanks." Emily smiled and purposefully held up her left arm.

Delia gave her an uncertain look and turned away to dump the coffee and start cleaning the pot.

"Don't you remember this?" Emily laughed a little. "Well, it was a long time ago, I guess."

"What?" Delia turned back.

"This," Emily said, moving closer to Delia. "It was my most favorite thing for so long."

Delia looked at the bracelet that Emily was displaying. It was a delicate ring of small blue glass globes, each decorated to look like an eyeball.

"Ah"—Delia nodded—"from Greece. From my visit. How old were you then?"

"I'm not sure, maybe four…?" Emily said. "It meant the world to me. My folks didn't let me have jewelry."

"They were always so careful about money." Delia nodded.

"Sure"—Emily shook her head—"but they were more worried about offending God. Always had a Bible quote ready. I could wear a cross, but never jewelry."

"I remember." Delia smiled. "But thankfully, I was cut from a different cloth."

"And this"—Emily fairly giggled—"This was pagan devil worship to them. Without your support I never would have been allowed to keep it."

Delia reached out and took Emily's hand and looked carefully at the bracelet.

"Matiasma," Silas pronounced slowly and carefully.

"My, my"—Delia laughed, sounding proud—"Trust you, little genius. How in the world do you know that?"

"Read it somewhere." Silas shrugged as he came over to look at his mother's bracelet. "Eyeballs. Eighteen of them," he observed. "Why eighteen evil eyes?"

"I don't know." Delia smiled at him. "But they are supposed to ward off danger."

She turned to Emily. "I hope it always does for you."

Emily looked at her aunt for a moment and then hugged her. "Thanks."

"I'm going up to work," Silas announced, having lost interest in the bracelet, and went upstairs.

Emily walked over to the large window and looked at her bracelet. The bright sunlight made the blue glass globes sparkle on her wrist.

"Don't forget you're getting pizza for dinner tonight," Delia said softly as she watched her. "I've a meeting at seven."

"Someone picking you up?" Emily asked as she continued to study the ring of evil eyes.

"Yes," Delia confirmed. She looked worried for a moment and then added, "I'm sorry to leave you in the lurch."

Emily looked up at her. "No, it's important what you're doing, and I couldn't be more pleased." Then she smiled fully and added, "*Sobriety is a journey—*"

"*… Not a destination.*" Delia smiled back. "Fancy you knowing that one."

"Well, *I keep an open mind,*" Emily quipped with another AA slogan she'd learned from her aunt.

"All right, that'll do." Delia grinned.

"*We are only as sick as our secrets.*" Emily playfully threw in a last slogan as she left the kitchen.

Delia laughed softly.

*   *   *

Paul tied the belt on his robe, opened the door, and waited. There were no other apartments but his, here on the penthouse level. In the small foyer, the private elevator opened, and Ida Orsina marched out.

"This better be important." Paul sighed as he let her in and shut the door.

Roxie came in from the bedroom, gathering a robe around her naked body.

"I agree," she added with a smirk. "What's up?"

Ida remembered a time, not so many years ago, when Paul was hers. The power of him inside her, perfectly matching, thrusting… Then like an electric flash, her mind cleared, and she said,

"The cops have raided The School. The FBI is there, too."

Paul's jaw tightened, and his eyes narrowed, "When?"

"An hour ago. Fat Nicky called me," Ida reported.

Paul turned away and walked to the glass doors of his terrace. Outside, the last light of day was fading. The windows of the buildings far across Central Park were sparkling with light.

"How did this happen?" he asked quietly.

"We don't know," Ida answered.

"Fuck me," Paul muttered darkly.

Then he turned to Ida and screamed, "Fuck me!"

Ida brushed her fingers nervously through her page-boy red hair. "Does it matter so much?"

"Yes, it does," Paul growled, his eyes flashing dangerously at her.

"Why?" She sounded confused. "What's to find there besides some chairs and candles?"

Roxie moved closer to Paul and touched his arm. "What is it Paul? What will they find there?"

Paul pulled away from her and sat on the sofa. He closed his eyes for a moment, relaxed his shoulders, and breathed out slowly.

Roxie looked to Ida, who shrugged in response.

"Find Paula DeVong," Paul opened his eyes and said evenly to Roxie. "Tell her to get a crew down to The School. It's time for our wonder girl to have another breaking story. She'll say the usual thing: she got a tip from unnamed sources."

Roxie nodded but looked uncertain. "I'll send Moira Weyland to cover it. If Paula shows up there, someone might connect her. You know, it's going to come out sooner or later, that Paula's in your class."

Paul nodded once. "I know." He could hear the fear in Roxie's voice. He got up and firmly took hold of her shoulders.

"It'll be alright"—he smiled at her—"If that ever happens, Paula will say that she joined the class as an undercover investigator. You'll need to make a file that creates a paper trail for her."

Roxie took this in for a moment before she whispered, "Yes, Paul, whatever you say."

"And that file has to be kept safe until we need it," he added.

"Of course," Roxie nodded.

"Okay, Paulie," Ida's commanding voice broke in. The familiar use of his name made him turn and look at her.

"Undercover investigator?" Ida said sarcastically. "What the fuck is going on here?"

Paul quietly said, "Another piece stolen from the Gardner Museum has been found."

Roxie and Ida stood stunned for a moment.

Then Ida said softly, "Oh Paulie... How fucking stupid are you?"

Paul took in a slow breath, walked over to Ida, and without warning slapped her hard across her face.

Roxie flinched and covered her mouth with her hands.

Ida took the hit without a sound. She touched her red cheek and looked at him stunned.

"The Feds don't just show up." Paul's voice was dangerous. "So, I have a question. Tell me Ida, who do you think it was that betrayed us?"

Ida felt the power of his strange lavender eyes burning into her. She swallowed once before she spoke.

"I don't know, Paul," she managed to whisper. "I really don't."

Paul stared at her a long moment more. Ida watched as the fierceness in his face dissolved and quiet control returned to his handsome, almost feminine features.

"You okay?" Paul asked softly.

Ida nodded once.

"Alright then," he said.

Paul turned to Roxie and directed, "Tell Greg, Paula, and Deni that classes are canceled until further notice. I expect you to keep them in line."

"Yes, Paul," she answered and headed off to the bedroom to get dressed.

"And you"—Paul turned back to Ida—"can keep your sister in line."

"Yes, Paul." She nodded.

"Where is Lucille?" Paul asked.

"I haven't a clue," Ida said simply.

"Okay," Paul said, dismissing her.

Ida went to the door, but before she opened it, she turned back and said gently, "You'll have to call your mother about this. You know that, right?"

"Shit," Paul muttered and sat back down on the sofa.

"She hates surprises." Ida looked at him with sad understanding. "It'll be better if she hears this from you first, and not on the news."

Paul looked up at her, and his eyes flashed with anger.

"Just think about it," Ida added kindly before she opened the door and left.

Paul looked to the glass doors of his terrace. Night had come.

"Fuck me," he whispered.

He got up and went to make sure that the bedroom door was closed. He went to the bar and poured himself a drink. He took a gulp, picked up his cell, and punched in a number. After a second, the call went through.

"I have something to tell you," Paul said with quiet respect. "And you're not going to like it."

* * *

By nightfall, the wind was up and the air colder. On the edge of Chinatown, the low buildings of Doyers Street were lit by flashing blue-red lights of a dozen police and FBI cars. Outside the lines of yellow barrier tape, Clayton Collins and Makani Kim stood with a handful of local people, asking for information. As usual, no one wanted to get involved, and they were learning very little.

Mak and Clayton ducked under the yellow ribbon, held up their ID's and passed the cops standing outside the old building. The rusted security gate that protected the entrance had been pushed up, and the heavy wood door was open. Inside, FBI and NYPD were working. Mak stopped inside the door to look at a large, colorful illustration painted on the wall: a fierce three-headed sea serpent. He knew that they had already photographed this, but he took out his phone and took some shots.

He made his way past a long wood bar that was moldy with age. Behind it were equally rotted wood shelves and a yellowed, splintered mirror. Past the bar and around a corner, a door was open. Bright light from below showed a flight of worn, irregular stone steps. Mak went down carefully and entered a vaulted stone cavern.

Here, more FBI agents were at work, taking photographs. The lights on stands, which the police had set up, revealed the great height and age of the large room. Six dark bronze standing candelabras surrounded the center area, where six gold folding chairs were set in a half circle, facing a low wood platform. On the platform was a heavy metal chair with a leather seat and, next to that, a small wood cabinet. And on top of that cabinet was the object that was the center of attention. It was a metal chalice, about eleven inches tall.

"I'm done," the FBI photographer said to Ray Gaines and stepped away.

Ray looked to Artemis and nodded.

Artemis reached down and took the chalice into his nitrile-gloved hands. It was surprisingly heavy. It was shaped like a small trumpet, with ancient Chinese markings on the dark patina.

Artemis knew for certain what it was. He again felt the link with his parents, who were killed so that this object would never be found. He realized he was holding his breath.

"Not the slightest doubt of it," he pronounced quietly. "This chalice, called a *Gu*, is from the Shang dynasty, twelfth century BCE and is most certainly one of the thirteen objects stolen from the Gardner Museum."

Drew Sweeney moved closer. "A ceremonial drinking cup…?" she asked.

"Yes, exactly," Artemis answered softly.

"We're getting there, son." Ray smiled at him. "We really are. Two Gardner Museum finds in less than a week."

Artemis nodded at him, the fire in his eyes growing. Still holding the chalice, Artemis sat carefully on the large leather covered chair on the platform. He looked at the gold chairs before him. He lifted the chalice up, smelled it, and smiled.

"Do you suppose this is a stage or an altar…?" he asked aloud. "Someone has recently been using this ceremonial chalice. Heavy red wine." He looked up to Mak Kim.

"We'll have that checked out." Mak nodded.

Artemis carefully put the chalice down on the table and turned again to take in the room. He saw six large dark marks on the vaulted ceiling, from years of candles burning. He let his eyes wander freely, waiting to see what caught his attention. Then something did. It was the numbers.

"Six below, and one above," he said, looking at the design of candles on one of the standing candelabras. "Six gold chairs. And one throne-like chair here on the altar."

"Sacred class? Esoteric school…?" Mak wondered.

"Could you send me pictures of all this?" Artemis asked. "The candles, the chairs, the whole set up?"

"Sure."

"And that painting on the wall by the entrance upstairs," Artemis added. "The three-headed serpent."

"Yeah, that got me, too." Mak smiled.

Ray stretched and groaned softly. "Damn, these days don't get any shorter, do they? Were you able to trace the call?" he asked Mak as he eased himself down on one of the gold chairs.

"No, sir," Mak answered. "It was from a burner phone, could have been purchased anywhere."

"Figures." Ray nodded and turned to Artemis. "So, any more thoughts on who she is?"

"She called herself Lucille," Artemis answered. "And was probably once a student of mine."

"Probably?" Ray said.

"She called this place *The School*," Artemis listed, "she called me Professor, and she said that she knew how important the Rembrandt recovery was to me."

Drew, wearing latex gloves, carefully lifted the *Gu* chalice. "Yeah, the Gardner robbery has been your only lecture topic forever," she said with a smile.

"Well, not the only topic"—Artemis shrugged—"but my favorite. But assuming her name really is Lucille, she couldn't have been a student for long, or I'd remember her."

"My guys are coordinating with Columbia University," Drew said as she studied the markings on the chalice, "and if she was ever there, we'll find her."

"And this place, *The School*"—Ray turned to Mak—"what do we know about it?"

"The building was supposed to be deserted," Mak opened his notepad and reported, "It was a speakeasy during Prohibition, but it's been empty a long time now. So far, we've learned that the last occupant was that bar upstairs; it was called *Necropolis*, and they've been gone a long time, maybe nine, ten years. We're checking."

Artemis's eyes flashed, and he smiled a little, to himself.

"Get anything from the neighbors?" Ray asked Mak.

"No. They're all shop owners: souvenirs, hair and nail salons. When they finish a day, they roll down the security gates and head for home. Nobody lives on this street. It's too run down, too dangerous late at night.

"No New Yorker has ever seen anything, ever." Drew shook her head in disgust as she gently put the chalice back on the table.

Clayton came down the stone steps and made his way to them.

"The press has arrived. We're keeping them back, of course, but they're being a real pain in the ass," the young man reported.

"How in the hell did they find out so fast?" Ray growled.

"I don't know"—Clayton shook his head—"but so far, it's just one reporter and her crew from TVNews."

"Which reporter?" Artemis looked up with interest.

"Moira something," Clayton said. "Sorry, didn't really hear the last name."

"Hell," Ray grunted as he got up. "I guess I better go make an informed statement that tells them absolutely nothing."

"Ray?" Artemis said, stopping him. "What if you do tell them what we found? News of the Rembrandt shook the trees, just like as you said it would."

"And maybe this thing"—Ray looked at the dark bronze chalice—"could really light a fire under somebody's ass...."

Ray considered for a moment before he said, "Alright. But I'm not the guy to speak to the press."

"That is so true." Mak smiled at his boss.

For a second, Ray looked like he might be angry. But then he coughed out a short laugh. "Bastard. I guess everybody knows it. So, Artemis...."

"I don't want to talk to the press ever, about anything—" Artemis started.

But Ray cut him off, "Look, I hate talking to the press, and it shows. But you're used to lecturing, and all that. And you know everything about this cup here and where it came from…."

"Ray…" Artemis appealed.

"I know, son. I do." Ray looked at him kindly. "But I need you on this. And that's official."

Artemis looked at him for a moment and sighed. "Okay, Ray. I'm with you. Let's get it done."

As Artemis and Ray stepped outside the building, the bright lights of the news crew came on. A young, eager-looking, attractive woman pushed through the cops to meet them. She and her crew were stopped at the yellow barrier tape.

"It's all right, officers," Ray said with authority. "We'll talk with them."

The woman's cheeks flushed pink with excitement, and her eyes grew aggressively bright.

"Thank you, sir," she called out. She nodded to her cameraman, ran her fingers quickly through her short, curly-red hair, and held up her microphone.

"This is Moira Weyland, TVNews. I'm standing outside an abandoned building on Doyers Street, in the Two Bridges district of Lower Manhattan. Here with me are Special Agent Ray Gaines and Dr. Artemis Bookbinder of Columbia University."

Ray was impressed that the young woman knew who he was and that she knew that the building was abandoned. Artemis was bothered, as always, to hear himself referred to by his doctorate title.

Moira turned to Ray, pushed the microphone under his chin, and asked, "What can you tell us, sir, about what you've found here?"

"Acting on an anonymous tip, we were directed to this building," Ray began stiffly. "Here, in the basement, we have recovered, what we believe to be, another stolen piece of art from the Gardner Museum in Boston."

"And this time it's not a painting, is that correct, sir?" the reporter asked pointedly.

Ray looked at the girl. She was young enough to be his granddaughter. "And how do you know that, Ms. Weyland?" he asked.

"Like you, I can't reveal my source," she said almost gleefully. "So, it's true, then?"

Ray hated being put on the spot, and he hated reporters asking questions, and he hated being on camera.

"This is Dr. Artemis Bookbinder, and he will tell you what we've found."

Like a hungry piranha, Moira Weyland turned to Artemis. "Doctor…?" she said as she pushed the microphone at him.

Artemis blinked a few times as the hot, bright light on the camera turned on him. Moira seemed to take pity on him, and she gave him a second to collect himself, by asking:

"I understand that you're working as a special consultant to the FBI on this case?"

"Yes." Artemis relaxed a little and began. He told them about the chalice they'd just recovered. That nothing yet had been learned about how it came to be here, but investigations were just getting underway. He went on to describe the piece, its history, and its great value.

"Isn't it true, Doctor, that your own father, an NYPD detective, was killed many years ago in connection with this same museum case?"

Artemis looked at her, quietly stunned. A wave of black pain squeezed tightly around his chest, and he found it difficult to take a breath. He thought of his family. Then, and now. Silas. Emily.

What have I done?

Moira saw the worry in his eyes, and she felt suddenly protective of him. This was an entirely new sensation for her. She again found herself trying to help him.

"I mean, Doctor," she said, changing the question, "could you tell us something about the robbery itself."

Artemis looked at Moira and smiled a little.

"Well, it happened thirty years ago," he said and then gave a short outline of the known events of the museum robbery.

Moira turned to the camera and signed off. The lights went out, and her crew started away for their van. She turned back to Artemis.

"Thank you, Doctor. That was great."

"Call me Artemis, please."

She smiled. "This will be on tonight, on Paula DeVong's show. You'll be pleased."

"Great." He nodded once.

"And congratulations on the find. You must be feeling pretty proud," Moira said sincerely.

He watched her walk away and wondered why he didn't feel proud. Or excited. Or happy. He just felt worried. He felt the presence of illness everywhere; the coronavirus was here and growing in New York City. And no one seemed to care.

He wanted to be home, protecting his family.

Chapter Seven

Thursday, March 5th

The morning sun in Halesburgh was bright, but the air felt cold. Outside their home, as always now, three dark cars were parked across the street. The night crew of FBI agents had been relieved by Bert Rocca and his team.

Artemis sighed and turned away from the window of his first-floor study. He was grateful for their presence, but it was hard to get used to. He sat at his desk, which was covered with neat piles of paperwork: well-worn pages from his father's old Gardner Museum files. On top of one of these files was a picture of the dark metal chalice they had recovered last night. Artemis pinned it in the center of the note-covered corkboard, above his desk. Next to it was a picture of their first find, Rembrandt's *Storm on the Sea of Galilee*.

Artemis settled back in his desk chair and looked at the two pictures.

Once again, he wondered about the odd assortment of things stolen from the Gardner that March night, so long ago. Some were priceless masterpiece paintings, some sketches, and two strange objects. One of these, they had recovered last night: an ancient Chinese ceremonial goblet. And the other one was even stranger: a gilded bronze eagle finial, which once decorated the top of a flagpole carried by Napoleon's Imperial Guard.

What they took seems so completely random. But was it…?

He focused on the Rembrandt picture. The figures in the scene were foundering in a ship. He thought about Raphael Sharder's missing boat, the *Khloe*. And the ship's wheel hanging on the wall of the pool house. And Artemis wondered why, of all of the thirteen pieces stolen from the museum, why did Sharder end up with that particular one.

Artemis rubbed his eyes, trying to clear his thoughts. It had been hard to get to sleep last night.

"I thought you could use this," Emily said kindly as she came in with a coffee and handed it to him.

"Thanks." He smiled, sipped a little, and set the mug down in the exact center of a square coaster on his desk.

Emily watched him, amused. She stepped behind him and laid her hands on his shoulders. "You okay?"

"Yeah."

"Want me to rub your feet? Come, lie down on the sofa...," she said simply.

It was something she did for him when he was too obsessed or worried or tired. It was so kind of her, and he loved her for it. "No, I'm okay. It would just put me to sleep. And there's so much to do. Thanks, though," he said.

She could hear the worry in his voice and feel the strain in his body. She had come in to tell him something that she'd noticed, something that bothered her. But she decided then not to. He had enough on his plate already.

"You heading back to the city today?" she asked and gently began to rub his shoulders.

"Yes, I'm going to Drew's office. Her computer has more access..." He closed his eyes and felt the comfort of her touch. "That feels great," he murmured.

"Good," she said softly. "You should see Silas before you go. He's upstairs working on his computers, on something about the case." She could feel his shoulders tensing at the thought. She stopped massaging and leaned her face close to his ear.

"It's alright," she whispered, "I think you were right. We can't stop him, and he truly needs to be involved. A little research from the sidelines is probably for the best."

She lightly kissed his ear and left the room.

Artemis smiled. He got up, grabbed his coffee, and headed up to see Silas. As he went up the stairs, he could hear Delia in the kitchen cleaning up the breakfast dishes. As always, there was a great deal of banging going on. He was glad that they had bought durable dishes.

"Great coffee, Big Dee," he called out, almost laughing.

"Quit that Big Dee stuff, and you're welcome!" her strong, loud voice called back.

Upstairs, he stood in the doorway of his son's bedroom, watching him work his three laptops at once. Silas was focused on the middle one, where he was navigating a link and taking a virtual walkthrough of the same Necropolis Bar, on Doyers Street, that had been raided last night.

"Where'd that come from?" Artemis asked as he sat down next to his son.

"Google Maps. Someone posted this. I'm not sure when, yet. But the place was still open. And that was years ago, right?" Silas pushed his heavy glasses back up on his nose and continued finding his way around the bar.

"Yeah, it closed maybe ten years ago. Nice work," Artemis said sincerely.

"And this is still there?" Silas asked as he stopped on a picture of a three-headed sea serpent.

"Yes. And I've been doing some work on that, too." Artemis suddenly sounded like he was talking to a colleague. "Can I use this?" he asked, indicating the laptop in front of him.

"Sure," Silas said.

Artemis rapidly worked and found another picture of a three-headed sea serpent.

"What do you think?" he asked.

Silas looked at the two screens for a second and smiled. "They're the same. Or pretty close. What does it mean…?"

"I'm not sure, yet"—Artemis shook his head and pointed to the image he'd found—"but this one is an ancient Etruscan wall painting that was found not too long ago, in Tuscany, in a town called Sarteano. The serpent is the guardian of the underworld."

"A necropolis," Silas said, understanding.

"Exactly." Artemis nodded. "Do you think you could find out when that bar opened?"

"I'm sure I can," Silas answered confidently. "Why?"

"Well, this"—Artemis pointed to his screen—"is from the *Tomb of the Infernal Chariot*, from the fourth century BCE. But it was only discovered in 2003."

"I get it." Silas smiled a little. "So, I'll be looking to find out who's listed as owner of the bar, and maybe, see if they come from Italy."

Artemis was simultaneously proud of his son and worried for him. "Just research the opening date. Leave everything else to me, okay?"

Silas looked up and saw the seriousness in Artemis's face. "Okay, Dad."

"Good," Artemis said, took a sip of coffee, and got up to go.

"So, track finals today?"

"Yes"—Silas nodded as he turned back to his computer—"but not for a while."

"No, I mean, I'm glad." Artemis watched him working. "Good luck today."

But Silas was too involved with his research to even know that his father was still in the room.

*   *   *

Lucille had walked across Central Park to the Upper East Side. Even here in the city, the bright morning air was fresh and breezy. She stood on the sidewalk, outside of Paul's office. She took off her sunglasses, put them in her purse, and braced herself.

I can do this.

She leaned her weight against the heavy glass door and pushed her way into the small marble foyer. She reached out her delicate hand and pushed the button on the intercom.

Nothing happened. She pushed it again. Then, she heard the inner door being unlocked. Paul opened the door. He stood looking at her, saying nothing.

"Ida said to meet you here," Lucille said, "I got here as fast as I could."

"Did you?" he said quietly and then opened the door wider. She carefully stepped past him, into the reception area. He closed and locked the door behind her. They were alone, and the lights were off. Without a word, he led her into his inner office.

It was brighter here, with daylight filtering through the large window. Lucille stood in the middle of the wood paneled room. Paul closed the inner door, went past her, and stood behind his large mahogany desk. He turned away from her, pushed aside the sheer curtains, and looked at the crowds of people across the street, in front of the Metropolitan Museum.

"Did your sister tell you that I've canceled classes?" His voice was low and dangerous.

"Yes, she did." Lucille watched him.

"And did she say why?"

"No, Paul," she answered clearly, "but I saw what happened at The School on the news."

Paul turned and looked at her. The light from the window behind him cast his face into shadow, so she couldn't clearly see his expression. But she could feel the coiled power of his body, ready to strike.

"Where's your azurite necklace, Lucille?"

"I think you have it," she said unflinchingly. "And my diary, too. I'm here because I want them back."

"Good for you, Lucille." Paul smiled darkly.

This one is such a challenge.

He reached into his jacket pocket, took out the dark-blue stone pendant, and held it up so she could see it clearly.

"But this azurite gem is not yours. It was a gift from The Voices. And now that classes have ended, they said I should take it back."

Lucille considered this for a moment and then said, "Okay."

Paul came around and sat on the front edge of his desk. He breathed out slowly and said, "You know, I thought you were going to take The School more seriously."

"I did, I have—" she began, but Paul stopped her with a sharp wave of his hand.

"I helped you to get clean," he said softly, "and to have some respect for yourself again. I spent time with you, personally. And that meant so much to me."

Lucille remembered the power of his body, the force of his hips, the feel of his kisses.

"I'm sorry, Paul. I really am."

His eyes shot up and fiercely focused on her. His jaw clenched. "Are you? Do you have any fucking idea what you've done?"

The force of his anger startled her. And her resolve wavered.

He knows. He knows it was me.

"I never meant to hurt you." She swallowed.

"But, Lucille, you have," he said.

And then his body relaxed, his eyes grew kind, and that almost feminine attractiveness returned to his face.

"So, at Columbia, you loved going to Professor Bookbinder's lectures on art, right?" he said pleasantly.

She didn't answer. But it was at those lectures that she'd learned about the thirteen pieces of stolen art. Artemis had often talked about them and showed slides—slides of an ancient dark-bronze chalice, with very distinctive markings. A chalice she'd recognized when Paul drank wine from it during class.

"You remember," Paul continued, "I told you that I know Professor Bookbinder."

"Yes, but you said that you were just testing me...."

"I was"—he smiled—"but, in fact, I really do know him. We go back a long way. That's why I was so concerned that you were even thinking of hurting his wife."

"But back then, I was—"

He cut her off, "I know, it was just something you wrote to let off steam. I understand."

Paul got up and went behind his desk, and from a drawer, pulled out Lucille's diary.

"Why did you take that?" she asked simply.

"I wanted to read it more carefully. I only had that quick look at your place." He came around the desk and stood in front of her.

"Here." He held out the diary. She took it in both hands and looked up into his strangely powerful eyes.

"I am sorry, Lucille. From my heart, I am." His tone was sad and sincere. "I think you and I could really have been something together."

She summoned her courage and said, "I think Roxie Lee wouldn't like that very much."

Paul reached up his hand, brushed his fingers lightly across her neck, and tenderly touched her pale cheek. He slowly leaned to her and kissed her lips lightly. She felt a visceral rush of energy up her spine and across her chest. She leaned back away from him.

"Truth be told," he whispered clearly, "I don't think Roxie and I have much of a future together."

Lucille's eyes grew wider and she wondered if she could believe him.

"She's all about herself and conquering the world of television, all the time. It gets kinda boring. And the truth is, I need someone who can be more about me." He laughed softly at himself. "I know, it's selfish, and something that I'll never really find. But I've always been searching for a person who would put me first. For that person, I would open the doors of my soul."

"Is that the truth, Paul?" she whispered.

"Yes, and I swear it."

Lucille leaned into him, and he slowly wrapped his powerful arms around her. She closed her eyes and breathed in his scent.

"Oh, Paul, this is all I ever wanted," she confessed.

"I'm always too much about me," he said softly. "It has caused me so much trouble."

He lifted her chin and kissed her lips again, this time harder. His hand pushed easily into her breasts and then slid down the front of her shirt, under her belt, into her pants. His fingers slowly found their way inside her, and Lucille gasped and surrendered.

"Fuck me, Paul," she whispered urgently. "Please fuck me now."

* * *

At the 19th Precinct, the south-facing windows on the fourth floor were open a few inches, letting in the fresh air but also the constant sounds of traffic below.

Artemis was sitting near one end of the long conference table when Mak and Drew joined him. Mak closed the door, sat opposite Artemis, and opened his notes. Drew took three coffees from a brown paper bag and handed them out.

"Thanks," Artemis murmured as he automatically arranged where the cup was in relationship to his laptop.

The morning news had been mostly about politics and sports. An article about COVID-19 warned that the elderly were at greater risk, and that the Centers for Disease Control had made more testing available. There was a picture of the mayor of New York riding the subways to show how safe they were.

Artemis looked at his cup of coffee and sighed. "So, what have you found out? Was Lucille ever enrolled at Columbia?"

"We don't know yet," Drew said as she sat down at the head of the table, next to her cousin.

"Why not? Did the university say you need a warrant?"

"No"—Drew shook her head—"they're okay. But there was a small fire last night, in their records office."

"That's suspicious," Artemis said softly. "What time?"

"Somewhere around midnight. Clayton is there now with a tech team. We should be able to access school records in a few hours."

"Interesting timing." Artemis nodded. "Just a delay, then."

"Yeah, seems like it." Drew took a gulp of her coffee and turned to Mak. "Where's Ray?"

"Not sure," he answered. "Last I heard, he'd gotten a tip that Taki Fukuda had been seen somewhere in northern New Jersey. I think he went after that."

"Where in Jersey?" Artemis looked up sharply.

"Sorry," Mak said, "he didn't tell me."

Artemis nodded and opened the lid of his coffee to let it cool. "Anything new on Beth Schaefer?" he asked his cousin.

"We know that she took a flight to Montreal, midday Friday, from LaGuardia," Drew reported. "She didn't have a reservation; she just showed up and bought a ticket."

"Which brought up all sorts of international security flags." Mak nodded. "Our people are working on finding out what happened to her once she got to Canada."

"What's all this?" Drew leaned to see what was on Artemis's screen.

"Oak Bluffs," he answered.

"Um"—Drew shook her head—"the rehab place that Sharder left his money to…?"

"Yes, in Connecticut," Artemis confirmed. "I've been searching their database to see if I can find any record of a patient named Khloe. But there's nothing." Artemis took a careful sip of coffee.

"We have two recovered Gardner pieces," Mak said quietly. "One found in Southampton; one downtown. So… what is the connection between Lucille and Raphael Sharder?"

"I'd like to go back downtown," Artemis said after a moment, "and take a fresh look at the school and see what we can find out from the shop owners."

"You coming?" Drew smiled at Mak.

"Absolutely."

*   *   *

The light was soft and felt sweet to Lucille as she lay naked on the sofa in Paul's office. He stood before her, pulling on his pants. He smiled at her, satisfied.

"I've missed this," he said softly.

"Me, too," she whispered. And then she giggled, "And I feel so much better."

She reached down to the floor, retrieved her jeans, and pulled them on. She got up and picked up her diary, which had been left where it was dropped, in the middle of Paul's office.

Paul watched her with open admiration. "You know, I think I should be jealous of Artemis. The way you go on about him, in that book." He smiled.

"But I told you"—Lucille laughed softly—"that was forever ago, and I was out of my mind. I don't feel anything for him anymore."

"You know"—Paul, still shirtless, sat on the edge of his desk—"I've got a way to find out for sure. And you can do something for me at the same time."

"Okay, so, what can I do for you?" she said suggestively as she came to him and rubbed her hands across his bare, muscular chest.

"You'd be surprised," he softly joked.

"I would love to help you, Paul," she said warmly.

"But it will take a few hours of your time, right now. Still willing?"

"Try me." She nodded.

"Great." He got up and went to the back of his desk and from a lower drawer, lifted out a large manila envelope. He held it up so she could see the printed label: *Artemis Bookbinder* and his address in Halesburgh.

"Could you take this to Professor Bookbinder, at his home in New Jersey? He needs to get this right away," Paul said.

"… Take that… to Artemis." Lucille shook her head slowly. "I don't understand."

Paul smiled kindly at her and explained, "These are some personal papers that I promised would get there by the end of the day."

The confusion in her face was plain to see as she pulled on her shirt.

"But I know this is a lot to ask," he said, "so, if you think it's too much, I'm sure I can get someone else to take it."

Then Lucille's face cleared, and she said, "Oh, I see. You're testing me."

"Am I?" he said playfully.

"Yes"—she almost laughed—"to see if I really am the person who can put you first. And yes, Paul, I am. I'll be happy to do this for you."

"Thank you, Lucille." Paul smiled widely and admitted, "And you're right. It feels great knowing that I can depend on you."

He came around the desk and handed her the envelope. "And you'll have a chance to speak face-to-face with Professor Bookbinder. I think that might do you a world of good."

She wondered if that was true. Maybe seeing Artemis again would help. Maybe, if her dark, confusing world ever spun completely out of control, he could be the person to set her right again.

"So, what's in here?" she asked as she felt the weight of the envelope. "Papers?"

"I'm afraid I can't tell you. Doctor–patient confidentiality, and all that." He shrugged.

"Not a problem," Lucille assured him but wondered what could be so important that it needed to be delivered today. And did this mean that Artemis was a patient? Or maybe, they were working together on something? She looked at the address.

"But how do I get there? I don't have a car in the city, anymore."

"I know," Paul answered as he pulled out some cash and counted out four-hundred dollars in fifties. "There's a rental place, just a few blocks from here, on Third. Do you know it?"

She did. It was next door to the shop where she'd purchased the burner phone. She nodded.

"Good. Rent a car for the day. You'll have to use your credit card, of course, so here's enough cash to cover it and anything else you need." Paul handed her the money and gave her directions. He checked the time on his Rolex.

"So, everything clear?"

"Yes, Paul. And getting clearer all the time." She pulled on her jacket and gathered her purse and diary. "I'll call you later, when I'm heading back to the city."

She started to go, but he stopped her. He reached into his pocket and carefully pulled out the silver pendant necklace. The azurite gem sparkled dark blue. He reached his arms over her head and fastened the chain around her neck. She looked up at him.

"Did your Voices tell you to give this back to me?" she asked softly.

"No. This is from me."

She leaned up to him and kissed his lips. "Thank you, Paul. This means more to me than I can ever tell you."

He smiled and walked her through the reception area to the outer door. He leaned close to her ear and whispered, "I will never forget what I owe you."

Paul unlocked the door and let her out.

Feeling pleased with herself, Lucille walked away quickly and headed east, toward Third Avenue.

*   *   *

"And remember," Delia started.

"To lift my knees and run hard," Silas confirmed, but he looked worried. He pushed his heavy glasses back into place and zipped up his jacket.

"You'll be great." Delia nodded.

"Yes, you will," Emily said warmly as she came into the kitchen. She got her keys and purse and headed for the back door.

"We'll see you later," she called to her aunt. "And if you think of anything we need, just give me a call."

Delia walked Silas out and watched as he and his mother went down the back steps to the car.

As Silas got in, Emily turned and waved to the FBI detail waiting for them at the end of the driveway.

Delia shook off a worry, closed the door, and headed upstairs.

Across the street, Bert Rocca and his two agents were standing together near their cars. Following the usual protocol, one agent got into her car, pulled out onto the street, and waited for Emily to line up behind her. Bert turned to the man next to him.

"Follow me, Flip," he said.

The young agent, Steve Filipowski, known to his friends as Flip, had worked with Bert just long enough to be comfortable questioning this order. "What about Delia?" He nodded his head toward the house.

"She'll be okay," Bert answered. "But we're going to have our hands full at the school. So, I want you there to help us watch these two." Bert indicated Emily and Silas, who were stopped at the end of their driveway, waiting for his signal.

"Yes, sir." Flip nodded, and they got into their cars.

Bert smiled and waved to Emily. She pulled into formation behind the lead car. Bert pulled up behind her, and Flip followed him. Bert gave a command into the mic clipped on his lapel, and the four cars headed out along the quiet suburban street.

At Silas's school, classes were done for the day, but the gymnasium stands were crowded with parents. In the center of the arena, a large group of students were gathered, waiting to hear which events they'd been assigned to. Coaches separated the group into various teams: the sprinters, the relay-racers, the jumpers. Silas found himself herded into the largest and last picked group, the cross-country runners. In accordance with school policy, everyone who tried out made the team. But the thought of running long distances, across muddy fields, in March, usually had an effect. Most of the group decided to quit and walked off to the locker rooms, grumbling. Silas sadly made his way over to his mother, who was standing with Bert.

"Oh, Silas," Emily began. She was going to say how sorry she was but opted instead, "So, are you still up for this?"

Silas looked up at her and shrugged.

"Don't worry about it, kid," Bert's Boston accent made his gruff voice sound kinder. "Cross-country is great. You're gonna like it."

Silas looked up at the old man in the dark blue suit. Unconvinced, he nodded once.

Emily looked to Bert. "And what about you? Can you keep him safe?"

Bert waved one of his agents over and smiled. "I'm definitely not up for a long-distance run anymore. But Flip loves to run. Does miles and miles, every morning."

Agent Filipowski laughed. "It's true." He nodded and looked to Silas. "If you want to do this, I'll be there step for step. We have you covered."

Silas thought about it for a moment and then said simply, "Yep. I'm in."

A coach called the team back to the center of the gym. Silas went to join them.

"It'll be okay," Bert said to Emily.

She smiled and nodded her thanks.

*　*　*

Traffic leaving the city across the George Washington Bridge had been light, and Lucille was making good time as she headed up the Palisades Parkway. She had treated herself to a sporty, high-end rental. After all, Paul was paying for it. And she had missed driving: the feel of control, power, and speed. To her right she could see glimpses of the Hudson River below the Palisades and Yonkers beyond in the distance. Bright sunlight blinked through the branches along the roadway, and she smiled. Paul was right. This was making her feel better.

She took a quick glance at the seat next to her, where her purse and diary were. And the envelope addressed to Artemis Bookbinder. She wondered again what was in that envelope and why it had to be delivered today. It would be so easy to pull over and open it.

Lucille considered for a while and then she let it go. She reached up her hand and wrapped her fingers around the azurite gem hanging on her chest.

Paul trusts me. I never want to lose that again.

* * *

The afternoon was cold but sunny, and the coaches had decided to take the newly formed team for a workout on the outside track. Some kids were stretching, some were running wind sprints. Silas stood alone in the center of the large muddy oval, looking off at a passing jet, high above.

Bert stood near Emily, by the bleachers, where a group of parents sat watching. Bert signaled across the field to Agent Filipowski, who nodded and moved closer to Silas.

Emily sighed. "Sometimes I wonder if Silas even knows we're here."

Silas was studying a group of tiny midges, amazed that they had come to life so early in the year, and wondering why they were called *no-see-ums*. He could clearly see them.

"So, you wanna run a little?" A friendly voice brought Silas back.

"What's your name?" Silas asked simply.

"My friends call me Flip."

Silas smiled for the first time that day. "Good name. Sure, let's run."

Across the field, Emily sighed as she watched Flip and Silas start off together on the track. Her cell phone rang, and Bert stepped away to give her privacy.

"Bert," Emily said as she finished the call, "I have to go home for a minute."

"Not a problem," he answered as he came back. "I'll follow you, and these two will stay with Silas."

Emily looked at the woman agent standing guard at the far end of the track and then at the large, fit man trotting along with her son. Silas looked so small and out of place.

"They'll take good care of him," Bert said quietly.

She nodded. Bert walked her to her car and through the mic on his lapel, radioed instructions to his agents. He got into his car, signaled to Emily, and they drove away.

*   *   *

In lower Manhattan, bright daylight had brought Doyers Street to life. The gates on the shops were up, and the little street was busy. Artemis came out from a shop and saw Mak standing across the street, lighting a cigarette.

"I thought you were giving that up?" Artemis said as he approached.

"I'm always giving it up." Mak smiled at himself. He dropped the cigarette and stepped on it.

"You get anything?" Artemis asked.

"Nothing." Mak shook his head. "You?"

"Not yet." Artemis turned toward the shop he'd just come out of. "But the owner told me that the barber who works for him lives up there." He indicated windows, on top of the old three-story building.

"Lives here at night? He must know how to take care of himself," Mak said, impressed.

"Herself," Artemis reported. "And her apartment is perfectly placed to see anything that happens here." They were standing just a few feet from the entrance to the Necropolis Bar. The old gate was rolled up, and an NYPD cop was standing guard.

"So, can we talk to her?" Mak asked.

"No, she's in Hong Kong, visiting family."

"And the borders are closed there, right?"

"Right." Artemis sighed. "She's stuck there. Where's Drew?"

"Downstairs, in the classroom."

Mak held up his ID as they passed the cop and stepped into the old bar. Artemis stopped, just inside the door, to give his eyes a chance to adjust. Sunlight cut an angle across the wall painting to his left. Artemis looked at the strange three-headed sea serpent and its fierce, dark eyes. A wave of dread washed over him, so strong that he got dizzy. He stepped away from the picture and wrapped his arms around his chest.

"You okay?" Mak asked kindly as he came near.

It was a moment before Artemis could answer.

"I don't know," he said quietly. "Something isn't right. Let's find Drew."

*　　*　　*

Finding the place had been easy. Lucille parked in the driveway, near the front entrance of the Bookbinder home.

She picked up her purse and the envelope. She got out of the car and took a breath to slow her racing heart. It was quiet here. There was a car, parked in the driveway at the back of the house, but no one in sight.

She wondered what she would say if his wife opened the door. Emily. That very pretty woman, whose image had so bothered her not so long ago.

Maybe this is why Paul wanted me to do this.

Lucille looked at the fine old house, with blue clapboards above and solid stone walls below. Everything here felt so protected and clean. It was the kind of place she could only dream about. Her life had become so much about the city. But why? Maybe, someday she could have this. And be with someone worthwhile, somebody like Artemis Bookbinder. She looked at the envelope in her hands.

She gathered her courage and walked across the yellow lawn, past the fallow gardens, up the wood steps to the covered porch. She rang the bell.

As she waited, she looked across the street at the nice houses, fences, and yards. It was lovely. And strange. There was no one anywhere.

She rang the doorbell again. And noticed that the door was actually open, just a little.

After a moment she knocked. And when no one answered, she very carefully pushed the door open.

"Hello?" she called out. "Hello, is anyone home?" She stood in the open door, unsure what to do.

"Professor Bookbinder? Are you here?" she called louder. "I've got something for you from Paul Marin...."

This was weird. The door was open, and no one was here. She called out again. And then stepped into the foyer, leaving the front door open behind her. She noticed all the care that had gone into this place. Then she saw herself in the hall mirror.

I look so scared.

She smiled at herself. She rubbed her pale cheeks with her fingers to bring up some color. Pleased that she looked more presentable, she turned and walked slowly into the house. She felt curious sensations being alone in this house: dangerous and exciting.

"Professor Bookbinder?" she called out again as she passed the foot of the stairs.

She made her way around a corner into the kitchen. Through the large window she could see the sunlit backyard. Then she saw something wrong. On the floor, past the counter, was the body of a woman.

Lucille moved closer and carefully knelt down. There was a small pool of blood on the white tile floor.

She held her breath and gently brushed the hair from the woman's face. It was a beautiful face. One that she'd only seen in photos. A face that had haunted her.

"Mrs. Bookbinder...?" she whispered.

Lucille reached out, gently touched her cold cheek, and knew. Emily Bookbinder was dead.

Somewhere outside, toward the front of the house, a car door slammed shut.

Lucille flinched, and her mind jammed in panic. She tried to get up, but her legs felt weak. She reached up, grabbed the edge of the counter, and pulled herself to her feet.

I shouldn't be here.

She backed out of the kitchen, turned, ran the length of the foyer, out the still open door, across the porch, and the lawn. She fumbled in her purse to find the key. She opened the door of the car and froze.

There, on the driver's seat, was a small, black metal gun. Her breath came in ragged, shallow gulps. She picked up the gun, threw it toward the house, got into the car, started the engine, backed into the street, and started to drive.

She had no idea where she was heading, but she forced herself to keep the car under the speed limit. She came to a stop sign and turned right. She came to a blinking red light and turned left. She went down a steep hill and past a small group of stores. She drove until the houses became fewer. She saw a sign for the Halesburgh Reservoir and turned. After a half-mile, the dirt road ended by a trail head into the woods. There was no one here. She parked at the edge of the trees, turned off the engine, covered her face with her hands, and started to cry.

And then she wondered.

On the seat next to her, by her dairy and purse, was the envelope from Paul. She picked it up and controlled her trembling hands enough to tear it open. Inside were six pages of white paper. They were all blank.

And then she knew.

She reached up and undid the clasp of her pendant. She held the chain in her fist and lifted the pretty blue azurite stone so she could see it clearly.

"God damn you to hell, Paul Marin," she whispered.

She dropped the necklace on the seat beside her, opened her purse, and took out her cell phone. She scrolled her contacts and found his name. She hit the button.

"Hello," she heard him say, "is this Lucille?"

"Yes, Artemis, it is." Her voice was trembling, and tears flowed down her face. "Your wife…," she started, but her voice failed her.

"What about her?" Artemis demanded loudly. Drew and Mak heard the fear in his voice and came nearer.

"Your wife, Emily," Lucille forced herself to say her name, "… is dead."

"What…?" he whispered.

"At your house, I was just there, but it wasn't me, I swear it," Lucille said in a ragged rush. "She was dead when I got there.…"

A sudden impact into her car from behind jolted her head back and then slammed her chest into the steering wheel. She screamed and dropped the phone.

Another impact rammed her, pushed her parked car forward, and pinned it against a large tree.

Overwhelmed with adrenaline, Lucille forced her door open with her shoulder, got out, and ran blindly along the path and into the woods.

Agent Bert Rocca got out of the car that had pinned her. He pulled out his gun and ran after her. But she was young and fast. And soon, the old man was out of breath.

"Fuck me!" he screamed in anger as he pulled out his cell and hastily dialed a number.

*   *   *

That day was indelibly stained on Artemis's memory. Like a nightmare, some things were lost in shadows, but some were incredibly sharp and painful.

Drew got them to an NYPD chopper, and the flight seemed to take forever. Through headsets, Mak reported that Silas was safe. But Delia had been hurt.

They landed in an empty baseball field in Halesburgh. The sun was down, and it was getting dark. The local police, with sirens and lights, drove them to the house. The street was crowded with neighbors, being held back by cops. Two ambulances were in the driveway.

Artemis walked to the front porch. Ray Gaines was sitting on the top step, looking broken and old. He saw Artemis and stood up.

"I need you to get a good grip on yourself, son," he said sadly.

Artemis walked past him, into the house. Mak stayed on the porch with Ray. Drew followed Artemis down the hall, into the kitchen. There, an FBI photographer was working near Emily's body.

"Jesus," Drew whispered, and she leaned against the doorway.

The agent saw them and backed off. Artemis sat on the floor by his wife. He leaned close to her.

I'm so sorry, Emily...

Even then, he couldn't stop his mind from gathering facts and cataloguing information. The wound on the back of her head was close range, from a small-caliber bullet. Most likely, 9mm. Just like Raphael Sharder... The thought of that, the warning note, and the way he'd failed her became too much. Artemis sagged to the floor next to Emily.

When Artemis came to, he was lying on the sofa in his study. Drew was sitting nearby on the coffee table, and Mak was standing in the door.

"You okay?" Drew asked softly.

"No," Artemis said. "Where's Emily?"

Drew looked at him a moment before she said, "They're getting ready to move her body now."

Artemis nodded a little. Drew held out a glass of scotch.

"Drink this," she quietly commanded.

Artemis sat up and sipped a little.

"Silas is still at the police station?" he asked.

"Yes," Drew confirmed. "I'm heading there now. I just wanted to see you before I left."

"Thanks. I'll be there soon. Does he know what happened?"

"Yes," she answered. "No details, of course. But he knows."

Artemis rubbed his face with his hands, trying to clear his mind. He looked up at Mak. "9mm?"

"Yes, I'm sure it is," Mak reported. "We found the gun. It was dropped in the bushes out front. There's a little blood on the handle."

Artemis looked up, startled.

"From the hit that Delia took, I'm thinking," Mak said.

"How is she?"

"She's a tough old girl. She's gonna be okay," Drew answered. "They've been trying to get her to the hospital, but she won't go. Says she won't leave Emily."

Artemis took this in. "Where is she?"

"Her bedroom."

Delia had been upstairs, cleaning the bathroom, when she was hit from behind. She had fallen against the edge of the tub. The local police found her unconscious on the bathroom floor; her wrists, ankles, and mouth bound with duct tape. She had badly bruised ribs and a nasty cut across the back of her head.

Artemis found her sitting on the edge of her bed. Delia's head was wrapped with a white bandage, and her left arm was in a sling. Her face and wrists were still red from where the tape had been. A woman officer was standing nearby. She saw Artemis, nodded to him, and left them alone.

Delia looked up at him. Her eyes were red, and her cheeks flushed. She looked defeated. Artemis had never seen her look that way before. He sat down next to her. He started to say something, but his voice failed him. Tears filled his eyes, and he hung his head.

Delia looked at him and slowly pulled herself up. She reached her powerful arm around his shoulders and held him.

After a time, she said softly, "Drew says that we're going to be staying with her in Brooklyn…?"

"Yes," Artemis managed, "just like old times…."

It was a cold night. Mak and Ray stood together on the porch watching the ambulance with Emily's body drive away.

"What about that tip on Taki Fukuda?" Mak asked the senior agent.

"Nothing," Ray said with disgust. "Bert Rocca told me he'd gotten an anonymous call. Somebody saw a guy matching the description at a mall near here. But there was nothing."

"Where is Bert?" Mak asked.

"I haven't a fucking clue. Nobody does," Ray said darkly. "But when I find him, I'm gonna rip his goddamn balls off."

Mak sighed. He turned to look at the bare branches in the front gardens.

"It's Thursday," Ray muttered. "A week ago, Raphael Sharder was murdered. And now Emily."

"… And we've recovered two pieces of stolen art," Mak offered sadly.

Ray shook his head. "It's just not worth it."

"Sir"—an agent ran up the steps—"we've found the car."

"Where?"

* * *

Like his father, Silas would remember that bad day like strange glimmers of light. Still dressed in his muddy track gear, he sat waiting in a brown and blue cinder block room. On the metal desk was a forgotten cup of coffee and the Halesburgh Police logo on a laptop.

Drew arrived. She hugged him. And much later, when he could see the stars outside the high windows, his father and Delia came. They talked. And the more they said, the more the world changed.

Then they were in a car, riding for a long time. And no one said anything. Silence overloaded his ears until all he could hear was the hazy rush of empty air.

Chapter Eight

Friday, and beyond

The few next days and nights were part of the same un-waking nightmare. The investigators allowed them to return to their home and pack up what they needed. The house felt off-angle and sad. Emily was everywhere and nowhere.

Drew did her best to help them settle into her house in Brooklyn. Her father, Mathew, came up from Florida to be with them. On the street outside, there was a constant presence of NYPD cops.

Some days later, there was a funeral service in New Jersey. Some people sent their regrets, citing worry about the pandemic. But even so, the little church was full of neighbors, colleagues from Emily's school, AA friends of Delia, teachers from Columbia, and police officers in dress uniform.

Emily Twist Bookbinder was buried in Yonkers, in the same quiet cemetery where Artemis's parents were interred.

*   *   *

On the night of the murder, Lucille Orsina had used the cash that Paul had given her to get back to the city. She knew that she couldn't go to her own apartment. So, she waited outside of the building where her sister lived, on the Upper East Side. Ida found her shivering, sitting on a curb between two parked cars. Ida took her sister through the garage entrance to the elevator and up to her tenth-floor apartment, without anyone noticing.

Ida Orsina had been Paul Marin's closest friend and business partner since they went to college together. She trusted Paul and always believed that he trusted her, too. He had shared so many secret, personal details about himself. But after Lucille told her what had happened, everything changed.

*　*　*

It was Thursday, the twelfth of March, and the early morning skies over Brooklyn were dense with threatening clouds. Delia, still tired from another uneasy night, looked at her cell and scanned the news: With more than one hundred thirty-four thousand coronavirus cases worldwide, the United States banned all travel to and from Europe. In New York City, the mayor had declared an emergency and closed all restaurants, theaters, and museums.

Delia put the news down and turned her attention back to the stove.

"You're up early," Mathew Sweeney said as he came in.

"Yes." She shrugged. "There's coffee."

"Thanks." Mathew poured himself a cup and sat at the large kitchen table.

Mathew, like his daughter Drew, was a powerful figure. He was close to seventy but still ruggedly handsome, with a full head of close-cut white hair and a friendly face. His eyes reflected his clear mind and a determined good humor.

"Perfect coffee, Delia," he said appreciatively as his daughter came in.

"Morning," Drew said to both of them.

"Coffee?" Delia nodded as she stirred a large pan of scrambled eggs.

"You don't have to do that, you know," Drew said.

"I know"—she smiled—"but it helps."

Silas came in and looked around.

"Morning, Silas." Delia smiled kindly at him. "Breakfast is almost ready. Have a seat."

Silas didn't seem to hear her. Instead, he went over to the coffee and poured himself a cup. He sipped it, and sat at the table across from Mathew. The older man nodded to him.

Artemis was the last to arrive. He was shaved and dressed in his standard outfit: black jeans, vest, and tie. But his usually clear eyes looked distant and vague. He sat down carefully, almost as if he were afraid to touch the table.

Drew put a mug of coffee in front of him. He nodded his thanks but didn't touch it. She took the seat next to him.

Delia served out plates of eggs and toast and sat down. Silas looked at his plate uninterested and sipped his coffee.

"Get any sleep in that cubbyhole?" Drew asked her father, in an attempt to distract them all.

"Oh, fine"—Mathew nodded as he chewed—"I've slept there before."

"Yes, but you should be in your old bedroom," Drew said.

"That's where you sleep now. And I'm okay with that," Mathew said, with friendly finality.

"Eat a little something," Delia said to Silas. But again, he didn't seem to hear her. He poured a little milk into his coffee and watched the way it swirled in the cup.

Delia turned to Drew and Mathew. "This house is beautiful." She, too, was making an effort. "When was it built?"

"Eighteen ninety-four," Mathew said before Drew could answer. She seemed used to that. She smiled a little and took a large bite of her toast.

"It was completely renovated just before we bought it, some thirty years ago. Jesus, time goes so fast." Mathew smiled a little.

"And you keep it up nicely," Delia said, turning to Drew.

"Well"—Drew shrugged—"I just have to maintain it."

Delia looked across the table at the older man. "I know I still miss my husband. How long has your wife been gone now?"

"Well, Muriel died, I guess"—a sad look crossed Mathew's face— "maybe fourteen years ago." He looked to Drew for confirmation, and she nodded.

Delia decided to change the subject. "Drew told me that you were quite something on the police force, lots of awards. Were you there long?"

"Forty years," Mathew said and gave a warning look to his daughter. Drew shrugged. She knew that he hated talking about himself. But Delia Twist Kouris was a hard person to keep information from.

Artemis sighed. He reached slowly for his cup, but his fingers trembled. He pulled his hand back.

"That cup's not gonna bite you," Drew said quietly.

Artemis sharply turned his head to her, his eyes hot with anger. Then, in an instant, it faded. He nodded a little and fixed his eyes on his cup. Making an effort, he tightened his fingers around the handle, slowly lifted the cup, and took a sip.

Silas looked up at his father with worry. Aunt Delia carried on. She asked Mathew about Florida and if he missed living in Brooklyn. He told her that he missed police work but that life down south was good. There were other retired cops there, and he liked the weather.

"Except in the summer," he said. "That's when I like to come back and stay with Drew. But not for too long, I don't want to cramp her style."

Drew gave him a knowing look. "You are always welcome, anytime. This is still your house, you know."

"And it's your life," Mathew toasted her with his coffee cup. Drew smiled.

"And it never snows there, and that matters some," Mathew returned to Delia and the topic of Florida. He held up his large, gnarled hands. "I've got a little arthritis, you know."

"And you drove all the way up here." Delia sounded impressed.

"Well, yeah… I couldn't fly with this," Mathew said as he opened his sweater and revealed his service revolver, holstered below his arm. "I thought we could all do with a little more protection."

"I agree, Uncle Matt. Thanks for being here," Artemis said. Then before anyone could respond, he picked up his coffee and left the room.

Silas watched his father go. Then he got up and went back upstairs to his room.

Delia sighed. She stood, gathered the dishes, and started to clean up.

"Hey, that's my job here." Drew got up.

"No." Delia sounded strained. "I'll do it."

"Okay, thanks," Drew said. She turned to her father and met his eyes. Mathew nodded, and she went out after Artemis.

She found him in the living room, by the bar cabinet. He was pouring scotch into his coffee.

"Kinda early for that, cousin—" Drew started.

"Mary Drew, don't fuck with me," Artemis cut her off softly.

Usually, Drew would have retaliated to hear him use her old, discarded name. But today…she let it slide.

"Just saying, they'll all be here at three."

"I know." Artemis looked at her. "Don't worry. I'm always ready."

She smiled sadly at him and left him alone.

Upstairs, Silas had been given his own small room on the third floor, in the back of the house. He sat by the large window looking out at the courtyard below. The mossy garden and the high stone walls looked gray and sad under the cloudy skies. Silas adjusted his glasses and turned his attention back to a search he'd begun earlier on his laptop.

He'd been looking at some of his father's lectures at Columbia that were available on YouTube. This one was from about four and a half years ago. He hit play.

It was shot from a phone, probably set on a desk toward the back of the lecture hall. Silas could see the students sitting in the first few rows. In front of them, Artemis was talking about the art pieces stolen from the Gardner Museum, his favorite topic, with illustrations on the wall behind him.

Silas scrolled forward to the end of the lecture. He was hoping for something he'd seen before. Sometimes the camera kept recording even after the class was over and everyone had left.

He hit play and watched as the lecture ended. Some students came up and talked to his father. Then they went. Artemis packed his notes and left. And the recording continued of the empty room.

And then Silas saw what he'd been searching for. A young woman entered the shot from the back of the hall. She stood by the desk, where his father had been. She was pretty and very thin. She sat on the edge of the desk, like Artemis had. She smiled but seemed nervous. No, more than that. She looked afraid. She heard someone coming and quickly left the room. The recording ended.

And Silas was sure that he had found her. And her name was Lucille.

Delia, her kitchen work finished, walked up the old wood staircase to the third floor. She winced. She no longer wore the sling on her left arm, but her ribs were still far from healed. Her head wasn't bandaged anymore either but still ached, especially after an exertion like climbing stairs. She took a few long breaths and looked out the window on the landing. On the windy street below, she could see the parked patrol cars and cops standing on the corner.

She went quietly down the hall to check on Silas. His door was open, and he was staring at his laptop so intently he didn't notice her. When she had first come to this family, not so many years ago, little Silas was just like this. Always far away, lost in his thoughts, never speaking, never smiling.

Delia sadly turned and made her way back toward the front of the house. She knocked on Artemis's half-open door. But he didn't answer.

She straightened her shoulders and went in. Artemis was sitting in a chair by the window, looking out.

"At least they're cops this time," he said, without turning, "not the FBI."

He reached for the bottle of scotch and refilled his cup.

"You know," Delia said, "in the program we have a saying—"

"Don't do that shit right now," he said firmly. "It doesn't help."

"Sorry," she said and moved closer. His body tensed, and his jaw tightened.

"Maybe you're right," Delia said softly as she backed up a few steps. "I'm not going to start drinking again, that's for sure. But God knows you've got enough reason to."

She reached up and touched the wound on the back of her head. The pain helped her focus.

"But you know," she continued. "Silas still needs his father. A loss doesn't have to crush you. It can temper you, like steel, and show you how to survive."

Artemis continued to stare out the window.

"Think about what Emily would want," Delia said but instantly knew she had gone too far.

"Please get out," Artemis whispered.

Delia shook her head and left, closing the door behind her.

* * *

At ten o'clock, Ida Orsina buttoned up her jacket and went out her lobby door, onto East 84th Street. The noise from the near corner of Madison was loud, as always, with traffic. Despite the coronavirus news, the sidewalks were still full of people. She considered getting a cab but shrugged it off. She always liked walking to her office. She did her best thinking in motion. And today there was so much to think about.

At the corner, on impulse, she looked north. A half block away, a very fat man ducked into a recessed doorway, trying to hide. But his large stomach stuck out. It would have been funny, but she knew who the man was. Fat Nicky was a business partner of Paul. And she knew he was dangerous.

Fat Nicky realized that she'd seen him. He rolled around the doorway, leaned against the wall, and smiled darkly at her.

Ida had known him a long time, too. His presence was a sure sign of trouble for her and for her sister.

She started walking south, toward her office. She looked back and saw that Fat Nicky was following her. She smiled a little.

At least, they don't know where Lucille is. Yet.

Fat Nicky was keeping his distance. As Ida crossed 80th Street, she pulled out her cell and hit a number.

In her glass-enclosed office, on the eighth floor of the TVNews building, Paula DeVong saw who the caller was and lifted the phone on her desk.

"This is an unexpected pleasure. What's up?"

"It's private. Are you alone?" Ida said as she continued down the sidewalk.

"Hang on," Paula said and waved an imperious hand at the frumpy, little woman, sitting across the desk. Like a faithful dog, Anna Canneli got up, gathered her notes, and headed for the door.

"And shut that," Paula commanded.

Anna closed the door and went into her own adjoining cubicle. Unlike her boss's office, this space was tiny and windowless. It was also hidden from the wide outer office by solid walls.

Anna sat at her little metal desk, lifted her desk phone, carefully pushed a button, and listened in:

"I need a favor. A big one." Ida sounded agitated.

"Of course," Paula purred, "What can I do for you?"

* * *

A little after three o'clock, Artemis stood up, straightened his tie and vest, and made his way downstairs. He found the group already seated around the long oak table in the vintage dining room. He saw where he was supposed to sit but decided to stay standing. Across the table, Mak Kim nodded once. Next to Mak, Clayton looked at Artemis with equal sympathy. Artemis felt exposed and sick. He nodded back.

Ray Gaines was sitting on the other side of Mak. He was dressed correctly, as always in a dark suit. He was clean shaven. But he looked old and broken. Artemis looked at him with clear distrust. Ray took this in for a moment and then looked away.

Mathew had been watching Artemis carefully. "Something to eat?" he asked quietly.

"No thanks, Uncle Matt," Artemis managed. "Where's Silas?"

"I'm here," Silas announced as he came in and sat at the table, next to Drew.

"You should be upstairs," Delia sounded alarmed as she entered from the kitchen with a fresh pot of coffee.

"No, Auntie," Silas said firmly. "I belong here, where I can help find the people who killed my mother."

Delia looked at him amazed. "Artemis?" she quietly appealed.

When Artemis was twelve, Silas's exact same age, his parents were killed. And then, he had come to live here, in Brooklyn, with Drew and her parents. And Artemis had spent all of his life, since then, trying to find those people. And he had failed. Emily was gone.

"You shouldn't make my mistakes," Artemis said very quietly to his son.

Silas answered, "I have to do this."

There was something in the calm way Silas spoke. He sounded older and determined.

Artemis weighed his options and then nodded.

"All right," he said.

Delia sucked in a short breath, frowned with disapproval, and turned away to her work at the sideboard.

"So, where is Bert Rocca?" Artemis began the meeting.

"We found his car parked at the shipping docks in Newark," Ray growled. "We've matched the dents and paints. It was his car that crashed into the perpetrator's."

"And"—Ray shifted uncomfortably—"we have a reliable witness that says he saw a man fitting Bert's description boarding a small boat and heading out into the harbor."

"That night?" Artemis stared at him.

"Yes, before midnight on Thursday," Ray answered.

"So, where is he?"

"We think he might have gotten aboard a tanker, out in the harbor. We're checking."

"And what has the rest of Bert Rocca's *team* told you?" Artemis asked darkly.

"Bert ordered both agents to stay with Silas," Ray answered. "While he alone escorted Emily back to the house."

The sound of her name stopped everything for a moment.

"And there's something else." Ray sighed. He turned to include Silas.

"I've known Bert for most of my life. I trusted him. And I was wrong. I failed you both. And I'm so sorry."

Silas nodded once.

"And what about Lucille…?" Artemis pushed on.

"We know she took a bus late that night to the city. The driver is sure it was her," Clayton answered as he handed out copies of her photograph. "We got this from her student records at Columbia."

Silas studied her picture.

"From the rental car place we got her license," Clayton continued. "It's the same woman: Lucille Orsina Prons."

"Prons…?" Artemis looked at the gentle face in the photo.

"Her married name, we're working on that," Drew explained. "Do you remember her?"

"She never said much"—Artemis nodded slowly—"She always sat in the back of the hall. She wasn't there long."

"Right," Clayton said, "She dropped out near the end of her first semester."

"I found her online," Silas said, and they all turned to him.

"On YouTube, one of your lectures, about four and a half years ago," Silas explained to his father. "I think it shows that she really had a thing for you."

Artemis nodded. "Okay…"

"That fits with the diary we found in her car," Mak joined in. He threw a quick look at Silas before he continued. "She was obsessed with you, Artemis. And she hated your wife. The book is full of threats and fantasies of how Lucille would get rid of her."

Artemis shook his head. "I hardly even remember her."

"We have a definite match of her fingerprints on the gun," Mak added.

"Lucille has a record," Drew explained. "A drug bust at a downtown party some six years ago. She was let off with a warning."

"And the bullet is a match," Mak continued. "We're certain the gun is the murder weapon."

"Is it the same gun that killed Raphael Sharder?" Artemis asked softly.

"Yes," Mak affirmed.

"And it's the weapon used to attack Delia," Ray said as he gave a reassuring nod to Delia. "We tested the blood on the handle against a sample of hers. It's the same: AB positive."

"Anything to help." Delia smiled weakly. "There's fresh coffee here, if anyone needs," she added and went back to the kitchen.

Artemis wrapped his arms around his chest and took a long breath.

"Okay," he said, "anything else?"

Drew turned to look at him. The strain in his voice worried her.

"What about the blue gem necklace?" Silas asked.

"We don't know much about it, except," Mak answered and referred to his notes, "the chain is sterling silver, and the gem is called azurite."

"Azurite comes from copper," Artemis said softly. "And it's rare in a gem form. And she left it behind in the car."

"I don't think it was her," Silas said as he looked at Lucille's photo.

Artemis turned to his son. "Why not?"

"It's too much," Silas said. "Who drives around with an incriminating diary on the front seat?"

"I agree." Artemis nodded. "Lucille called me from her own cell phone. Not a burner. To tell me that she didn't do it."

"And you believe her?" Mathew asked. Like his daughter, he spoke with quiet authority.

"Yes," Artemis said slowly. "Silas is right. She's not the killer."

"But her prints on the gun…?" Mak asked.

"I don't know." Artemis looked at him. "But, there's too much evidence. She's been set up."

Silas got up and poured himself a coffee. Artemis watched him and was afraid for him.

I can't let it happen again. Not ever again.

Artemis started breathing in short, shallow breaths, and he stopped listening to the meeting. It seemed the walls of the house were melting, and endless darkness was seeping in everywhere.

His cousin Drew knew that he was in trouble. She got up and stood next to him. She was careful not to touch him but wanted him to know that she was there.

As the discussion at the table continued, Drew whispered, "Are you okay?"

Artemis whispered back, "Nobody's listening."

"I am," she answered. "I hear you."

Artemis turned to her. "No, not you… them… outside. Nobody is taking this fucking virus seriously."

Though he spoke quietly, everyone heard the fierceness in his voice.

"Sorry," Artemis said to the group. "I'm… I'm a little tired. I'm going back to my room. Carry on without me."

With his arms still wrapped around his chest, Artemis carefully left the room and went upstairs.

"Just like before," a sad voice murmured, and they all turned to look at Mathew Sweeney staring at his folded hands.

*   *   *

It was half past two, the darkest part of the night. A cold rain was falling outside his window, and Silas couldn't sleep. He got out of bed and quietly made his way down the hallway. He passed a door where he could hear Delia's loud snores. At the end of the hall, he found the door to his father's room opened a few inches. He could hear soft, ragged breathing. He pushed the door open and saw Artemis, still dressed, sitting on a chair by the window, staring out into the darkness. On the window sill was a nearly empty bottle of scotch.

"Dad?" Silas said softly. But Artemis didn't seem to hear him.

"Artemis?" Silas said a little louder. But it had no effect.

Silas watched him for a while before he left, closing the door behind him.

* * *

By three the rain had stopped, but the night sky was still thick with clouds that hid the waning moon. Ida and Lucille carefully made their way down to the garage and out to 84th Street. They flagged a cab at the corner of Park Avenue and headed downtown.

Lucille sat quietly, her head down, her arms wrapped protectively around herself. But Ida was being hyperaware for both of them. She looked back often to make sure that no one was following them. They got out near Penn Station and flagged another cab. They changed cabs for a third time near Gramercy Park and continued downtown.

The apartment was in a mid-century, brick building, in the East Village. There was no doorman, but Ida had a key to the outside door. She let them in and took Lucille up to the seventh floor, which was as high as the elevator went. They got out on a small landing, with three apartments. Ida led her sister through a door and up a flight of stairs. Here, on the top floor, was only one apartment. Ida opened the door, let them in, and switched on the ceiling light. The place was a simple studio: an additional space that had been added to the top of the building. It was clear that no one had been here for a long time. A layer of dust was thick on everything. Opposite the entrance, large double windows showed the rising valley of buildings and lights to the north. Ida pulled the heavy canvas curtains across the view.

"Whose place is this?" Lucille asked, her voice quiet and constrained.

"Paula's," Ida answered as she put down a bag of groceries on the small kitchen counter. She sniffed at the stale odor coming up from the drain and ran water in the sink.

"Paula DeVong lives here?" Lucille looked incredulous.

"No, she hasn't been here for years. But this is where she lived when she first came to the city. Her daddy bought it for her, and she's kept it. We've put out-of-town guests here sometimes."

Lucille wondered who that was… but decided not to ask. "Does she know I'm here?"

"Yes," Ida confirmed as she shut off the water and went over to the bed.

"Do you trust her?" Lucille asked simply.

"Yes," Ida said again as she took off the bedspread and gave it a vigorous shake. Dust flew up in a hazy glow toward the ceiling light. "Paula owes me. For everything. She will not betray me."

Like everything Ida said, this sounded like a sure pronouncement. But Lucille wondered.

Ida remade the bed, switched on a table lamp, and put her hand over the radiator to make sure the heat was coming up.

"Do not open the door to anyone but me," she commanded as she handed Lucille the keys. "Do not go out. Stay away from the windows. I will be back tomorrow night. You'll stay here until we can figure something else out."

Lucille nodded vaguely at her sister.

"You're gonna be okay." Ida put her hand on Lucille's shoulder. "Just stay quiet, and give me some time to figure out what to do. Okay?"

"Yes." Lucille looked at her older sister's determined eyes. "Thank you, Ida."

Ida nodded once, quickly hugged Lucille, and went to the door.

"Lock this after me," she ordered and left.

Lucille locked the door and turned to look at the room. It was nice enough for a prison. She turned out the ceiling light, went over to the bed, and turned out the table lamp. She found her way through the darkness to the curtains, pulled them open, and looked out at the city. The buildings across the street, and for a few blocks around, were as low, or lower, than hers.

She tried to lift a window, but the wood frame was stuck solid from years of overpainting. She tried the second large window, and with effort, it gave.

She felt the cold, moist air on her face. She heard the noise of traffic nearby. Lucille leaned out and saw that the apartment was set back a few feet from the building's edge. She buttoned her coat, sat on the window sill, swung her legs over, and stood up on the roof.

Here, protected by the night, was a strange world of shadow and darkness. She made her way to the foot-high wall that edged the roof and carefully looked down. Even here, on a side street, Alphabet City was alive with sounds: a dog barking, people laughing, cars honking.

A slow-moving figure, eight stories down, caught her attention. A young, thin woman walked alone in the street, along the row of parked cars. The woman staggered a little and then looked around to see if anyone had noticed. But no one had. She slowly continued on as if she wanted to be ignored and forgotten. She rounded the corner and disappeared, like a passing ghost.

Just like me.

Lucille hung her head in despair.

Why am I still alive in this vengeful world?

*   *   *

His head felt all wrong. He opened his eyes and saw a dropped ceiling, with fluorescent rectangles above. He was in a very small bed, in a little room. The walls were pale green. There was one high window. It was dark.

Taki Fukuda tried to sit up but couldn't. His arms were belted to rails on the sides of the bed. An empty IV bag was connected to his left arm. He tried to call for help, but his voice was weak, and his words muffled. He tried to clear his mind but couldn't.

"Ah, you're awake at last." An elderly woman, in a dark blue nun's habit, was watching him from the doorway. She came closer and looked down at him. "How are you doing there, Mr. Fukuda?"

"Taki," he whispered, "everyone calls me Taki. Where... are you from...?"

The old woman was smiling at him, but her eyes looked dark.

"... You sound a little," Taki tried to explain, "like my best friend, Raphael. I miss him so much..." He swallowed hard. "Am I in a hospital...?"

"Don't you know?" she said pleasantly as she started to change his IV bag.

"What...? No, I...," Taki mumbled, "was I hurt?"

The nun chuckled quietly, "There's nothing to worry about, Mr. Fukuda. You're in good hands here."

Taki struggled to wake up. It seemed that he could smell the ocean nearby. Like his home in Southampton, tossing donuts to seagulls circling overhead... His mind was swimming, but he forced himself to focus on the woman. "Where am I...?"

"There, there," she said as she finished hooking up the bag. "You should be able to sleep now."

"No," Taki said weakly, "I have to go..."

"Go where?" she spoke to him as if he were a child. He fought to stay awake.

"I... I want to feed my seagulls," Taki whispered sadly. He surrendered, closed his eyes, drifted away, and in the darkness of the void, he called out to Raphael for help.

*　*　*

Through the night, Artemis had enough scotch to make anyone pass out. But he didn't. In the morning, Drew found him sitting at the antique desk in his room.

225

"Same room. Same reason," Artemis said sadly.

It was true. The last time Artemis moved in, he was twelve years old and his parents were dead. Drew sighed and put a mug of coffee on the desk.

"I'm heading to the precinct, you wanna come?" she said.

"No, I'm good here."

"I'm worried about you. My dad, too," Drew said.

"Don't worry, I got it handled."

"Yeah, I can see that," Drew said pointedly.

Artemis took a sip of coffee and focused on her. "Are you really okay if we stay here for a while?"

"As long as you need," Drew assured him.

"Thank you." Artemis nodded and leaned back in his chair. "I had thought to move us back to the condo in Manhattan. Our renters will be out by the end of the month. But with all that's going on"—he made a vague gesture toward the window—"I just don't think this is a great time to be making a move."

"Couldn't agree more," Drew answered.

"I'm not going back to Columbia." Artemis sounded like he was reading off a list. "My classes are all canceled anyway."

"I heard they're gonna be doing everything online." Drew watched him. "You could work from here. From this room."

"No"—Artemis shook his head—"I'm done. Been done for a while, I just didn't know it."

Drew considered him for a moment. "Okay. So, what now? Will you stay on the case?"

Artemis looked down. "… I'm not sure."

"You know." Drew paused, unsure how this would go over. "What Emily said was right. This thing has no end, until we find these people. And make them pay for what they've done. She'd want you to finish it."

Her words hung in silence for a moment. Artemis drank some coffee, stood up, and went to look out the window. On the street below he could see the NYPD still on the job.

"They've canceled the St. Patrick's Day parade," Artemis said quietly.

Drew shrugged. "You hate crowds, what do you care?"

"No, not that. It's an anniversary. The night of the parade, thirty years ago in Boston, the Gardner Museum was robbed." Artemis dropped his head, took a long breath, and said, "I need to carry a gun again."

"You want to rejoin the force?" Drew asked.

"No."

"So, what then? I really don't see you as a private investigator."

"I know," Artemis answered, "but it means I can legally carry again."

Drew understood. "The license won't be a problem. Both Dad and I will support your application."

Artemis turned to his cousin. She was always so strong, dependable… and ready to help him.

"Thanks" was all he could say.

"Call me if you need anything," she said and left.

*   *   *

By midafternoon, the weather had improved and turned warmer. The Brooklyn Botanic Garden had been closed to the public because of COVID-19, but FBI Special Agent Ray Gaines had no trouble getting them in. He and his old comrade-in-arms, Mathew Sweeney, were walking slowly together on the path that ran along the pond in the Japanese Garden. Here, the sounds of the city were muted by the gentle waterfalls and the breeze rustling through the still bare trees.

"Today's the thirteenth"—Mathew smiled—"fuckin' Friday the thirteenth. Seems we've had enough bad luck already, you know?"

Ray nodded as they walked past the large cinnabar-colored gate in the water.

"Muriel and I used to take Artemis here, you know," Mathew said. "Not at first, but after he got a little better and could tolerate being outside the house. Be nice to get him here now."

"Yeah, that might help," Ray sounded tired.

"This is the place." Mathew led them up a few steps to a small grotto. On one side was a curved stone bench, and on the other, a stone wall inset with a large bronze decorative panel.

Ray groaned as he sat on the bench.

"Me, too." Mathew smiled as he sat next to him. "Nice that it's warmer. Should help everyone feel better."

"Not if we all have to wear gloves and masks like we're goddamn doctors or something." Ray shook his head.

"Nah, no one's gonna bother with all that," Mathew said. "Because it doesn't make a damn difference anyway, at least that's what I've read."

"Depends what you read," Ray said quietly. He looked around at the trees and sighed. "Ah fuck it, I'm too old to care anyway."

Mathew thought for a while before he said, "It's not your fault, Ray. I knew Bert Rocca a long time, too. He had everyone completely fooled."

Ray shrugged and looked at the bronze plaque. It was a relief of a mythic scene: a woman, with one arm around her child, reaching out to gently touch the leaves of a young plant.

"It was a dedication to the guy who paid for the park," Mathew explained. "It's Mother Nature showing her children how to appreciate all this beautiful stuff around us."

"Jesus, we've really fucked it all up, haven't we?" Ray's voice was thick with regret.

Mathew turned to him. "What's up?"

"What if this thing was made in a lab?" Ray answered.

"Are you asking me, or are you telling me?"

Ray shook his head. "I'm neither confirming nor denying. I'm just saying. What if this pandemic was engineered?"

"And released on purpose? Like a weapon?" Mathew rolled his eyes. "Bullshit. That online conspiracy shit is a hoax. Those are the people we should do something about. Causing panic and hurt, and for what?"

"That's the right question," Ray said quietly. "For what? What would be the purpose of all this?"

Mathew dropped his head to one side and cracked his neck. He stood up and stretched. "It's still too cold to be sitting on stone for long."

Ray smiled and got up. "I'm just talking, Matt."

Mathew nodded.

"What time is she supposed to be there?" Ray asked and looked at his watch.

"Three o'clock."

"Well, then"—Ray loosened his tie and opened his collar—"I think we have time to see some more of this beautiful place."

Mathew smiled and led them down the stone pathway, toward the Shakespeare Garden.

*　*　*

Drew had gotten a supply of medical masks from the NYPD. She slipped one on and opened her front door.

"It's nice to see you again, Mary Drew. It's been a long time," said the elderly woman standing before her, who was wearing the same kind of mask.

Drew winced to hear her old name but decided to let it go. "Good to see you, too, Leah. Please come in."

Drew stepped back, and the woman came into the foyer and closed the door behind her. She took off her gray wool coat and laid it carefully across a chair. She neatened her white hair with her hands, adjusted her heavy glasses, and took in Drew.

"You look fine and strong." Her voice was thin with age but warm. "You always did love to work out."

"Not so much now, but I swim almost every day," Drew answered. "And you look good, too."

"Don't let this mask fool you, girl," Leah laughed. "I'm as old as the hills of Rome."

"Is this her?" Silas sounded suspicious as he entered the foyer from the kitchen.

"Yes," Drew said as she moved closer to Silas. "This is Leah Carras. Leah, this is Silas Bookbinder."

"It's wonderful to meet you," Leah said. "You look like Artemis when he was your age."

Silas watched her and said nothing.

Leah stepped back a little and pulled her paper mask down so he could see her face.

"I was very sorry to hear about your mother," she said kindly.

Silas took this in before he said, "You're the one who helped him back then?"

"Yes," Leah answered. "Where is Artemis?"

"Upstairs," Drew answered.

"The same room?"

"Yes."

"Don't suppose you put an elevator in here?" Leah said lightly as she started up the steps.

"Afraid not." Drew was smiling as she took off her mask. "You gonna be okay?"

"Never better," Leah answered as she rounded the landing and headed for the third floor.

Outside of Artemis's room, she paused to catch her breath. She put her mask back on and knocked on the door.

"Come in," his tired voice said.

She opened the door and saw him, perfectly neat and clean, sitting stiffly upright on a chair, staring out the window. She stayed by the door, giving him as much space as she could.

"Anything interesting going on out there?" she asked quietly.

"Not so much," he murmured. "I wondered if they would call you."

"And if I was still living, you mean." She laughed a little.

"Thought you retired."

"I did." She watched him. "But I have lots of free time these days."

Artemis turned to look at her.

"I appreciate your wearing the mask, Leah."

"It's my pleasure."

"And thank you for coming," he said. "I think I could use a little help right now."

Coda: Birth of the Angel

On March 13, the United States declared a national emergency. New York City had ninety-five coronavirus cases, and the mayor was resisting shutting down the public schools. On the 14th, a woman in Brooklyn became the first New Yorker to die of the virus.

By Sunday, the 15th, there were five deaths in the city and three hundred twenty-nine cases. The mayor agreed to close the schools. On this day, the Ides of March, there were close to six thousand deaths worldwide.

Lucille was losing track of how many days and nights she had been alone in her rooftop sanctuary. Ida had faithfully come with groceries. But not with news. She had refused to say anything about what was going on in the outside world: news of the virus, news of Emily Bookbinder's murder, news of Paul Marin, nothing.

The day outside had been cool and clear. But Lucille had done what her sister asked and kept the curtains closed. But now, at night, with the lights off, she felt safe enough to open the curtains, lift the large window, and let in some air.

Lucille stood at the open window and listened. Even this late, the night was alive, murmuring constant city-noise. It was especially dark outside; the sky was covered with clouds.

At least no one will see me.

She wrapped a blanket around her naked body and stepped out onto the roof. She felt drawn to the edge, just a few steps away. The rooftop felt rough and cold beneath her bare feet. She moved closer to the edge and looked down to the concrete sidewalk, eight stories below. She stepped onto the low wall that bordered the roof.

Who can I turn to now?

She wrapped her arms around her chest and hugged the blanket tightly around her thin body. She thought of Paul, how she loved him, and how he betrayed her.

She thought of her sister, Ida, who looked at her with such pity now.

She thought about her ex-husband. Calvin Prons had once been proud of her, given her gifts, and treated her so well. But now? *Don't ever fucking call me again,* he'd said to her.

Her eyes grew wet when she thought of Artemis. She wanted to be with him and his son, Silas. She wanted to protect them from all the bad things in the world. Then she saw Emily Bookbinder lying dead, her blood red on the white tile floor.

And she knew that Artemis was just a fantasy. And there was no one else. No one to miss her if she was gone.

All I have to do is lean forward, and the pain stops.

Lucille closed her eyes, imagined herself falling into the dark void below, and she felt relief. She slowly leaned forward.

A siren suddenly pierced the world below. She opened her eyes and saw the flashing lights of an ambulance speeding past, on the street. It turned the corner and faded away.

And she realized something. She hadn't flinched, like she used to do.

And she wondered what that meant. A gust of cold air came up from below and swirled around her.

Then, a miracle happened. The clouds in the dark sky above opened a little, and a beam of bright, clean moonlight came through and found her on the edge of her solitary rooftop.

And she remembered her dream. A terrible, sad dream, when the savage light of a blue moon had broken through night clouds, touched her skin, and burned her flesh.

But this moon didn't burn her. And she wasn't dreaming. She was awake and alive. She looked up at the light in wonder and asked softly:

"Do you still want me to live?"

And then she felt it. The electricity of the city crucible beneath her feet, and the righteous light of the goddess reaching down from above. And she, Lucille, was where these forces met.

"You have been waiting for me to stop being afraid," she whispered to the light.

She pulled the blanket off her shoulders and let it drop. She stood naked under the light, tipped her head back, and breathed in.

She felt an entirely new sensation spreading through her chest like cold fire. She had lost everything and everybody, and yet she was still alive. And not a passing ghost.

"I will be afraid no longer," she said quietly to the light. "I will no longer be called Orsina or Prons or Azurite." She let these hateful names fall away.

"I will never again be a victim, a sex object, a girlfriend, a wife."

She reached out her arms, lifted them up, and opened her naked body to the vast night sky. And she felt free and alive, like someone who could control her own fate. And she was amazed.

Lucille looked up at the goddess Moon and asked, "What is my new purpose called?"

Vengeance, my dearest Angel. Righteous and holy vengeance shall be yours.

And Lucille believed what she heard. For it was clear in her heart, as strong and true as a birthright.

She was new at last. Remade, here in the cold wind, on the edge of death.

She shouted out to the vast dark sky:

"I am the Angel of Death and I will be feared!"

The story concludes in Book Two of
The COVID Murders Mystery: The Death of Television

Author's Note

The robbery of the Isabella Stewart Gardner Museum on March 18th, 1990, is a real event. But beyond that the story told in this book, of what might have happened, is entirely fictional. None of the stolen art pieces, including Rembrandt's *Storm on the Sea of Galilee*, have ever been recovered.

However, a vast amount of material is available about the actual robbery, the investigations, and the history of the truly wonderful Gardner Museum. I hope you explore further, and enjoy the journey as much as I have.

Conal O'Brien

The Characters in Birth of the Angel

Bookbinder Household:

Artemis Bookbinder – a young professor of art history, former NYPD detective, lifelong germophobe, and driven investigator.

Emily Twist Bookbinder – his wife, a dedicated principal of a special needs school.

Silas Bookbinder – their twelve-year-old, introverted, genius son.

Delia Twist Kouris – their live-in housekeeper, and Emily's aunt.

NYPD:

Drew Sweeney – she is Artemis's cousin, and a lead detective in the Criminal Intelligence Section.

Mathew Sweeney – her father, a retired captain, now lives in Florida.

Jerome Clayton Collins – a young Black detective and specialist in computers.

FBI:

Ray Gaines – a dedicated agent, has been on the Gardner Museum case since the beginning.

Makani Kim – known as Mak, a young capable agent of Hawaiian and Korean lineage.

Bert Rocca – a senior agent and longtime friend of Ray Gaines.

Frank Filipowski – attached to Bert Rocca's team, known to his friends as Flip.

New York City:

Paul Marin – a charismatic psychiatrist, specializing in drug treatment recovery.

Ida Orsina – a forceful woman, who owns and runs a successful dermatology business.

Lucille Orsina – Ida's younger sister, and a survivor of a bad marriage to Calvin Prons.

Ladimir Karlovic – also known as Ladmo, went to medical school with Ida and Paul.

Fat Nicky – so called because he is obese. He takes care of certain business concerns for Paul.

Beth Schaefer – the young manager of the 64th Street Gallery.

TV NEWS:

Calvin Prons – Head of Network, an aggressive misogynist, and Lucille's ex-husband.

Jock Willinger – Executive Producer, an older gaunt man from Liverpool.

Roxie Lee – Supervising Producer, a respected showrunner.

Paula DeVong – an ambitious newscaster, who has succeeded in getting her own show.

Anna Canneli – Paula's devoted assistant.

Greg Schaefer – a handsome openly gay man, Jock's assistant, and Beth's brother.

Deni Diaz – a young news writer, and close friend of Greg's.

In Southampton:

Raphael Sharder – a wealthy octogenarian art dealer.

Taki Fukuda – the manager of Raphael's gallery on Main street.

Patty Figgins – Raphael's housekeeper of many years.

Barbara Borsa – Raphael's lawyer.

Maddy Griffin – owner of the Primrose restaurant, and good friend to all who come there.

Morty Singer – owner of the oldest gem and jewelry shop in town.

Toby Brown – a tough old sailor, owner of a yacht for hire in Sag Harbor.

Sheila Brown – Toby's granddaughter, runs the marina in Southampton.

Go to conalobrien.com to learn more about this book and other Bookbinder Mysteries.